SONG OF
Draupadi

Also by Ira Mukhoty

Akbar: The Great Mughal
Daughters of the Sun: Empresses, Queens and Begums of the Mughal Empire
Heroines: Powerful Indian Women of Myth and History

SONG OF
Draupadi
a novel

IRA MUKHOTY

ALEPH

ALEPH

ALEPH BOOK COMPANY
An independent publishing firm
promoted by *Rupa Publications India*

First published in India in 2021
by Aleph Book Company
7/16 Ansari Road, Daryaganj
New Delhi 110 002

ISBN:978-93-90652-24-2

5 7 9 10 8 6 4

Printed at Parksons Graphics Pvt. Ltd., Mumbai.

For all the unrecorded voices
For the furious, the untamed, the dispossessed,
and the voiceless
For the women of India

Contents

VIII
LEGION

Family Tree

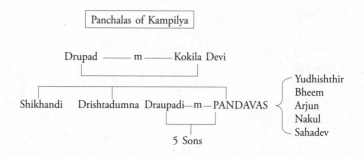

Panchalas of Kampilya

Drupad —— m —— Kokila Devi

Shikhandi   Drishtadumna   Draupadi — m — PANDAVAS

5 Sons

Yudhishthir
Bheem
Arjun
Nakul
Sahadev

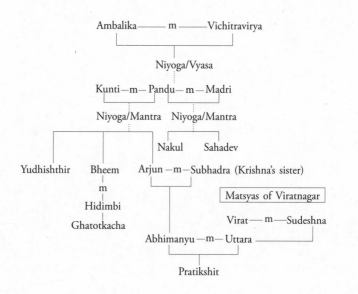

Ambalika —— m —— Vichitravirya

Niyoga/Vyasa

Kunti — m — Pandu — m — Madri

Niyoga/Mantra   Niyoga/Mantra

Nakul   Sahadev

Yudhishthir   Bheem   Arjun — m — Subhadra (Krishna's sister)

m

Hidimbi

Ghatotkacha

Matsyas of Viratnagar

Virat —— m —— Sudeshna

Abhimanyu — m — Uttara

Pratikshit

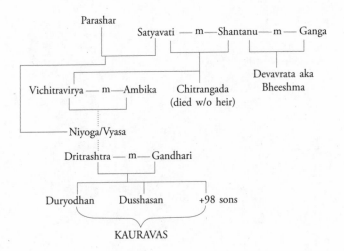

Kurus of Hastinapur

Parashar

Satyavati —— m —— Shantanu —— m —— Ganga

Devavrata aka
Bheeshma

Vichitravirya —— m —— Ambika   Chitrangada
(died w/o heir)

Niyoga/Vyasa

Dritrashtra —— m —— Gandhari

Duryodhan   Dusshasan   +98 sons

KAURAVAS

Author's Note

~

To anyone growing up in India, the stories of the Mahabharata form the cadence to which the seasons are set. They are at once intensely familiar and often deeply obscure. This is because the Mahabharata is not a homogenous text, composed in one setting or even in one era. Scholars now believe it to have been composed over at least eight hundred years, from approximately 500 BCE to 300 CE with successive layers of redactions and interpretations, regional variations, and didactic meanderings.

The Mahabharata also comes to us at various stages of our life, as our horizons change and our quests emerge. I have always been interested in the depiction of women in the text, in the polyphony of female voices that struggle to be heard against the crashing background of male concerns and the strident call to war of the conch shell. My personal quest, in *Song of Draupadi*, is to recover these muffled voices and examine the many ways in which they were able to express defiance and claim justice for themselves in what was in essence a profoundly patriarchal world. I have centred my story around a handful of these women, trying to understand the subtlety of their rebellion and the grief in their whispers. Readers may therefore be surprised to find that the action turns its back away from the endless battles of the text to observe the way in which the women navigate these dangerous waters too.

In the late nineteenth century, an attempt was made to make chronological sense of the gargantuan mass of writing which makes up the Mahabharata, so as to access the earliest possible version of the epic. This project took fifty years to complete at the Bhandarkar Oriental Research Institute, Pune, and the final work is called *The Critical Edition of the Mahabharata*. The English translation of the *Critical Edition* by Bibek Debroy is the text I have most often consulted for *Song of Draupadi*. Readers will find that as per the *Critical Edition* some beloved instances from the text are omitted, believed to be later interpolations, such as the presence of Krishna during Draupadi's disrobing. Other social practices are included, such as the custom of Niyoga, or levirate. Niyoga was the transference of a husband's conjugal rights to his kinsmen for the purpose of procreation. This could have the effect of transforming women into the property of their husbands, practically wombs on rent. This was the case for Ambika, Ambalika, and Kunti. In other instances, I have examined the custom of natal alienation, a practice which still exists today and is exoticized, for example, through the excessively maudlin bidai genre of singing. Draupadi, Kunti, and Gandhari all suffered the deracination of natal alienation.

In addition to the *Critical Edition*, I have also used C. Rajagopalachari's and K. M. Ganguly's versions of the text. For a greater insight into feminist interpretations of the texts I have consulted Shalini Shah's *The Making of Womanhood: Gender Relations in the Mahabharat* and Kumkum Sangari and Sudesh Vaid's *Recasting Women: Essays in Colonial History*. I am also greatly indebted to the great Irawati Karve's *Yuganta: The End of an Epoch*. For a greater understanding of the conditions that may have existed at the time of the Mahabharat, I have used Jeannine Auboyer's *Daily Life in Ancient India: From 200 BC to 700 AD*.

While the scaffolding of the story of *Song of Draupadi* is based on these readings, and the important incidents depicted are as per the texts, this book is a work of fiction. Though many of the words the women utter in this book are from the ancient texts, others are not. I examine some of the women's motives, their decisions, and their desires, which are perhaps forever hidden from us.

I believe this study remains relevant as many women from the Mahabharata are used as role models for women even today. Whether it is the idea of Gandhari being a perfect pativrata because of the sacrifice of her sight for her husband or the unquestioned perfection of Draupadi's devotion for her five husbands, these women remain distant as goddesses while the patriarchy uses them to enforce stifling standards for women. What I wish to reclaim, instead, is the ferocious will of these women, their determination to extract justice, and even vengeance, for their righteous cause.

If there are indeed as many versions of the Mahabharat as there are people on earth, then this is the one that resonates best with me. A version in which the women are imperfect. In which they are noisy and railing and furious, rather than pleading or silenced. This, then, is a song set to these women's meter, to their many, clamorous harmonies.

Prologue
Fire and Ice on the Last Journey Home

~

Aeons have passed since the Woman began her journey with these five Men. New worlds have spun and coalesced out of nothingness and now, at last, her once incandescent rage has forged her into a shimmering, clean thing. They have journeyed before, for glory, for vengeance, and once for salvation, but on this final journey, they have come looking for death. It was the Elder's decision and the other four brothers stood alongside him without a murmur, as they have done all their lives. Except once, when the Second Eldest spat and snarled at the Eldest, but that was a long time ago.

It was surprisingly easy to walk out of the desolation of their echoing palace. To bow one final time before the sacrificial fires guarded by the flinty, austere priests who have kept the three fires burning their entire adult lives. Easy also to remove the gold earrings, waistbands, and necklaces, untie the fine silk dhotis and lay down at last the iron-tipped arrows and heavy wooden bows. They leave all this behind like a sigh, like a half-remembered dream. The Woman kept only her gold anklets with the little golden bells. She has a premonition that a time will come when its soft murmur will be her only solace.

For days, then weeks and months, they cross the marshlands and forests to the north of their kingdom before arriving at the dense, deciduous foothills of the Himalayas. Here they turn away the last of their retinue—the ossified priests and the keening elderly maids. Only a dog remains with them, stubborn and optimistic, eyes filled with the unconditional love of a child. The five Men and the Woman remove their white cotton dhotis, their overgarments, and turbans and replace them with clothes of bark, reed, and wool—fibrous, organic garments more like a feral skin than clothes.

They walk for days up the mountain slopes, foraging for food and sleeping in the rough shelter of shallow caves. Conversation slips away and their movements become dense and slow.

They carefully gather fruits, berries, and roots which they eat raw, the taste a smoky earthiness that makes them feel light-headed. The dog disdains their leafy offerings and disappears on most days, returning triumphant and bloody with a scrawny hare or an indolent crow-pheasant in its deceptively lethal jaws.

Eventually they reach the high passes, where the sacred geography of eternal snow and subterranean mythical rivers beguiles and blinds them. Their footsteps are muffled now. The Woman's anklets are quiet as her feet sink deep into the freshly fallen powdery snow. The Men are fiercely gaunt, ancient scars from forgotten battles hidden among the folds of their now loose skin.

One day, after a bitterly cold night huddled in front of a faltering fire, they walk out before dawn onto an immense icy plateau at the top of the world. They walk silently for a while, as their breath foams and swirls around them and the stars silently fade into the opalescent dawn. Under the vaulting sky in this place where all stories end, the Woman suddenly finds she can't walk any more. Each step has been an agony of effort and will and now she can do it no more. She cries out in shock but as she slowly sits down on the frozen ground, she realizes that the Men are already far ahead, an indistinct smudge of shapes on the pristine snow.

She calls out to them once again, her voice husky from disuse.

She thinks she sees one of the Men falter and briefly glance back. She strains to make out which one of the brothers has been arrested by her call, and whispers a name. But the figures are now all walking away from her, their shadows getting smaller all the time.

Come back, she cries again, her voice strangled by sobs.

Don't leave me alone.

Her sobs make a painful, rasping sound but no one comes back for her. Not even the dog, who is an ungainly shadow next to the Eldest. Finally, after staring at the figures till her eyes burn, the Woman settles back against the cold embankment and looks away with a sigh. She pulls her blanket of coarse fur tightly around herself and hacks out a slight hollow to lean against with the wooden stick she uses for walking. She rubs her eyes roughly with the heel of her hand and pulls the blanket over her head, hiding her thickly coiled plait, still provocatively black.

She pulls out a small cloth bundle from the folds of her clothes and takes out a few rust-coloured dried goji berries. She eats these slowly as she looks around at her stark surroundings. She is alone at last, after a lifetime saturated by people and animals and the ebb and flow of constant movement. She wishes the dog, at least, had stayed behind with her. She would have gathered him into the folds of her fur blanket and his hot, musty animal breath on her face would have been a consolation.

The snow starts to fall gently, in sparse, economical drifts. The Woman gathers a few snowflakes in her palm and scoops them into her mouth, amazed at the clear taste, like eating a cloud. She looks out at the distant horizon where the sky glows pomegranate red in a suffused band behind the peaks. The first rays slice through the frigid air, incandescent and true, like the very first dawn of time. The woman closes her eyes as she feels the rays kiss her face. Behind her eyelids are striated patterns of gold and saffron.

As the snowflakes gather softly on her eyelashes, the crimson warmth of the sun awakens an ancient memory in the Woman. She feels her being scatter into nothingness and catapult through the meagre mountain air into the wide-open skies. She can sense that her body is still in the snow, shallow breaths barely lifting the rugs and skins as her other, spectral being rushes towards the fire and heat of an older, primal time.

⌒

Smoke, acrid and greasy, billows out in the air from the sacrificial fires and spreads like a malevolent thing through the ceremonial hall. The smoke smells of ghee and camphor and a spike of herbs. Priests are everywhere, gaunt and sepulchral, the tendons on their necks straining as they chant the mantras endlessly. Two priests— brothers—huddle before the main altar of baked tiles, sweat pouring down their faces in which the eyes are manic and vacant. The sweat trickles down their bare brown chests, soaking their janeus. They wipe their faces with the ends of the white upper garments as their vibrating, tremolo voices rise and fall in cadence. Marigold, champa, and mango blossom garlands, fragrant and fresh ten days ago, hang limply like disconsolate brides.

Heaps of offerings—rice balls, milk, yoghurt, honey, and fried barley balls—lie in rotting piles next to the flickering flames. No servant dares to step onto the consecrated grounds to clear up any more. Wispy rumours unfurl out of the hall and through the corridors of the unholy black-magic rites being performed by the vengeful king.

In the darkest corner of the hall, the earthen floor is dark with the blood of the sacrificed goats, first smothered to death then butchered following explicit rules. Their excrements are buried in the ground and the animals are dismembered, with select parts offered up to the priests and the devouring fire-god. The blood of the animals, collected in earthenware jars, is offered by a priest to

Ira Mukhoty

the legion of baleful, evil spirits. The sharp metallic smell of blood mingles with that of the incense sticks, rotting flowers, and food, and it smells like carnage.

The two brothers pour a final offering of soma into the fire which blazes up, sizzling and crackling into a raging inferno. Aghast, they step back from the fire, as the flames begin to singe the braided banana-leaf ceiling of the hall. The goblet of prasad glows red in the elder brother's hand, and he calls out loudly for the queen.

The rani! Call for the rani at once!

The king, who has been keeping a wrathful vigil these past ten days, turns to the cowering maidservants:

Go at once! Bring the rani here immediately!

Within minutes, the sound of running footsteps can be heard hastening towards the fire altar. The queen is rushing towards the priests, her long black hair cascading down her back, slick and wet from her interrupted bath. Her gold waistband and armbands glitter in the light of the sacrificial fires against her smooth nutmeg skin. The priest is almost screaming now as the prasad slowly singes his skin. He grabs the queen by the throat and presses the pot of soma between her lips. The queen swallows the soma and her eyes widen in fear for a moment before she faints in the priest's arms. He carries her out of the hall which is now ablaze from the flames of the main altar and lays her down gently on the ground under the clear sky. All thirty priests hurry over to the queen, abandoning their altars to the howling fire and the disintegrating bamboo structure.

The instant the queen faints, the Woman, who has been observing the proceedings with a puzzled detachment, feels herself hurtling towards the unconscious figure. She tries to scream and fight the falling sensation but it is inexorable. She feels the world solidify and crush around her, forcing air into nascent lungs. As she approaches the queen's body, she is startled by the brushing presence of another being, jostling and kicking her. She tries to turn towards this other presence but she is held fast now in an ocean of pulsating red liquid and the only sound in the distance is the faint and steady throb of her mother's heart.

I

Black Magic and a Magical Black Girl

The Garland-maker's Daughter

~

In the bleached morning sunlight of a summer's day, two little girls sit in the shade of a mango tree. They are sitting on the bare floor, surrounded by coir baskets heaped full of fresh flowers: flaming marigolds, delicately scented champas, red hibiscus, and pearly jasmine. Smaller baskets shimmer with assorted feathers, beads, and dried berries.

Both girls are making flower garlands, teasing each flower with a wooden needle onto a length of fibrous cotton stalk. A small monkey sits on a low branch of the mango tree, chattering quietly to himself and peeling a raw mango with his tiny, sharp teeth. A pair of mynah birds hop anxiously on a branch nearby, fixing their glassy, unforgiving eyes on the small creature. Butterflies hover languidly while the bees make their staccato and precipitous way from flower to flower.

One of the girls is struggling with completing the first garland. Dressed in an indigo-blue pleated skirt, her skin is the colour of the blue-black jamun berry. Her friend Kamini is the malakar's daughter and her tiny, nimble fingers string the flowers expertly.

'Come on, Kamini, help me make breakfast quickly,' Kamini's mother calls out to her from the shade of the hut's small covered veranda.

'Choti Rani can have breakfast with us today.'

Kamini runs over to the small outdoor kiln and tucks her short

3

dhoti even higher so that it is out of the way as she works, and her two long plaits gleam on either side of her small head.

With the help of a bamboo fan, she quickly kindles the fire in the kiln and then places a pot of water on it. Once the water comes to a roiling boil, she pours in the rough short-grained rice her mother has pounded in a mortar. Not a grain of rice falls to the ground and Draupadi watches her friend enviously. In her home she is not yet allowed anywhere near the kitchen fires.

Draupadi loves being inside the one-room hut in which Kamini lives with her parents and two older brothers. It is like a doll's house—with everything the family needs stacked within its granular wattle-and-daub walls. A few small terracotta pots against one wall contain the family's groceries—short-grained rice, barley, a few condiments, salt, cloves, and peppercorns. Kamini's father's work implements are neatly lined up against another wall—a sickle, a hoe, brooms, and a collection of coir baskets.

As they eat their meal of boiled rice and mango pickle, Kamini tells her friend an important piece of news. Her father has gone to the market to buy a cow for the household. Draupadi nods appreciatively. She knows the value of cows. The large herds owned by her father are guarded by cowherds with bows and arrows and men have fought and died over them.

'Maybe I will get milk to drink every day now.'

'Hush, child,' Damini frowns. 'It is not good luck to talk of things which are yet to happen. You know it does nothing but attract the evil eye.' She gets up quickly to shoo away a squawking crow sitting at the entrance of the courtyard.

'Horrible birds, always bringing bad luck with their loud screeching.'

The squawking is replaced unexpectedly by a different commotion. As Damini stands on the threshold, she hears the sound of a woman wailing and children talking excitedly.

A middle-aged woman appears at the small wooden gate, surrounded by children chattering up at her. The woman is oppressively gaunt, high cheekbones emphasized by her taut, brown skin. She leans against the wooden post, thumping her thin chest with a fist.

'Hai! I am ruined, I am bereft. I will be cast out in my old age, where will I go?'

The woman's heavy gold earrings stretch her earlobes dangerously and she pulls the end of her white dhoti over her dishevelled hair. Her large, uneven teeth have wide spaces between them, like the stones on a crumbling wall.

Damini rushes out of the hut to stand before the older woman, bowing deeply.

'Please do not upset yourself, Maatrika Devi, the child is here with us. She is well.'

The clutch of children at the gate are delighted at this wholly unexpected dramatic performance. They are half-naked, wearing only ragged loincloths or dhotis with amulets around their necks and scrawny, bruised arms.

Draupadi and Kamini stand at the entrance to the hut in silence. The minute the woman sees Draupadi, she shrieks in alarm like a deranged bird and rushes past Damini to grab her.

'Hai!' she wails again, and her voice has a raspy, metallic edge to it.

'Look at your hair, what have you done to yourself? And where is your upper garment, child?'

It is true that her hair is in utter disarray, rebellious strands twisting out of the coiled plaits.

'We used it to play hide and seek and then I lost it, Mataji. I think Bhola hid it,' Draupadi replies sullenly, blaming the monkey. The enchantment of the morning is quite broken, the marigolds are crushed and the mango juice is spilled.

Maatrika Devi grabs her roughly by the arm and drags her through the crowd of scabby, grabbing children. They rush through the narrow gullies of the village past expectant cows and alarmed hens. In the distance, a peacock cries its disquietingly near-human call.

Through the gathering heat of mid-morning, as the dew evaporates off the waxy green leaves of the lotuses in the ponds, Maatrika Devi and Draupadi hurry out of the village on the outskirts of town.

The old woman covers Draupadi's head and face with the end of her upper garment and the two of them enter the city of Kampilya through the great vault of its main gateway. Through the main street full of determined merchants, scrawny labourers, and shoppers, they dodge past horse-drawn chariots and palanquins till they reach the palace.

The newly whitewashed palace walls gleam like Indra's elephant in the sunlight. They cross the unpaved floors of several courtyards, past the royal elephants' enclosure, the horses' stables, the war chariots, and the soldiers' barracks till they reach the inner courtyard of the women's quarters.

The corridors here are narrow, cool, and dark with smooth floors along which servants swish by on bare feet, carrying trays and baskets and clothes. At last, they reach the rani's chamber and Maatrika releases Draupadi before collapsing onto her haunches, head cradled in her bony arms.

'Here she is, Devi, this child will be the death of me. Do you know where I found her? In the malakar's hut, outside the city walls.'

Kokila Devi turns away from the large wooden birdcage in which two small songbirds are pecking at the barley seeds she has just given them. The queen is extravagantly beautiful, with smoky, flame-coloured eyes below straight black brows. Her hair is elaborately coiled and twisted into a high bun which sparkles with tiny gemstones. A slim gold braid circles the line of her brow then twists and coils into the braids on the sides of her head. A servant girl has just finished dressing her hair and leaves the room carrying a tray of combs, hair ornaments, gems, and garlands.

Kokila Devi gasps when she sees her dusty daughter and hurries over to hug her.

'Daughter, what a state you are in and look how you have upset poor Maatrika Devi.'

Thus encouraged, the older woman starts wailing anew, still squatting by the door.

'She is possessed, Devi Rani, it is the evil eye. You must have her exorcised immediately.'

Kokila Devi frowns. She doesn't like talk of the evil eye where her daughter is concerned, but the older woman is right. The yakshis and other malevolent spirits are everywhere. A moment's inattention and they are ready to defile a sacrifice, sicken a child, or snatch the foetus from a mother's womb. She shivers suddenly and waves at the servant who has just brought in a tray full of fresh garlands.

'Go bring the things necessary for the exorcising at once. And Maatrika Devi, gather yourself and bathe the child quickly.'

Suddenly invigorated by her task, Maatrika Devi rushes out of the room with Draupadi. When they return a short while later, Draupadi is wearing a clean new skirt and upper garment and her hair is dripping wet.

Maatrika Devi who is the resident expert in such matters, grabs the tray which the servant has brought in, bearing a small burning lamp, some red chillies, and a few twigs tied together in a bundle. Muttering the incantations under her breath, she holds the tray close to Draupadi's face, throwing the chillies into the flame and beating the space about the child's face with the little broom.

The stinging, swirling smoke brings tears to Draupadi's eyes and soon she is wailing aloud in pain and outrage.

'See how the evil spirit rages and fights! Begone, foul creature!' Maatrika Devi vigorously beats her broom in the air, hissing mantras under her breath.

'Enough, Maatrika Devi, enough.' Kokila gently pushes the older woman away and pulls Draupadi close to her. She takes the sobbing girl over to her large bed, covered by a soft white bedspread. Draupadi puts her arms around her mother's slim waist and feels the weight of the gold waistband into which Kokila has tucked the end of her red-and-white fine cotton dhoti.

Kokila holds her daughter's face in her hands. Her features are smudged by her tears and Kokila wonders distractedly if they will ever gain any symmetry. Draupadi's luminous eyes, though, are arrestingly beautiful, finely drawn, and slightly upturned like a wild leopard's.

'Beti, you are old enough to understand a few things now. You are the rajkumari of Panchala, the greatest kingdom in the world. You cannot run around like an urchin, eating food at anyone's place like a beggar.'

Draupadi is indignant. 'But, Ma, the food was delicious, and I didn't ask for it, Kamini's mother made me eat it.'

'Yes, and that poor woman must have gone hungry, having given you her share. Maatrika Devi, tomorrow you will give the malakar's wife this coin for her trouble.' Kokila Devi takes out a small silver coin from a wooden box and hands it to Maatrika, who has returned from disposing of her smouldering tray.

'I didn't know that, Ma, I thought there was enough food for everyone,' Draupadi is dismayed.

'You will be rani one day, Daughter.' Kokila gets up and goes over to a small table. 'It will be your duty to know what it costs to run your household, from the smallest, most insignificant expenses to the large yajnas. It is not for a king to worry about such things. He has to keep the kingdom safe from cattle raiders and wild tribals.'

Ira Mukhoty

She brings over a few small vials and boxes and places them carefully on the bed in front of Draupadi.

'Now play with these boxes while I dress your hair.' Kokila massages Draupadi's hair with coconut oil and then combs it with a small carved wooden comb. Draupadi opens each jar and vial carefully, smelling the sharp green fragrances. Her favourite is the tiny metal vial with the lip balm which her mother uses in the winter. It is a paste made of the jujube fruit mixed with milk and she dabs a small amount on her own lips.

'I wanted to play with my brothers this morning, Ma, but they say they are too busy to bother with me. Even Drishtoo.'

'You know they have started their weapons training now, Daughter. Archery, mace, and wrestling. Nothing of interest to you but your brothers will grow up to be warriors and must learn all these things.'

Draupadi sighs and thinks that she would very much like to wrestle with her brothers but knows better than to mention this. She misses their rough and effervescent company, especially her twin, Drishtadumna, and the gently teasing Shikhandi.

Kokila finishes combing Draupadi's hair and quickly ties it tightly into two thick braids which hang almost to her waist.

Two young servant girls, just a few years older than Draupadi, enter the rani's chamber. One girl brings two glasses of sweetened milk flavoured with fresh cardamom pods, and a pomegranate, which she places on a low table in front of Draupadi.

The second girl brings a selection of paan, spiced with a paste of lime, cinnamon, nutmeg, valerian, and clove. Kokila drinks the glass of cold milk then chooses a paan and tucks it at the back of her mouth. The mixture is sweet, sharp, and spicy, and flavours her breath all day.

Draupadi cracks open the pomegranate, its glassy seeds scattering onto the plate like rubies.

'Sushila, the paan is very good today. Take them to the king in the meeting hall.'

The young maid bows to Kokila, pleased.

Draupadi jumps up, stuffing a handful of pomegranate seeds into her mouth. 'Let me go with Sushila, Ma, I want to give Father the paan.' Without waiting for an answer, she gathers up the remaining fruit and runs after the young maid.

The two girls run out of the darkened room and corridors, stifled laughter bubbling out of them, and Draupadi gathers up her skirt to be able to keep up with Sushila. The young maid wears a simple dhoti tucked high and a breastband and her long single plait snaps from side to side down her back.

Draupadi throws a few pomegranate seeds to the pearly pigeons and stops briefly to pick up and hug a stumbling, erratic puppy.

'Come on, Choti Rani, we are almost there, put that dirty dog down.'

They arrive at last at the assembly hall where King Drupad is seated on a low bench among a gathering of visiting priests and scholars. The king is imposing, like a sarus crane, in a billowing white cotton dhoti and a white upper garment draped about his shoulders. His long hair is tied in a low knot and he wears a crown of gold set with coloured stones. He also wears a garland of fresh marigolds, brought in that morning by the malakar, and is surrounded by his councilmen—his senani, his charioteer, the royal priest, and the bard.

Sitting on the ground of the open assembly hall is a disparate group of men. There are a few grizzled ascetics, with haunted eyes and matted grey hair, wearing only wraps of bark and animal skin. Their emaciation is extreme, sinews and tendons boldly visible beneath their parchment skin. Then there are the itinerant scholars who retain the slightest veneer of respectability with barely scuffed upper garments and clean dhotis. There are priests present today as well, in addition to the familiar portly royal priest. They have long beards, grey or black, and long, matted hair tied in a knot on the top of their heads. They are all bare-chested, wearing only the sacred threads and holy rudraksha beads.

Draupadi creeps up quietly to her father and hands him a paan, which he takes from her with a sudden smile. He pulls her distractedly onto his lap and Draupadi breaths deeply of his beloved and familiar smell of musk and clove. She plays for a while with the long pearl necklace the king is wearing beneath the marigold garland.

A man is sitting in the middle of the assembly, a priest, and he is speaking to the king and the men with a uniform, intonating cadence that is both hypnotizing and soothing. His gaze is oblique and he rocks slightly back and forth as he speaks. Draupadi realizes he is quoting from the Vedas which she has overheard many times being taught to her brothers. Piqued now by her borrowed knowledge, she listens carefully to what the man is saying. All the men are listening too, though the old ascetics sometimes shout out a truculently incoherent word or phrase.

The man is speaking of the sacred duties of kingship and the dharma of a warrior. Of the need to take up arms to defend the kingdom against intruders, of the holy duty of a king towards his people. Draupadi knows that this is something her father agonizes about. There is an ancient story that lurches through the corridors of her father's palace. A story of a boyhood promise made on a golden summer's day when friendships are forever. Of a pledge redeemed and then broken when the boys had grown into men, their summer spent. Of honour lost and a kingdom cleaved.

Draupadi also has a simmering awareness of an expectation her father has, of her and her twin. A glittering, brittle hope in King Drupad's eyes sometimes when he looks at her. Draupadi knows this hope is related in some way to Drishtadumna's endless archery practice under the searing sun, the fierce, crazed ambition with which Drupad looks at his son swinging his spiked iron mace against his training partners.

What her role is to be, Draupadi doesn't know. Despite her pleadings, she is not allowed to touch the instruments of battle so her role lies elsewhere and she must try and understand what she must do. When the time comes, she must not fail her father.

'O Princess,' Sushila hisses up at Draupadi. 'Come along, we need to go back to the rani's courtyard. Your mother wants you to help with the meal preparations today.'

Draupadi sighs at the prosaic interruption and jumps off her father's lap. The girls run back to the rani's quarters. A clamour of women is settling down in the main inner courtyard to prepare the ingredients for a meal. It is to be quite an elaborate service, in honour of the erudition of the visiting scholars and priests.

In the shade of the deep verandas, women are pounding long-grained aromatic rice from its husk in cool stone mortars. Sitting on their haunches, their dhotis tucked up behind them, other women are chopping root vegetables and gourds and rubbing the glistening slices with spices—chilli, pepper, cumin, cloves, and salt. In the middle of the courtyard, an ancient peepul tree reaches up brokenly to the wide skies and groups of parakeets, lime green and gaudy against the dusty, dark leaves, devour their stolen meal of gleaned grain, fought for against the feathery, tumbling squirrels.

There are women of all ages in the courtyard. There are shy, fumbling slave girls, eleven or twelve years old, war bounty from distant lands. Draupadi hears them crying out at night, in sibilant and foreign tongues. They are the pedestrian spoils of war, carelessly gathered when the gold and precious stones are found wanting, on a footing with the horses and the weapons. They are given the simplest of jobs, removing the chaff from the fine white rice and the honey-gold barley.

Then there are the exuberant, scathing local women, maids to the rani of the greatest mahanagar in all Bharat. Tawny and impudent, their dark skins gleam as they sweat in the heat of the peepul's shade. They are busy making the rich, scented desserts— balls of rice coated with sugar, thin slices of coconut, and various spices, then fried in butter, the curds mixed with molasses, ghee, and pepper.

Older women, bleached and toothless, supervise the grinding of the spices in the exact proportions so that the brazen coriander does not overshadow the elusive cardamom and the peppercorns add as much fiery heat as required.

Once in a while, slim, young male servants wearing white dhotis and turbans come to the courtyard to bring more spices, fetch the desserts or to transmit a message from the cooks at the kilns. They are immediately surrounded by a cacophony of teasing, jeering phrases as the women size up the dark-skinned youth. The boys hand over the condiments and the messages, and fairly run out of the courtyard, unable to bear the devastation of the sidelong glances and the loud teasing.

Kokila Devi walks into the courtyard and the burble dies down momentarily. She stands over the different groups of women, tasting the spices and checking the plump whiteness of the grains of rice. She calls out to Draupadi, who is mixing jaggery into the thick, creamy curd, to follow her into the outer courtyard, where the cooks are hunched and labouring over their steaming, blackened kilns.

Today the cooks are frying slices of veal in ghee and roasting partridges wrapped in bitter leaves. A thick sauce of ghee, mango juice, salt, and pepper is bubbling in another pot to accompany the roasted meat. Kokila Devi makes Draupadi taste the gravy and then takes her to the large hall where the men are seated in rows on the floor, the first course of fried vegetables laid out on the banana leaves in front of them. The women remain in the antechamber, where they cannot be seen, and Kokila Devi points out to Draupadi the various dishes being brought out.

In between courses servant girls hand out spices—basil, ginger, and asafoetida to stimulate the palate. Milk and whey are poured into terracotta pots, which will be broken and thrown away after use. The men eat in concentrated silence, mixing the meat into the rice with their hands, occasionally wiping their sweating brows with the ends of their upper garments.

Then the desserts are brought—sweetened curd and honey. Luscious slices of mangoes signal the end of the meal, after which the paan is distributed. At last, the men get up to leave, satiated and rendered speechless and fragrant by the paan bulging in their cheeks. Draupadi is finally released by her mother, and she runs out into the walled orchard at the back of the palace where she knows her brothers will have gathered.

The boys have just finished their simpler meal of meat and rice and are limbering up in search of afternoon amusement. Draupadi rushes up to them and jumps into the arms of a slim, young boy.

'Drishtoo! At last! You have been out the whole morning.' Draupadi tightens her grip around her brother's neck as he hugs her quickly and then places her gently back on the floor. Though he is her twin, Drishtadumna is half a head taller than Draupadi already and his sinews and muscles move beneath his amber skin like a promise.

The children spend the afternoon amongst the mango trees and the harsingar, with its secret moonlight flowering. They are oblivious to the searing heat as they tumble and collide in the laden shade of the glossy-leafed trees. The palace sleeps, rani and maids alike, only Maatrika Devi remains to keep an eye on the errant rajkumari. She is stretched out and somnolent in a wedge of shadow on the veranda. An occasional, particularly loud cry, wakes her from time to time and then she resumes counting her rudraksha beads and muttering mantras angrily.

After a while, the children settle down under the ber tree to collect its small, tart red fruit. Some of the fruits are still yellow, not quite ripe, and their taste is sharp and green like a premonition of spring. Occasionally, Draupadi throws a fruit to a peacock that is tied by a long rope to the trunk of an ixora shrub. Its provocative cry is either threat or thanks, she is never sure. The mynahs, parakeets, sparrows, and hoopoes collude in keeping a detached vigil on the fruits the children scatter.

Drishtadumna stands up suddenly and stretches to shake off the torpor of the late afternoon. He rubs his head where the dove-soft fuzz of his hair has started growing again after his head was shaved during his upanayana ceremony the previous month. He straightens his sacred thread, which loops over his shoulder, and nudges one of his brothers with a toe.

'Come on, wake up, let us go for a swim in the pond.' The other boys throw away the remaining ber fruit and straighten their janeus and crumpled dhotis. Though they are all older than Drishtadumna, he is the unquestioned leader, organizing their aimless games and distributing rough and immediate justice. His brittle energy is stoked by the blaze of his father's denied ambition and he feels sometimes, in an incoherent and barely tangible way, like the goats and deer and buffaloes being led to sacrifice. It makes him fizz and seethe and he is impatient, often, at his slower and gentler brothers. Like the sacrificed animals, he senses it will end in blood, his blood, warm and viscous and glittering somewhere on a distant battlefield.

But for now, he is a boy amongst other boys and he is invincible in the gathering dust of this golden day. The boys run off, barefoot and raucous, scattering the mynahs and the parakeets into the looming sky.

'Not you, Chhoti Rani,' Maatrika calls out to Draupadi, who had hoped to make her escape for the second time that day. She sighs loudly as she gets up, arranging her upper garment around her head and shoulders. 'You will come with me to the herb garden and help me gather the leaves for the evening samskara. And instead of wasting all that ber fruit, bring it with you and we will use it to make that lip salve your mother likes.'

Draupadi follows the older woman into the small fenced-in garden where Maatrika tends to her herbs and medicinal shrubs. Despite her protestations, Draupadi quite enjoys accompanying Maatrika Devi into her garden with the pomegranate, neem, and mango trees in addition to the sweet-smelling champas and the spicy herbs and shrubs. She helps Maatrika Devi pluck the leaves of the tulsi shrub for the evening oblation. The older woman keeps up a constant stream of grumbling talk, partly to herself, partly to Draupadi, and partly to the inconstant and fickle gods, alternatingly pleading and exhorting, prosaic and lyrical.

'Hé Indra, may the rains come on time this year so that the paddy can grow and we do not starve. But do not send the rain too early, or the barley will rot. Surya, keep your rays strong so that the mangoes ripen, I really need the mangoes to make that chutney the king likes. Hé Devi, protect us, your wretched servants, keep Sarama, the evil bitch mother, away from our homes and our women, so that they may give birth to resplendent pundits and brave Kshatriyas who will sing your praises.'

Maatrika stops suddenly, remembering a more immediate concern.

'O Devi, the prayers, the evening samskaras! We will be late with the tulsi leaves. Come on, Chhoti Rani, we have to run.'

And run they do, an unlikely pair, through the courtyards and twisting corridors. The older woman with her long-limbed, egret-like stride and the slight girl, with her corkscrew curls resolutely undone.

When they arrive at the courtyard of the inner sanctum, they realize they have reached just in time. Raja Drupad and the royal priest are just about to sit in front of the holy altar of fire of the clan of the Panchalas. The raja has just had his evening bath and his loose hair glistens as it drips water down his bare back. He is dressed in a simple white dhoti, like the priest, and he has put aside his upper garment. The men sit on either side of the brick altar and glow in the dual light of the flames of the fire and that of the dying day.

Kokila Devi collects the tulsi leaves and the marigold garland from Maatrika without a word but with a single scathing glance that almost has the older woman weeping again. The rani has prepared all the items of oblation and sacrifice, the milk, the herbs, the ghee, and other condiments but she will not participate in the rite herself.

The priest starts the incantation in his familiar, sing-song vibrato, pouring the libations of ghee and camphor into the fire which hisses and smoulders. For a while all activity ceases and concentrates around this ancient fire, which is both a holy sacrifice and a vortex, a gateway to the gods. Draupadi and Maatrika sit beside the threshold of the courtyard where they are not seen. Maatrika repeats the hymns almost inaudibly under her breath, each phrase perfect in the pulse and swing of its cadence.

Draupadi must have fallen asleep during the prayers because the next thing she remembers is waking up next to Maatrika in the dark. Kokila Devi is busy with King Drupad's guests this evening so Draupadi is dispatched rather peremptorily. Maatrika gives her a light meal of barley gruel and whey and then the two of them go up to the roof of the women's quarters. She lays out bedding of kusa grass and blankets covered by a soft cloth and they lie down beneath the wide arch of the night sky. Draupadi can hear the sound of musical instruments, a flute, and maybe the veena. The sound is muted, though, and distant, and Draupadi feels closer to the glittering stars and the heavy, indolent moon. She yawns and stretches and turns towards Maatrika.

'Maatrika, tell me the story again, the story of my birth.'

Maatrika is stretched out comfortably next to Draupadi, rolling a paan to her specifications, with more lime and cinnamon, and a pinch of ginger.

'This Sushila, who does she think she is? Titch of a girl from nowhere, one praise from your mother and look how her head swells up!' Maatrika's querulous muttering is finally silenced when she places the paan carefully in the back of her mouth. She sighs, leaning back against the low wall of the roof terrace, and pulls Draupadi into her lap.

'So, you want to hear that story again. You know I don't like talking about it very much. Who knows what mischievous spirits are lurking around, eavesdropping on everything.'

Draupadi puts her arms around the older woman's waist and breathes in the familiar, sharp, peppery fragrance of ginger and lime. She knows she must contain her impatience and wait while Maatrika adjusts the thick cotton wrap around her head and shoulders.

'For a whole year your father tried to find a priest who would carry out the rites, but no one was willing. Naturally they were not willing, unholy and depraved black magic, who would want to corrupt themselves with such sacrifices?'

Maatrika starts shaking her head and pulls out her rudraksha beads and Draupadi knows she must orient her carefully or the older woman will spend half the night chanting propitiating mantras.

'But why did Father need to carry out the sacrifice in the first place, Mataji? You have forgotten the beginning.'

'Haan, the beginning, you mean you want to hear about your father's firstborn sons? Well, such a puny and sapless bunch, bless them, it was clear there wasn't a true Kshatriya between the lot of them. And your father needed a true warrior, to defeat Drona and his acolytes. And who is that Drona, a Brahmin, to question your father about kingdom and lands, I ask you? What does a Brahmin know about ruling kingdoms? What does he know about anything except tending to the altar of fire, you tell me?'

But this is a rhetorical question and Maatrika is off on one of her favourite tirades, and Draupadi must stop her again.

'Yes, yes, Mataji, you are right, of course. Drona was arrogant and ill-advised to come asking my father for half of his kingdom, all because of a silly childhood promise.'

'Arrogant, yes, that is the right word, Chhoti Rani. Drona was arrogant to send his acolytes to snatch away half your father's kingdom. His duty is to tend to the sacred fire, to look after the well-being of the gods and ancestors, not to lust after kingdoms. He has confused the duty of a Brahmin with that of a Kshatriya, which is what led to all this mess. So now your father needed a worthy son to fight his war and reclaim his kingdom.'

'And that is why he conducted the great yajna, isn't that so, Maatrika?'

'Yes, Chhoti Rani. After searching for a year, he finally found a priest, Upayaja, and his brother, who agreed to perform the yajna.'

'Why was it so hard to find a priest? Father often conducts sacrifices and yajnas, what was so special about this one?'

'Inauspicious, Chhoti Rani, not special, inauspicious.' Maatrika's mood has altered subtly and her voice is slow with dread. 'The sacrifice was conducted to bring about the death of someone, to invoke Yama himself. It is very dangerous and mischievous magic, to call upon the Lord of Death himself. There was so much heat generated from that powerful magic that the sacrificial hall burnt to the ground.'

'But it worked. The magic worked, Maatrika, didn't it?'

'Yes,' the older woman sighs. 'The prasad was blessed and given to your mother and she bore twins, splendid and strong twins.'

She smiles in the dark at Draupadi; this is the girl's favourite part of the story. 'They were expecting only one child, a boy, and they got him, of course.'

'But they also got me,' Draupadi squeals in excitement at the thought of her parents' surprise.

'That's right. They got your brother Drishtadumna, who will kill Drona one day as per your father's wishes, but they also got you, Chhoti Rani.'

Maatrika takes out a small brass jug which she has carried surreptitiously up to the terrace with her. She takes a quick swig of the liquid it contains and settles back against a cushion. Draupadi doesn't question her about this drink, she only knows it is Maatrika's special rice drink and she is not allowed to taste it. What she does know is that sleep follows quickly once the contents of the jug are consumed, so she must hurry if she wants to ask any more questions.

'But what is my role, Maatrika? If Drishtoo must kill Drona to avenge Father, what must I do? Must I also kill someone?'

Maatrika makes a hissing sound and quickly swallows a big sip of the liquid in the jug.

'No, no, child, no killing for you,' she puts her arms around the little girl and holds her close. 'Women are not meant to kill, only nurture and create.'

'But then why was I born during the abhicara sacrifice, the death-dealing sacrifice? I am scared, Maatrika, sometimes I have bad dreams that frighten me very much. I don't understand what they mean and Mother won't listen to me when I try and talk about them.'

Draupadi's voice trembles as she tries to control her tears and her confusion.

'Shush, child, quiet now. The great goddess will watch over you, don't be afraid. When the time comes, Devi herself will help you understand what you must do.'

Maatrika starts singing a low song—part lullaby part incantation.

'Maybe you are not linked to the sacrifice at all, just a beautiful, precious gift the Devi decided to leave behind.'

Maatrika whispers this to herself, but she doesn't really believe it. She falls asleep, shoring up the citadel of her mind against the legion of evil spirits.

Draupadi stays awake a little while longer, watching the wheeling stars. When she finally sleeps, she knows she will dream again of fire and blood. Of running feet and boiling fire. And then beyond that, surprisingly, of something dark and coarse and alluvial and when she wakes up, she will remember the lingering smell of grass.

The Clan of the Panchalas

~

Five years pass and it is monsoon season in northern Bharat. The storm front which has been building up over the Bay of Bengal has finally reached the mahanagar of the clan of the Panchalas. The unforgiving heat, relentless since the month of March, is slain by the rolling monsoon clouds. In the palace of Kampilya, the first fat drops of rain are falling in the courtyards, scattering the dust, the squirrels, and the birds.

Inside the palace, Maatrika Devi is mobilizing an army of servants as if for war. She is directing the raising of the beds with bricks, in anticipation of an unwelcome invasion of snakes escaping the rain, bringing in the caged birds so that they do not drown, ordering the sullen cooks to change the ingredients in the sauces and overseeing the preparation of a new batch of ointments and pastes.

Each season of the year has its own defined set of rituals and mantras, cosmetic preparations, and dietary requirements. The monsoon season, the fourth season of the year, with two more yet to come, is particularly important as a time of rejuvenation and Maatrika Devi has much work to do. She stops for a moment to berate an ancient woman, wearing a single white cloth, headed towards the rani's quarters.

'O listen here, Amma, I hope you have got the sesame oil for the rani's massage. No more cooling coconut oil now that the monsoon is upon us.'

The old woman mutters something back inaudibly which Maatrika decides to interpret as acquiescence of some form. One end of the old woman's dhoti is wrapped haphazardly around her bare breasts and shoulders, modesty abandoned along with youth and beauty. Her hands and wrists remain surprisingly strong, though, and Kokila Devi has retained her services as her personal masseuse despite the vagaries and ill-humour of old age.

'Hé child! What are you doing here?' Maatrika has almost fallen over a young woman sitting on her haunches on the steps of the outer courtyard. She is holding her head in her arms and doesn't look up when Maatrika questions her.

'Is that you, Sushila? What are you doing loitering here watching the rain fall, when there is so much work to be done. Go inside at once!'

But Sushila averts her face and pushes Maatrika's hand from her shoulder.

'I am afraid to go in, Mataji, I don't want to bring bad luck to the rani's house today. A braying donkey crossed my path this morning when I was on my way to the palace.'

'Hai! A braying donkey! An evil omen indeed,' Maatrika is horrified and draws back, fumbling for her rudraksha beads. 'Why have you come here at all? You should have turned around and gone back home right away, girl. Go home now, at once.'

'Why the commotion, Mataji? Why are you sending poor Sushila home in this rain?'

Draupadi is standing by the steps of the courtyard, smiling down at Sushila. Her hair is more elaborately done up than when she was a child, with many tiny braids woven into two gleaming, undulating plaits.

'And where have you been, Rajkumari, so early in the morning? Eavesdropping on your brothers' lessons, no doubt? Your brain will get soft and friable at this rate, women are not supposed to learn things like battle formations and chopping people's heads off.'

'Mataji, warfare is only a part of what they learn. Today, it was astronomy. The planets and the stars in the sky, and how they affect our lives.'

Draupadi adds this last bit quickly as Maatrika is glaring uncomprehendingly at her.

'And the pundit made no mention of braying donkeys at all. In fact, he said that this was a good time for our clan and that Father will return victorious very soon from his campaign.'

Sushila giggles despite herself, still huddled on the steps but Maatrika is enraged.

'That's right, you just make fun of me, Rajkumari. Don't come crying at the end of the day when nothing but bad luck befalls us all. And, as for your father's campaign, it doesn't take a pundit to predict this victory. The heralds arrived this morning bearing the good news that your father's army returns tomorrow.'

Draupadi steps up to the older woman and gives her a quick hug. Maatrika still towers over Draupadi, though the princess has almost reached her full height.

'That's wonderful news indeed, Mataji. Drishtoo will be returning too, then, along with Father. I am sure he will have fought bravely.'

King Drupad's latest campaign was more a tour of the territories of the Panchalas than an outright battle. There were ambitious warlords to appease, dutiful vassals to compensate and bristly chieftains to intimidate. This was, therefore, not a very dangerous mission yet there was always the possibility of a wound that wouldn't heal or a flux or contagion of some sort. Meanwhile, in the king's absence, Kokila Devi has been immaculately conscientious in maintaining the sacrificial fire with oblations morning and evening.

'Let Sushila come with me, Mataji. We will not go to the inner quarters but only to the minor reception hall. The gandhika is about to arrive with a lot of new perfumes and I want to choose something before Father returns.'

Draupadi pulls Sushila up by her hand, not really waiting for Maatrika to respond, and the girls hurry away through the corridor. Maatrika, irritated beyond endurance, sits down beside the young women pounding herbs for the rani's ointments and makes them repeat the secret recipes endlessly.

Inside her darkened bedroom, Kokila hears the girls' chanting voices and smiles to herself. Maatrika is putting her apprentices through their paces but she is a fair teacher and, if they please her, she will give them an extra ration of sweetened milk or her own special mango and sesame chutney for their mid-day meal.

The small window in the rani's chamber has been opened to let in the rain-bearing breeze after months of searing desert wind. The rani's caged songbirds and koels are unusually excited, sensing in the gusts of wind and the fierce raindrops a freedom they have lost forever.

Kokila is lying on her bed, wearing an oil-stained dhoti while the old masseuse rubs the warmed sesame oil between her hands and then starts massaging Kokila's soft belly. She knows that it is her assiduous massage which keeps the rani's belly smooth despite the birth of her many children. 'So Shanta Devi, what is the news from the town today?' The old woman lives in the shanty town on the edge of the capital, where the snarl of huts are huddled together and gossip ricochets across the narrow alleys.

The old woman moves to stand behind Kokila and begins to massage her forehead and her temples with her strong thumbs, smoothening out any incipient lines. When she speaks, her voice is broken and hoarse with age.

'The watchers on the towers have seen the dust rising in the distance. The raja returns.'

'Yes, Shanta Devi, the heralds started arriving two days ago.

The raja should be here by tomorrow.'

'The watchers have also seen a palanquin in the king's retinue.'

Kokila is silent for a few moments, then she sits up slowly and faces the old woman.

'What do you mean, Shanta Devi? Why should there be a palanquin in the King's retinue?'

Kokila's honey-gold eyes gaze steadily at the old woman. She wears no jewellery except for a pair of simple gold teardrop-shaped earrings and her beauty is stark.

Shanta Devi's eyes are aqueous and even her lashes are white. It is as if a slow frost has crept over her body. Though it is presumptuous for someone of her station, she is too old to care and so dares to show compassion when addressing her rani.

'A tribute, my rani, from one of the clansmen to the North. It is she who rides in the palanquin.'

The rani presses a palm to her belly, to still a shadow pain, though her expression doesn't alter.

'I see,' she whispers. 'You may go now, Shanti Devi.'

The old woman gathers her oils and cloths and leaves without another word, shutting the door gently behind her.

Outside in the courtyard, the rain has stopped suddenly, and the sun is shining clean and true. The garland-maker has just delivered his big bundle of garlands for the day and they are being carried by servant girls throughout the palace to the ladies of the house. Today the garlands are a mix of blue, white, and pink lotus flowers, spiked with jasmine. The massage women dawdle in the corridors for a while, exchanging gossip with the hairdressers and the bangle seller.

In the women's hall, Draupadi, Sushila, and a group of other women from the palace are siting on low-cushioned divans watching the gandhika lay out his wares on a white cloth on the floor. He lays out fragrant woods, sandalwood and agarwood, and roots like ginger,

Ira Mukhoty

galangal, and spikenard. He also shakes out spices—cardamom, saffron, cinnamon, nutmeg, clove, and pepper and spreads out the lemongrass, ginger-grass, citronella, and basil. A heavy, heady fragrance unfurls out of the boxes and jars, and combines with the smell of the rain on parched earth.

The perfumer is a bland and skinny middle-aged man in a dhoti and turban. His most surprising feature are his ears, which stick out almost perpendicular to his head. He talks continuously, in a soft, persuasive murmur, holding out the different jars and explaining their virtues.

'See here, Rajkumaris, this is a new body oil I have brought this time, a wonderful combination of jasmine, coriander, cardamom, tulsi, pine, saffron, and clove. Soothing and beguiling. And please see this chameli oil for dressing hair. Sesame and jasmine, best quality, you will not find any better oil for the hair.'

He hands out the jars to the women as he speaks, addressing all of them tactfully as 'princess' and keeping his gaze on the side of their faces, to avoid committing the indiscretion of looking straight into their eyes. The women open the jars and the boxes and dab a few drops of the perfumes onto the squares of cloth which they pass to one another, commenting on each fragrance. A couple of servant boys bring leaf cups filled with cold water spiked with mango blossoms and plates of thinly sliced red guavas.

'And, see here, ladies, these wonderful new drops to make the breath fragrant like the spring breeze—camphor, saffron, musk, cardamom, and cloves, all mixed together with mango juice. Delicious, and useful too. And also new, these wonderful sticks which can be used in rooms for fumigation. Smell, please, Rajkumaris, saffron, jamun, sandalwood, pine resin, and camphor, blended with honey. Burn them in the rooms and watch the insects disappear like magic.'

Sushila is sitting on her haunches on the floor, next to the gandhika. She picks up the sticks of insect repellent and shows them to Draupadi.

'These are good, Rajkumari, I think your mother will find them useful. So many insects during the monsoon.'

'Yes, Sushila, take them. Let us get some more boxes of laksha as well. And I like this lotus fragrance very much. I will ask Mother if I can have it. She should have been here by now.'

Just as Draupadi looks up from the boxes and jars, she sees her mother step in from the courtyard into the hall. Kokila is simply dressed, in a white dhoti and breastband and her hair is tied up in an austere bun. She wears no jewellery apart from her gold earrings. This is how it has been during the entire period of Raja Drupad's absence, a mock widowhood, a paring down of all adornments. Draupadi knows that this withdrawal from the world of coquetry and sensuality is quite normal for a woman whose husband has left the home on a long absence. Yet there is an exposed and ravaged quality to her mother that Draupadi hadn't noticed before.

She gets up quickly, with the pots and jars that she has selected, and goes to stand beside her mother. The two women are now of the same height, rather smaller than the average. They both have slim wrists, small feet, elegant necks, and sudden curves. The perfume-seller sweeps sidelong looks at the women, darting and covert, as it would not do to be caught staring at the rani of Panchala and her beautiful daughter. Whereas the rani has the complexion of a honeycomb glinting in the sun, her daughter's dark skin, like the shade of the gulmohar tree, catches the light in disturbing, warm ways. The white of Draupadi's dhoti is more startling, her golden waistband more flushed against her starless, night-sky skin. The perfume-seller looks away quickly, clearing his throat and displacing his boxes aimlessly. The other women, gathering their purchases, seem insubstantial in comparison. The stories about the startling beauty of the rajkumari of Panchala were not exaggerated.

Kokila has approved of her daughter's selection but there is something more important that she wants to discuss with her.

'Beti, you are old enough now, I have a task for you. I want you to oversee all the arrangements for your father's homecoming. You know all you have to do, don't you? The homecoming puja, the food preparations, bedding for all the returning soldiers, the counting and distribution of all the tribute.'

Draupadi is startled, but very pleased. She has never been asked to do this before though she has helped Kokila on numerous occasions.

'Maatrika Devi will help you, child, and, of course, the chief cook has begun preparations a week ago, the minute the first herald arrived. I am not feeling very well, I will remain in my room today.'

Draupadi is now too excited to remember to ask the rani about the fugitive sadness she saw in her eyes.

'I will not let you down, Ma, please return to your room and rest.'

The rest of the day passes by in a flash while Draupadi and Sushila check on all the arrangements for the raja and his retinue. They instruct the family priest about the homecoming puja to be performed at the palace gates, before the king and his sons enter the palace. Draupadi gives him leave to order the milk, cake, ghee, and butter he may need for the oblations.

They go to the kitchen courtyard where the head cook is tormenting his assistants in the rising heat. Hunters, poachers, and fishermen have returned with fowl, partridge, deer, and fish. Bleating goats, unaware of their fate, spend their last day tethered in the steaming courtyard. The cook is checking each sauce for taste and consistency, and is quick today to dispense sharp slaps and twist ears when faults are found.

The girls also make sure there is enough rush grass for bedding, give instructions for the temporary housing of transiting soldiers on the outskirts of the town, mobilize the animal doctors for the treatment and care of the returning horses, cattle, and elephants.

It is late at night, and the monsoon clouds are gathering again, by the time Draupadi falls asleep and dreams of war elephants, chanting priests, and her bleeding brothers.

The raja arrives at last, under an iridescent dawn, the air charged with moisture and colours. He stands with his sons at the threshold of the palace as the chief priest offers thanks to the merciful gods.

Draupadi is standing with a cortege of women, holding the garlands delivered before dawn. She has especially asked for her favourite lotus and jasmine garlands in addition to the marigold ones. She looks out at the throngs of city-dwellers, early risers who have come to exult in their conquering raja. She tries to squint past the rising camphor smoke from the sacred fire to catch a glimpse of her beloved twin brother. She thinks she sees him, sun-burnished almost to her night-sky complexion, thinner and taller, more sombre too. Draupadi is distracted by a pulse of colour right at the end of the retinue. A scintillation of reds, ochres, and gold amongst the bronzed, beaten bodies of the soldiers. It is a small, huddled group of women in strangely tied clothes, their lower garments wrapped like long skirts rather than twisted into the dhoti shape of Panchala. In the midst of them is a figure in a fine gauze veil and Draupadi realizes that she is staring into the face of a young girl with frightened brown eyes. She turns around to point her out to Sushila but at that moment the priest finishes his blessing with a final sprinkling of water on the men and Draupadi is swept up in the forward tumult of the women.

It is late evening by the time Draupadi realizes she hasn't seen Kokila all day. The men have been welcomed and feted. They have washed away the red clay that stained their feet and feasted on roast pheasant, braised fish, and fried meat. The tribute has been collected and counted in the ceremonial hall. Glass beads, fine bolts of cotton, sacks of fragrant rice, a few clinking gemstones. The clans have given what they could, or what they thought they might get away with. Musicians and entertainers have filled the palace with swirling sound again after two months of a tomb-like containment.

Now the last of the revellers have stumbled off to sleep, Draupadi decides to report back to her mother, who must be very ill indeed not to have attended to the travellers at all. As she rushes through the darkened courtyards, in which tiny clay lamps flicker snugly in alcoves in the rain-bearing breeze, Draupadi feels a wisp of panic begin to build in her. The peepul tree is swaying wildly and lightning flashes on the distant horizon. Draupadi navigates her way through the puddles in the courtyard and through the corridors, where the oil lamps cast monstrous shadows.

When she reaches the corridor leading to the Rani's bedchamber, Draupadi slows down to catch her breath. As she rearranges her upper garment carefully around her shoulders, she hears a disorienting, feral sound.

Draupadi walks silently up to the small window and looks through the wooden slats of the screen placed against the opening. At first she cannot make sense of what she is seeing and thinks that perhaps her mother is laughing. The sounds she hears are coming from her but it is not laughter. Kokila is lying face down upon the white cover of her bed and her long black hair is completely undone. Draupadi gasps when she sees her mother's hair like this. Never once in her entire life has she seen the rani with her hair in this kind of disarray and she is filled with a smouldering shame for her mother. Once in a while Kokila lifts her head from the bed, her face a shadow mask, and howls, tearing at her soft hair with her hands. Jewellery lies in violent heaps on the floor, armbands, bracelets, waistbands, and necklaces of gold. Raja Drupad stands a few paces away from his wife and from the way his shoulders are hunched and his arms limp at his sides, Draupadi senses his baffled dismay. He takes a step towards the rani and then steps back again, as if approaching a poisonous snake.

'Take this also,' Kokila hisses, hurling a last slim bangle at the raja. 'Give this to your whore as well, since I am cast aside I have no need for ornaments. Give them all to her, the new young rani of Panchala.'

'Rani, calm yourself, I beg you. I had no choice. To refuse the child would have been an act of war. This is only a matter of keeping the peace, nothing else.'

But Kokila has lifted her head to the monsoon clouds and is howling her rage again. Draupadi cannot bear to look at her mother like this any more. She is a monstrosity, a desecration of the mother she knows, a primal being torn screaming from the maws of hell itself. She turns away from the wooden screen and runs back through the gathering storm to her own quarters.

For the next few days, Draupadi stays away from her mother. She feels a smear of shame at the thought of looking at her mother in the clean and washed sunlight of these rain-filled days. The palace is bustling with jobs to be done now that the army has returned and Raja Drupad is kept busy meeting with his local council. Draupadi seeks out the company of her brothers, grown suddenly into men after their crusade, with their soft moustaches and sudden, reticent silences. She tries to find out more about the strange girl with the frightened eyes but no one will say anything directly to her though the palace hums with rumours and whispers.

Finally, on the third day, after a night of incessant, wearying rain, when the red ants form soldierly lines through the corridors, abandoning their waterlogged, underground homes, Kokila reappears in the women's hall. The goldsmith has come to visit the palace women, bringing his clinking store of rubies, cat's eyes, sapphires, corals, and crystals.

The rani is wearing her favourite necklace of pearl and lapis, a thick gold waistband, and diamond pins in her elaborately coiffed hair. Her delicate feet are stained with red laksha paste and her golden eyes are thickly outlined with kajal. Her face is smooth and unlined and her white-and-red fine cotton dhoti rustles softly as she walks. Draupadi looks at her mother from behind a pillar in the hall and is awed at her transformation.

'Rajkumari, come along quickly, I want to show you something,' Sushila tugs gently at Draupadi's upper garment and leads her up the narrow, dark staircase to the second-floor ramparts. Sushila points to a small gathering at the back of the palace walls, towards the exit used by the servants and the labourers. Draupadi can see a small palanquin swaying as it is led away, followed by the group of long-skirted women she had seen on the day of the king's return. Under the looming black clouds of a foreign land, the girl with the frightened eyes is being taken away, into the countryside filled overnight with grasses and rushes and throbbing with flying insects. Draupadi knows she is being taken to the quarters where the illegitimate, the dispossessed, and the forgotten members of the family are housed. Close enough, so no disrespect can be claimed by visiting clan heads, but cast out nonetheless.

'Come on down, Rajkumari, what in the name of heaven are you doing up here?'

Maatrika Devi, with her unerring instinct for tracking down Draupadi, is standing on the ramparts and holding her side while she catches her rasping breath.

'Your mother requires you in the hall at once, she is choosing the jewellery for your swayamvar.'

II

Twin Rivers

Myth and Magic

~

Poised on the threshold of Draupadi's swayamvar, it may appear that the scene is set and the die cast for the inevitable unfurling of the banners of war that were to figure so prominently in Draupadi's life. But it is farther back in time, half a century or more, that the first small subterranean tectonic shifts occurred. Each action seemingly insignificant at the time and yet leading with a shearing and grinding movement to the cataclysmic events that were to take place.

And so it was that, somewhere in the dense forests of northern Bharat, west of the territories of Panchala, on the outskirts of the Kuru capital of Hastinapur, a rustling and a crackling were heard in the leaves of the peepul and kachnar trees. A ripple and a crepitation within the warp and weft of the very air itself, followed swiftly by a muffled bump and a subdued intake of breath as a beautiful, young girl fell, glowing and flailing from heaven, through the air and onto the soft, alluvial humus of the Gangetic soil.

Or perhaps not. Perhaps a baby girl was born to one of the tribal communities that lived on the margins of the forest and of civilized society. A community of hunter-gatherers and subsistence farmers who dressed in animal skins and wove red hibiscus flowers into their hair. Who lived away from the tyranny of the fire altar and worshipped instead the rich red earth and the warm summer rain. Into this society the girl was born, abandoned perhaps by an unwed mother or orphaned by a flash flood. And because she was born under a full moon near the river, and because her complexion was the golden burnished colour of ripe wheat, they named her Ganga. She grew up tall and strong and beautiful.

A Ganges River Dolphin

~

Under the clean and clear sky of a spring day, the young Raja
Shantanu is getting his horse-drawn chariot ready in the main
courtyard of Hastinapur palace. His grooms are bustling around,
harnessing the king's favourite chestnut horse to a light two-
wheeled wooden chariot. The king's armourer rushes up with a
quiver of iron-tipped arrows which the king fastens around his
torso with a leather thong. A young boy, a cousin, stands quietly to
the side, holding Shantanu's wooden bow.

'Shall I come with you, Bhai? I can ride fast too.' The boy is
smooth-skinned and eager but the raja smiles at him and shakes
his head.

'Another time, Kartik. You look after the training of the new
horses, I am counting on you.'

With a quick tousle of the boy's hair, the raja takes his bow
and leaps easily onto the chariot. His long hair is tied in a low
knot and he wears gold studs in his ears. He snaps the reins and
leans backwards, balancing on the heels of his feet as the horse
leaps forward in a single fluid motion, a silken, russet thing of
beauty and grace.

The grooms watch the raja's chariot till it is a crackle of dust
on the horizon, at the edge of the fields and villages where the
unknowable shadow of the forest begins. They know he will not
return before the end of day, perhaps not even for a few days. There

are rumours in the town that the raja of Hastinapur is trying to outrun his fate, his destiny even, and the old men in the town shake their heads disapprovingly as they throw the first clinking dice of the day.

'Well, now,' the old men susurrate, their gums barren and red-stained. 'He is not like his brother Devapi. Now there was a real raja.'

The old men have wrapped coarse cotton shawls around their wasted shoulders and their turbans are twisted in voluminous folds around their heads and ears. In this early spring morning, they must guard against the devious ghouls that flutter by in the wispy wind, ready to crush a man's chest with their icy fingers.

'A wise and kind man, that Raja Devapi. But these muttering priests must have their way, with their endless chanting and doomsday predictions.' Pulling his turban further down on his head, the old man who has just spoken spits a crimson jet of betel juice onto the dusty ground, to further emphasize his disdain for the priests.

In the distance, Shantanu feels the oppressive weight lift off him the further he draws away from Hastinapur palace. The drumming of his horse's hooves is an intoxicating heartbeat, a meditation that helps him forget his endless duties and responsibilities as raja of Hastinapur, greatest and oldest of the mahanagars of northern Bharat.

It stills befuddles him to realize he is raja. The youngest of three sons, born late to his parents, his was to have been an effervescent destiny full of gambling and hunting and fighting. Kingship, with its rigours and expectations, was for his older brothers. And so it was for a long time, while his beloved brother Devapi was yuvraj. Shantanu adored his elder brother, who was more like a youthful father to him than a brother. While Shantanu tumbled and played with his cousins in the palace gardens, Devapi was already a young man, tall with steady eyes and an easy manner that made him accessible to all. He was a solace to the old raja and rani, who were content, at last, to hand over the increasing responsibility of leadership to Devapi.

Which was why, when Devapi first experienced his symptoms, he kept them to himself, not wanting to believe that anything could come in the way of his golden destiny. By the time the first scars appeared, on his face and hands, it was too late for the family physician to try any treatment, however ineffective. Devapi's father, the raja, was fierce in his refusal to accept the verdict of the appalling kustha, the eating-away disease.

'There has never been any kustha in this house,' he railed, while his advisers stood by, bewildered. 'Cure my son, I beg of you,' he implored the physicians, the healers, and even, it was whispered, the dabblers in black magic.

But there was no cure for kustha, that great defiler of a disease, and its progress was implacable as the scars thickened over Devapi's handsome face and the tingling in his fingers became a constant misery.

Finally, one winter's day, a huddle of priests arrived at the palace gates and their ruling was trenchant and heartbreaking.

'Devapi cannot be raja.'

And despite the raja's howling grief and rage, the priests declared Devapi unfit, the disease a mark of some ineffaceable sin. The young yuvraj laid down his golden crown and walked into the forest, preferring banishment forever to a slow descent into decrepitude in front of the pitying and fearful eyes of his subjects.

Bahlika, the second of the raja's sons, had long ago dedicated himself to defeating a distant rival and had disappeared from the kingdom for several years. This was how the raja's baleful stare now fell upon Shantanu. The young rajkumar was dragged in an instant from the happy anonymity of youngest son to the constant appraisal of yuvraj. His resentment was seething but silent, the ancient line of the Kurus depending on him and so he began a lifelong habit of escaping every few weeks the cloistered and dusty confines of the palace for the empty and unknown forests and plains around Hastinapur.

Now, as Shantanu rides out of the palace, he is surprised, as always, at how rapidly the palace, Hastinapur itself, and the small cluster of mud-hut villages at its edges disappear, replaced by the grazing grounds and the few fields around the township which are cultivated. Very soon the fields give way to unchecked scrub, babool trees, marshlands, and then the jungle. The ground is dusty and stony and even the forest looks parched after the sharp, dry winter. Shantanu rides on till he is past the small bit of the forest which is reserved for the raja's pleasure, his personal hunting grounds, and stops only when he reaches the teal and uncharted forest.

Shantanu jumps off his chariot and tethers his horse to a tree before walking down a thorny path under the low branches. In the sudden silence he hears a plaintive bird cry and looks up to see an eagle swooping effortlessly on the rising thermals. His footsteps crackle and snap on dead leaves and now he can see that the forest is not dried up at all. Everywhere there are signs of the wanton spring—in the tiny, curled, sap-green leaves and each gust of breeze that sloughs off the last remaining dead leaves onto the dusty earth.

Shantanu can't help but remember that it was in just such a forest that he saw Devapi for the last time. For after Shantanu was crowned king, there was a period of many years in which the rains failed and the crops dried up. A terrible, mystifying time of anxious waiting and growing suspicion. For as the months became years, and then a decade, and as the earth grew parched and cracked and the cattle lay down and died under the relentless sun, whispers reached the palace of a curse on the land. A curse that the capricious gods had brought about because Shantanu had been crowned raja instead of Devapi. Worn down and harried, his eyes hurting from scanning

Ira Mukhoty

the skies every day, Shantanu gave in to the advice of his priests and sought out his reclusive brother to obtain his help in pacifying the gods. Shantanu knows he will never forget the sight of his brother in the forest till his dying day. His cascading terror and pity when he saw the blistered face of his beloved brother, the stumps that were now his fingers, the living desecration that was Devapi. He was living in a cave, like an animal, but the dark brown eyes were still steady in the livid face. Devapi agreed to help his brother. Shantanu had the holy fire brought to the forest from Hastinapur, and the brothers performed the fire rituals for days. It did rain that year, hot, splattering drops that made the old men and the young girls walk out into the night and stand under the racing clouds. Shantanu returned to Hastinapur and never saw his brother again.

He walks now for a long while in the forest before finally coming out into the open sky and tall bulrushes at the banks of a river. The sun is low on the horizon and it is suddenly much cooler, a reminder that winter has not been gone long from the northern plains.

He walks along a bend in the river and realizes that there is a group of young women in the distance, collecting water from the river in earthen pots. Shantanu slows down and edges behind a tree where he remains unseen. The girls are shouting out to each other as they fill their pots with water and bind up bundles of kindling with twine. One of the girls is sitting on her haunches, sifting through a basket of wild jujube berries. They are dark-skinned and strong, stepping lightly through the gorse on their bare feet. They wear short wraps of antelope skin and spiky yellow jasmine in their hair. One of the girls laughs, her glossy head angled back, the soft camber of her dark neck exposed and tender. Shantanu is mesmerized. These girls are unlike any women he has seen in the palace, who are furtive with their smiles, soft and languid in their limbs.

There is one young woman who stands slightly apart from the

group. She has walked into the river till the water reaches her thighs and stands there quietly while the roosting birds sweep and dive all around her. She holds out an earthen pot and lets it skim the surface of the river, where it creates small eddies and swirls in the rushing water. She finally fills the pot with water and turns around to walk back to shore. In the slanting rays of the evening sun her complexion is cinnamon, with a terracotta sheen to her dark skin so that she seems to be ablaze. Shantanu sees her and is undone by the curve of her hip, against which she rests her pot of water.

He steps forward towards the group of girls till he is standing in front of them. They have stopped talking amongst themselves and are standing quietly in guarded, watchful appraisal. They see his fine-spun cotton clothes, his burnished gold waistband, the leather thongs on his feet and they know him to be an outsider, a plainsman, unfamiliar with this secret forest.

'Take me to your tribe headman,' Shantanu tells the women simply. 'I wish to marry this girl.' A tiny gesture towards the russet-skinned girl.

At this, there is a slight shuffling and shifting amongst the girls and one of them steps forward. She is smaller than the others but wide-hipped with slanting slate eyes.

'That's our Ganga you want to marry. She is our lucky charm, you know, some say she is the spirit of this river.' The girl's eyes are full of mischief, and something else too, a guileless mocking.

Shantanu shrugs, and the girls gather their pots, their kindling and their baskets of scavenged fruit and set off rapidly on soundless feet through invisible paths in the forest. Shantanu stumbles as he tries to follow them, his leather thongs chafing and bucking against the stony ground. In the gloaming, the twisted branches of the thorny trees reach for him like spiteful friends. It is almost dark by the time he is standing in front of the tribe headman, who still has his spear in his hand after a day spent hunting in the forest.

Shantanu has never been so deep in the forest. This is the realm of witchery and unknowable terrors. He looks into the fierce, proud eyes of the chieftain and reiterates his wish.

'Ganga is a child of the village. She has no parents but, in a way, we are all her guardians.'

Wordlessly, Shantanu takes off his golden waistband and hands it over to the chief who looks down at the smelted weight of it in bemusement. He would have preferred cattle as dowry, or perhaps iron-tipped arrows.

'She is a good woman, and knows all the ways of the forest. But she is also somewhat different. Do not come back here later if you are dissatisfied with her.'

And so the deal is struck and Shantanu leaves the forest with Ganga that very night. It is the first time in her life that Ganga has ridden on a chariot, or seen a horse from so close, and she laughs aloud at the thudding hooves and the rapacious wind in her hair. Shantanu holds her against him as he flicks the reins of his foaming horse and smells her earthy, spicy scent, like ginger and tuberose. Under the vast vault of the sky, with its crackling stars and a glossy moon, the future is full of promise.

They get married rapidly, though the people of Hastinapur are not impressed by this bride, who brings neither cattle nor gold nor land. Ganga moves into the women's quarters in the palace and, for a while, it seems like the blight on the palace, the stupor that weighs down the very air itself, might finally lift. The old women of the palace rouse themselves from their torpor to show Ganga the ways of the house of Hastinapur. The younger women gather around the bride to discuss jewellery and the intricate weave of fine-spun clothes. But it is not long before these efforts give way to disappointment, thwarted by Ganga's tribal language, which the older women are quick to dismiss as gibberish. It is foiled also by Ganga herself, and her complete lack of interest in the management of her household and her disinterest in all things worldly. They are disconcerted by the way she has, when they are trying to explain to her the use of ground masoor dal and honey as a face pack, of looking past them into the high blue sky at the spikes of migrating cranes in their mysterious flyways.

After the first few tender months of happiness, Ganga finds herself increasingly sunk in a gloom of isolation and incomprehension. She stumbles over the singsong diphthongs of palace speech and is hurt when the other girls laugh at her, elaborately hiding their smiles behind raised palms. The Vedic rituals, which she must attend to at the fire altar three times a day, terrify her. The ascetic priest glares at her and she fumbles while bringing the freshly drawn milk or the heated ghee.

After a lifetime of walking for miles in the forest, Ganga's loose-limbed, swinging walk is unseemly in the confines of the palace, where she is constantly benighted by doorways and steps. She tries to sit down companionably next to the malakar girls and help them string flowers onto twine, but finds she is not welcome. She is upset by the frigid stare of the caged birds and sets them free, only to have them snatched up by the plundering eagles. She is nauseated by the butter-rich sauces and forages in the storerooms for raw fruit and root vegetables, while the greasy cooks look on in contempt.

Ganga's one solace is a daily trip to the river which flows just outside Hastinapur. Without fail, and in all weather, after the morning ritual of the fire altar, Ganga and her entourage leave the palace and cross the wakening town till they reach the grassy lands by the river. In winter, the fog hangs low over the grasslands and fields, burning the tender ears of wheat. While the other women huddle in sullen silence, heavy cloths wrapped around their heads, Ganga walks into the water unmindful of the cold, and raises her palms to the rising sun. In summer, Ganga swims out to the middle of the river, where the current is strong, and lies on her back while the river holds her like a mother. She watches the kites circling in the sky and can hear, muted, as the water fills her ears, the croaking of countless frogs and the raucous chatter of the parrots in the mulberry trees. She is never lonely in the river, in the languid sub-aquatic company of the slow-swimming turtles and the catfish.

Shantanu, meanwhile, is helpless and dismayed by his wife's deepening unhappiness. Haunted always by a sense of inadequacy, Ganga's sorrow becomes another burden he needs to escape and he resumes his old habit of disappearing for days on hunting expeditions and, it is whispered, to search out the undemanding company of laughing tribal girls.

Eventually, however, there is a change in Ganga. Her easy, striding walk slows down and becomes guarded and close. The sharp angles of her face smoothen out and her gaze no longer swings up towards the sky but becomes watchful and secret. The older women are quick to notice these signs and rush to inform Shantanu of the imminent arrival of a son and heir. For the next few months the palace fizzes with excitement as the entire machinery of the household prepares for the birth of a prince. The menu of the rani is altered, stimulating ingredients are banished, as are overpowering fragrances. Nourishing potions are prepared and auspicious mantras chanted. As her pregnancy advances, the vigilance with which Ganga is watched over makes her breathless. She is repulsed sometimes by the thought of this second beating heart that has taken over her body and her mind, making her thoughts opaque and indistinct, filling her with a searing effervescence, like drinking soma juice.

At last the baby is born, in a rush of pain and blood that devastates Ganga. While the palace jubilates in the arrival of the prince of Hastinapur, Ganga is assaulted by a sorrow so great she is confounded and she tries to speak to the midwives and masseuses who tend to her. Instead they give her warm, restorative drinks and gently massage her swollen belly. When they bring the baby to her, gleaming and smelling of mustard oil, she is revolted by his weathered and puckered skin and his high, thin wail. Obediently, she follows the midwife's instructions and holds him to her swollen breast and cries tears of shame and anger. The midwife misunderstands her tears and removes the baby after a while to allow her to sleep and Ganga gives in to an exhausted sleep so deep it is like death.

A few days later, when the baby is found dead by the rani's side in the clean, rinsed morning light, everyone blames it on the evil prowling spirits who haunt the four corners of the earth, eternally famished for newborn flesh. The palace mourns but the rani is young and healthy, they console each other, there will be more babies.

And there are more babies, several more, wailing and lusty boys but each one dies within a few days. The sympathy and sorrow for the rani is replaced by dull bemusement and finally a truculent suspicion. A sightless soothsayer is brought, and then a gaunt, squalid black magic practitioner. They cast sidelong glances at the rani and sidle up to Shantanu, whispering unspeakable things. Shantanu dismisses them all, he will not have them call his wife a witch, but he goes instead to speak to Ganga.

Ganga is sitting on a low cot which has been placed in the courtyard in the dull, splintery shade of a gulmohar tree. She has a plate of crispy sesame and honey balls, which she crumbles and throws to the clamour of pigeons flapping their wings in impatience in the gathering heat. They rush in with noisy self-importance while the smaller birds, the sparrows, the babblers, and the black-crested bulbuls, wait in the branches of the gulmohar tree.

She looks away and will not answer when Shantanu questions her, sitting on the edge of the cot, a supplicant. Instead she nibbles at a sesame ball and smiles at the small monkey who is tied to the leg of her cot and who is standing on his hind legs chattering earnestly at her.

Ira Mukhoty

Shantanu holds his head in his hands an instant and then gets up. He is amazed at the way Ganga has now adopted the sedentary life of the palace princesses. Her languor has slid into indolence and her quiet reserve into apathy and a sullen inertia. But he has seen the telltale swelling of her ankles and the lassitude in her limbs and he will watch over this pregnancy like a hawk.

When the time comes for Ganga's confinement, he moves into her quarters, to the shocked disbelief of the midwives but the ghosts of the dead princes linger in the dark passageways and no one dares to protest too loudly.

When the baby is born, swiftly and with little fuss, the raja is the first to see him, after the midwives have cleaned him and rapidly checked him for any signs of malevolence. Shantanu carries his son carefully over to the window. A crackle of lightning in the distance, the earthy smell of approaching rain. The baby is tiny, his head fitting entirely in his father's palm. His skin is the same ochre colour as his mother's. He opens his opaque, old-man eyes and yawns toothlessly at the sight of his father.

Shantanu maintains a relentless, ferocious vigil. He will not allow this child to follow his brothers into the endless silence. At night, he stays awake, listening to the crashing rain and the sudden, panicked crying of the baby waking up hungry. He stands over as the child is massaged with mustard oil, the nurse using just the tips of her fingers to plump up his tiny, gesticulating limbs and rub his swollen belly.

Several weeks pass by and Shantanu is scoured and raked by his sleepless watch. His eyes burn constantly and he feels a choking delirium overcome him. He knows he will not last much longer without proper sleep but he needs to wait just a little while yet before he can wean the child away from his mother.

One early morning, he gasps awake to the dull, staccato sound of a door banging somewhere in the palace. The strong monsoon wind brings with it the salty smell of the faraway ocean. The light spilling in from the tiny window is saturated and crimson and Shantanu notices immediately his missing wife and child. He rushes out into the courtyard wearing only his crumpled dhoti, the wind whipping at his bare skin. He follows, by some feral instinct, an invisible trail and runs out of the palace, stepping over sleeping maids and somnolent guards. He slips along the wet, muddy path leading to the edge of the town, down to the marshy land by the river. The brittle red clay of the river delta is dark and glossy and sodden with rain now. The river itself, the Ganga, has been transformed by the monsoon into a roiling, thundering menace. The water foams and seethes, threatening to flood its banks and disgorge its rich, alluvial sediment.

Shantanu sees a figure hunched on the grey slippery rocks by the edge of the river. He calls out to his wife and she turns around, perplexed, holding a small bundle just below the surface of the water.

'Ganga, stop! Please, give me the baby,' Shantanu stumbles up to the edge of the river, his voice husky with dismay. Ganga gets up slowly, holding the baby, who is spluttering and coughing, his wail strangled by the loamy river water. He is slick and brown and glistening, like the Ganges river dolphins that swim in the deep pools that form downstream from where the rivers converge.

'I was only bathing him, Raja, the holy water is good for him, and will make him strong.'

Ganga holds up the baby but her gaze is cold. When Shantanu tries to edge forward, she frowns and steps back, slipping a bit on the wet rocks.

'Just give him to me, please. See, he is cold and shivering, and needs to get back home.'

The rain has started again, oblique ropes of water sluicing down Ganga's face. She looks at the raja slyly and Shantanu realizes he has lost forever his forest bride with the swaying walk and open, limpid face. But as he stands there with his head down, his grief keening hopelessly within his chest, Ganga steps forward suddenly and thrusts the baby into his arms.

'Here, take him then, look after him,' she whispers quickly, before turning back towards the water. Shantanu grabs the baby, stupefied, as Ganga steps swiftly over the wet rocks, the water frothing like churned milk. Whether she jumps or slips, Shantanu will never know, but suddenly she is in the water, limbs flailing and mouth filling at once with the brackish water.

Shantanu screams his wife's name into the lashing wind but the river seethes and bubbles and the churning current carries away Ganga's body in an instant. Shantanu runs along the river's edge, clutching the baby against his shoulder. He searches desperately for the small brown shape, twisting and twirling like a macabre puppet. But the river is grown huge and monstrous, like the ocean, like a many-limbed goddess, and soon the dancing brown shape disappears. Shantanu stands for a long time by the river, watching the heartless river and then turns slowly back towards the palace.

For Shantanu from this day on his infant son will be the quiet anchor in the maelstrom of his life. He calls for a legion of nurses, teachers, priests, theologians, and warriors to look after and instruct the prince. He is tonsured, anointed, and given the name Devavrata. Later in his life he acquires a different name, a more terrible one, but for now he is the blessed one, the cherished and the resurrected one.

Devavrata grows up strong and tall. He has his mother's bronze skin and the angles and shadows of her face but his father's high stature and broad brow. He is taught the Vedas by wandering mystics and the martial arts by craggy, weather-beaten archers. He is taught political science by frugal teachers with fraying dhotis and lustrous voices. He is prepared in every way to step into his destiny as yuvraj of Hastinapur, inheritor of the ancient line of the Kurus. But there is one nameless area of his life that remains unknown and full of wraiths. It is the hinterland of his heart, the tiny, unmanned back door through which fear and hatred will crawl through. For when Devavrata, from a tiny boy, enquires about his mother, Shantanu falters in his vigilance and strays from the incorruptible path.

'She was very beautiful,' he says, which was true.

'She loved you very much,' he adds, which he is not really sure about and which no one will ever know.

'She was a divine being, a celestial nymph sent to earth for a short time,' he says. 'She was the goddess Ganga herself, the spirit of the river, now returned to heaven to fulfil a higher destiny,' he adds, to which the maids and aunts concur with eager, bright faces. For no one is keen to expose the tender prince to the truth—the rustic, foraging background and the unspeakable infanticides.

So Devavrata absorbs the lies and the half-truths and they sink to the bottom of his soul, where they fester and foment for a long time and, slowly, one insidious step at a time, infect every fibre of his being till finally his every adult action is tainted by the original sorrow and rage of his mother's rejection.

The Fisherman's Daughter

~

In the pale, faltering dawn of a spring day, the birds of the twin river basin are abandoning the marshlands of the Yamuna as if sensing a cataclysmic end approaching. In a great blaze of strumming feathers and beating hearts, the huge flocks of fawn and teal geese and mallard ducks leave the grassy marshlands and the sal and rosewood forests in swirling and weaving synchronicity. They will disappear completely over the course of a few days, alerted by the gently lengthening daylight, scattering seedpods and feathers. Like seasoned mariners, they will decipher the topography of the earth, the mountains, and valleys and estuaries. At night, they navigate by the light of the low-slung moon and the scattering stars. They are abandoning the north Bharat plain to its rising heat in search of their ancient summer grounds. But to the people of the plains, they are the spirit and memory of long-vanished ancestors. Every year, they arrive like a miracle, to bring their blessings to their toiling, earth-bound kin and then return to more celestial pastures.

The fishermen and the hunters watch the birds fly away with raised palms, praying for their safe return. They make offerings of flowers, wheat, berries, and grain, bound up in leaves, and float them gently on the glassy river, in praise and thanks.

The birds skim the surface of the river one last time, flapping wingtips a breath away from the dark green water. In the swirling, muddy depths of the river, the long-snouted gharial swims slowly, waiting for the heat of the day to spark his dormant, reptilian speed. For now, he has to content himself with watching the silver carp and the sweet-fleshed mullet, his alien, ochre-yellow eyes glinting through the settling mud.

The native birds remain, the rotund partridges, the flashy peacocks, and the emerald parakeets. The smaller warblers and sparrows peck at the seeds of the spear grass and perch, swaying, on the soft white plumes of the kans grass, tiny funambulists.

The mist, which gathers on the river and surges and swirls between the blades of the spear grass, blurs the boundaries between the dark water and lightening sky. It is only as the sun burns away the fog that the islands and channels emerge from the river, a complex and nebulous water kingdom.

For the girl rowing the ferry through the narrow inlets and streams, the river is an old friend, familiar and comforting in its meandering geography. The older couple and the adolescent boy that she is ferrying across, however, are speechless with fear. They are sitting on their haunches in the middle of the boat, bundled up in coarse cotton clothes. They cut sidelong glances at the shadowy, unknown shapes skimming through the river and at the sudden fizzing burbles and hisses at the surface.

'Are there any magarmach in this river?' the man whispers.

'Oh no, Baba, not in this river. Only delicious rohu and mahseer. All very tasty, you should take some from our fishermen for your journey,' the girl chatters on cheerily, the lie light, not deeming it necessary to tell the travellers of the children who are killed every year by the monster of the river, the gharial.

'Ma, you must be so excited to see your daughter after so many years,' the girl carries on talking. The older woman smiles despite herself. She is nervously stroking an amulet around her throat and her glass bangles clink softly.

'Yes, I haven't seen her since she got married fifteen years ago and I haven't seen any of my grandchildren. This is the tenth child she is expecting and at last I will be able to help her. We have been saving a very long time for this journey.'

The sun has risen while they have been talking and the mist is almost completely gone. The river is thrumming with life as dragonflies hover and dart over the surface of the water, wings like crushed diamonds. Kingfishers swoop in an iridescence of blue and falcons hover over the banks, searching out the floppy-eared hares. On a rock by the river, a long-necked snakebird is immobile, huge black-feathered wings stretched out languidly to absorb the warming rays.

Finally they reach the riverbank, and the girl's village clustered haphazardly by the edge of the forest. Women are sitting on the sandy banks, repairing straw and hemp baskets. The fishermen are laying out the first catch of the day and tiny, horned shing fish have been spread out to dry on a bed of straw. Naked children, festooned with amulets, play among the baskets of fish.

As the travellers get off the boat, they are struck immediately by the smell, which is like a pulsating, live presence. It is an organic smell, tinged with something corrupt and fetid. It hangs in the air and coats every surface, the smooth, dark skin of the fishermen and their glistening hair, like an invisible, viscous presence.

There is a group of travellers waiting for the ferry, self-absorbed merchants with soft bellies and jewelled turbans but the girl signals to them to wait. She walks up to a group of girls talking animatedly by the edge of the fishermen's village.

'Ey, Satyavati,' one of the girls, white teeth large in a tiny, angular face, calls out to her. 'Madhu here saw a group of hunters when she went foraging in the forest this morning. They were asking for food and we are to take them a meal. Your father says you must come with us.'

Madhu, with her gentle smile and lurching walk, after a

childhood disease spared her life but shortened a leg, turns to Satyavati. 'Baba, what a fright I got! Huge, hulking foreigners with muddy looking skin and long, long hair. Loud voices like crows, I dropped my basket and lost all my berries.'

Madhu has tiny, nimble fingers and gleans berries and plants all year round for her fishing community. Tiny red jujube berries, gleaming black jamun berries, wild plums, and gooseberries. She looks distraught now, without her basket at her hip, her limp more noticeable.

'Don't worry, Madhu, we will find your basket when we go to give them their food. Wait for me, I will be back by midday.' Satyavati turns away from her friends and hurries back to her boat, where the merchants are fussing with bales of cloth balanced on the heads of young boys with limbs like twigs.

By the time Satyavati has completed her round of ferrying, the sun is high in the sky and heat coils like a snake in the shade of the rosewood trees, a premonition of the blazing summer. She goes over to her friends and helps them collect food for the strangers, fish roasted with salt and red peppers and barley flatbreads. Together they set off for the forest, accompanied by two adolescent boys, nominal chaperones.

They walk through the forest a long while, fallen leaves crackling underfoot. One of the girls stops to pick up a sprig of mauve kachnar flowers which she twists into her hair. Eventually they hear voices and stop just before a clearing, all of the girls in a huddle. Satyavati steps forward a little, watchful. In a small clearing between the rosewood trees, a handful of men have set up a makeshift encampment with bamboo posts, matting, and stretched cloth. But what shocks Satyavati is the air of careless carnage all around. The men have been hunting and there are broken partridges, soft-bellied hares, and gallant, fierce wild boar lying in bloody heaps on the ground. Most shocking of all, a beautiful, honey-gold chital deer, white spotted fur like drops of rain, lies dead and bleeding on a structure of rough-hewn wood. Satyavati can see from the gently curving belly that the doe was pregnant and she feels a spike of hatred towards the men who have been so wanton. The doe is still bleeding, dark drops falling onto the loamy soil. The carcasses have been there a while and the men haven't even started dressing the meat so as to preserve it. Mixed into the glutinous smell of blood is something darker, a hint of decay, and Satyavati knows that most of these animals will be left to rot. This inexplicable waste is a perversion. For the people of the forest and the rivers, the jungle is a mother and a goddess and no one is careless with a mother's gifts.

The men in the clearing seem overwrought and are talking too loudly, clapping each other ostentatiously on the back. Their clothes are splattered with mud and blood and they are grimy with sweat. There is another smell mixed into the stench of blood and dirt, something sharp and forbidden. Satyavati notices a jar of some unknown liquid in a large earthenware pot from which the men are drinking in large, thirsty gulps.

Satyavati and her friends step into the clearing and lay the food that they have brought on a clean cloth that they spread on the forest floor. Sun-dried and spicy shing fish, delicate whole trout roasted in banana leaves, roasted yam, barley bread, and salted barley gruel in small pots.

The men whisper to each other as the girls unpack the food. They nudge one another and one of them makes a remark in an aside that has them all laughing loudly and slapping their thighs.

Satyavati steps forward once the food is ready. 'This food has been sent from the fishermen's village, as requested,' she tells them in their language. 'We hope it is to your liking.'

Satyavati has learnt a few phrases of the plainsmen's language from her years spent ferrying people speaking a medley of languages across the Yamuna and the men are visibly amazed.

'You speak our language!' One of the men steps forward, curious and staring as if a pet monkey had suddenly shed its chain and started conversing.

Satyavati nods. 'A little only. Please let me know if you need more food for tonight or tomorrow.'

The man looks at Satyavati as she speaks. His thick, long hair grows low on his forehead and under his dark, straight brows, his eyes are tawny and avid, a rapacious golden eagle. The man takes out a few small coins from a cloth bundle and hands them to Satyavati. Another man whispers something to him and he smiles and takes out another coin.

'And please accept this for the pleasure of your company. Our raja asks that you stay back with us awhile.'

Satyavati's gaze snaps up and she notices for the first time a man sitting slightly apart in the shade of a flowering lilac kachnar tree. He is sitting on a makeshift seat of logs covered with a clean red cloth and the chequered shade of the butterfly leaves cast coin-shaped shadows on him. He sits upright and there is an air of quick vitality about him but Satyavati now notices the silver in his long hair. Something dissolute also about the soft girth around his waist and the appraising evaluation of his stare, like the fishermen gauging the catch on their lines.

Satyavati steps back quickly into the safety of her friends.

'We will bring more food tomorrow,' she tells them and the group of girls disappears into the forest on nimble feet that step easily between the stones and the gorse.

The next morning at dawn, when Satyavati arrives at her boat, she is not very surprised to see the group of strangers standing there, waiting for her.

'I want to go on a tour of this river.'

The raja steps forward and hands her a coin. He is tall, taller than his companions, and he has wrapped a covering of fine white cloth shot through with threads of gold around his shoulders.

Satyavati pushes her boat into the river and as soon as the raja has sat down in it, starts rowing into the deep water with strong, even strokes. At the edge of the river, fishermen in white loincloths and simple twists of cloth on their heads are wading into the water, shadow puppets. Herons and egrets prance in staccato motion on extravagantly long legs, keeping an indifferent, voracious gaze on the fish under the surface.

'You speak our language well, for a fishergirl. It is very rare to find a jungle-girl who can speak so well.'

The casual bigotry of the remark is so expected that Satyavati finds nothing offensive about it.

'I have been ferrying people since I was eight years old. Plainsmen and hill folk as well as forest dwellers. Merchants selling bolts of fine cotton or spices or gems. They speak to me of their travels and their homes, their towns and families. So I learn a little of their language.'

As she speaks, Satyavati slants a quick look at the raja. In the spreading light of the morning, she sees that he is older than she had thought. There is a slackness in the line of his jaw, a smudging of his features around the etched skin of his eyes.

'And for a fishergirl, you are very proud. I made you a fair offer yesterday, did my kinsman not explain that I am raja of a great city?'

'You may be raja in your city, but here this river is my kingdom, and I am rajkumari of all this.'

With a slight, graceful gesture of her eyes, Satyavati includes the world around her, the silver, scalloped scales of the fish, the breeze in the swaying spear grass, the russet-gold of the bee-eaters' feathers, the soft, loamy clay in the sediment of the river.

The raja watches her as she rows, the short white dhoti pulled high on her outstretched thighs and her feet bare as she grasps the floorboard with her toes. She pulls back on the oars with an arcing motion of her back which pushes her bosom up against her breast band. Her dark skin glows from within as if she has swallowed a star and the raja is entranced by the geometry of her collarbones, the fragile bones a scaffolding of triangles and angles.

He reaches out to grab her wrist and his voice is a husky whisper.

'I am not used to being denied by girls like you. But don't worry, I am not a thief, I am willing to pay for what I take.'

Satyavati stops rowing and the boat glides gently between the grassy islands in the middle of the river.

'Be careful, Raja. I told you I am the rajkumari of this river. No one knows the Yamuna like I do. I could leave you on one of these islands with their man-eating gharial and poisonous water-snakes and no one would find you again.'

The raja lets go of her hand, a shadow of uncertainty flickering across his face.

'Very well, then, take me back to shore. I will speak to your father, since you are clearly a foolish girl who doesn't know any better.'

When they get back to shore, the raja gets out of the boat without a backward look and stalks off with his waiting clansmen, sullen and flustered. Satyavati fastens her boat securely and walks towards the village to look for her father.

In the evening, when the strangers return, they are ready. Satyavati's father is waiting for them. He is a small, slight man with an amulet around his neck. He is braiding a length of twine as he waits and he gets up when he sees the Raja approaching with two of his clansmen.

Satyavati is standing just out of sight, leaning back against a gulmohar tree. She can hear the men talking, her father gruff and halting, a solitary man more used to interpreting the chromatic washes of the evening skies or the riff of the brainfever bird.

'I don't think you realize who I am,' the raja is saying. 'I am

Raja Shantanu, of the Kuru kings of Hastinapur.'

'You are welcome to our village, Raja, to our food and our hospitality also. But my daughter is free to do as she chooses.'

'I am willing to make a generous offer, ask what you will. Cattle, gold, slaves. Name your price.'

'I am a poor man, only a fisherman, raja. But I do have my honour, and my daughter is my honour. I cannot agree to what you ask for all the wealth in the world.'

And so it goes on, back and forth, between Raja and fisherman. Shantanu's patience begins to wear thin and he glowers at the fisherman, his face suddenly surly, and takes a step closer to him.

'I have been patient, fisherman, do you realize I could just take what I want instead of wasting my time?'

Shantanu's two kinsmen step up to him at this point and one of them whispers a quick phrase. Shantanu looks around and notices for the first time all the fishermen standing around, apparently aimlessly. They are standing with their fishing spears and hooks, with their vicious-looking sickles and arrow-heads, apparently unconcerned. But there is something in their watchful stillness that is menacing and Shantanu takes a step back.

'So what is it that you want, fisherman? Speak your mind freely.'

'You are a rich man, Raja, marry her. You can easily keep several wives and our honour will be saved.'

Shantanu is taken aback and he turns to consult with his kinsmen. What the fisherman says is true, he can easily consign Satyavati to a dim apartment at the back of the palace, with a title of official concubine. His kinsmen are not pleased, they prefer it if the king restricts his excesses to the forest and jungles, where the laws of society are pliable and opaque. But the raja is adamant, he will have this river girl with her sloe-black, slanting eyes and astonishing fragrance.

'I agree to your proposal, fisherman, I will marry your daughter.

Now ask her to get ready and I will take her back to Hastinapur tonight.'

Satyavati hears this and holds her breath. Will her father remember their pact or will he be swayed by the heft of the king's clinking gold coins and whispering gems? For all his talk of honour, Satyavati knows that her destiny balances on a whim as fragile as a blade of ripening wheat. She sees the women near the river, sitting on their haunches and scaling the fish for the evening meal. Time seems to slow down and she thinks she can see each scalloped scale fly like scattering glass. She subdues with a ferocious will her overwhelming desire to rush out and accept the raja's offer and escape forever the suffocating smell of dead fish.

'There is one more thing, Raja, one last whim my daughter has.'

'Speak, fisherman.'

'My daughter desires that any son born of her should be raja after you.'

Shantanu's kinsmen are so startled that they step forward and hold the king by the arms. Shantanu himself looks dazed and shakes his head in confusion.

'But I already have a son, the Yuvraj Devavrata.'

The fisherman lifts his hands, palms outwards, demonstrating helplessness.

'What can I say, Raja, my daughter is insisting, just a foolish girl's wish I know, but she is my only daughter.'

'Come away, Shantanu, these people are trying to trick you, can't you see?'

Shantanu's kinsmen are furious. They shake him by the arms and lead him, stumbling, back into the jungle.

Satyavati lets out a long breath. Her father has done as she has told him to and now the dice is thrown and she must wait to see if she was won her freedom from the tyranny of the river or lost everything.

Satyavati looks out to the river where the setting sun crinkles molten gold onto the water. If she is strong now, it is because once she was weak. Once, many seasons ago, when she was a very young girl who had bled for the first time in her life. When the fearsome, matted-haired Sadhu Parashar had come to the shores of the Yamuna. He had taken one look at the graceful, lambent-eyed ferry girl and had gruffly ordered away the other passengers. It was a late winter's evening and the cloying fog had cascaded down the river's length. Parashar ordered her to take the boat to one of the islands far from the village. Young as she was, Satyavati saw in the sadhu's frenzied eyes what his intentions were. When she realized that her tears would have no effect, she pleaded with the sadhu.

'Please, wise one, my father will kill me if he finds out. He is an angry man and will not tolerate this slur on his honour.'

But Parashar was quite unmoved and Satyavati stifled her sobs so that no passing riverboat would hear her cries, too late to help. When it was over and Parashar went to the river to bathe, Satyavati had stopped crying. She swore upon her pain and her humiliation that she would never be weak again. That she would crush that part of her that was tender and trusting and would keep only the steel framework of her being. She rearranged her clothes and her hair with trembling hands and walked back slowly to her boat. As she rowed the sadhu to the other bank, there was a single thought that goaded her incessantly like an angry wasp.

'What will I tell my father, and my family? My honour is lost, what will become of me?'

Parashar looked at Satyavati in surprise at this.

'Don't be foolish, child. Everyone has heard of me in these parts. I am feared and respected everywhere I go. If I say that there has been no dishonouring of you then no one will dare to question me.'

He looked at Satyavati more closely.

'I have seen the omens and read the stars. A great and learned soul is to be born soon and I believe he will be born to you. You will hide your pregnancy easily during the winter months and when your time comes, find a reason to come away to this island. I will send for my son and I will raise him to be a powerful sadhu.'

Satyavati rowed silently for a little while, and then could contain herself no longer.

'So, like a thief, you take what you want, and just walk away? And what do I get, nothing? Just the burden of bearing a child, so that you can do what you like with him?'

At this the fierce and irascible Parashar threw back his head and laughed.

'So, you have a tongue on you after all, and a fiery one at that. I am no thief, child, ask for anything you want and I will give it to you. No gold, I am not a rich man, but any mantra or blessing you ask for is yours. As for the child, what do you have to offer him? Neither learning nor wealth, I think. But I can give him knowledge and power and I promise to tell him who his mother is so that you can call on him if ever you should need him when he is a man.'

They reached the bank of the Yamuna and after Parashar got out of the boat, Satyavati stood before him with folded hands.

'Bless me, so that I find a strong and powerful husband. Bless me, so that I am the mother of rajas, never again subject to the random whim of fate.'

With the fog now swirling densely around them, Parashar lifts his hands over the girl's bowed head.

'Remember, what I say will come true and cannot be undone. Be prepared to live with the consequence of what you ask for. May you be a rani amongst women and may your sons be rajas. You are beautiful enough already to beguile any man. But this smell of fish that suffocates your village and all of you village folk may be too much for a raja. I have fragrant herbs from the mountains that you must wash your clothes and hair in every day and you will never smell of fish again.'

So Satyavati rowed back to her village with a bundle of dried herbs and a child in her belly. In time she did as the sadhu had instructed her to and handed her newborn son to two tranquil young acolytes of Parashar who were waiting on the island in the middle of the Yamuna.

Years passed and Satyavati searched the fluid and changing horizon every morning so that when Shantanu's hunting party stumbled into the kachnar forest of the Yamuna river valley, she was waiting for him.

✧

As the short, illusory north Bharat spring spins into summer, Raja Shantanu slips into a despondency so pervasive that his courtiers and clansmen begin whispering of enchantment and sorcery. The heat rises and bleaches the sky, the earth, and the soul of the people of the river valleys. The gentle charm of the madhavilata coils and scatters on the gentle spring breeze. The residents of Hastinapur sprinkle their streets with water in the early mornings, feeble efforts at containing the heat and the dust while in the forest and pleasure gardens of the palace, the red silk cotton tree explodes with colour, ferociously blooming in the rising heat.

Hastinapur is a besieged city, its attempts at checking the heat derisory. Cooling pitchers of water are placed in the palace and hung from beams to evaporate and cool the scorching rooms. Bamboo shades are hung in front of all the windows so the palace remains in perpetual dusk. The songbirds are brought indoors and covered with cloth to spare them the sight of the endless, scoured sky. Amla and bel juice laced with mango blossoms or crushed cumin are carried through the palace corridors all day by young boys with burning eyes.

The one consolation of the endless summer is the mango, which is not so much a fruit as a benediction. The hot desert breeze starts blowing in April, bringing a shearing, grating dust that blows over from the west in great, red, tsunami-like waves, slithering under the doorways and the awnings to fill the mouths of sleeping babies and settle like grit in the water pitchers. But the heady fragrance of the golden, red, and green mangoes is a constant provocation. The servant girls pound the fruit to make chutneys mixed with spices and ginger. They chop it into curries which will be added to meat, pickle it with salt and lemon to make preserves, and slice it into slim, sweating segments to be eaten raw.

All activity ceases by midday, which is no longer a marker for time but a state of being, of suspended animation. Splayed-toed lizards run away from the burning stones into cool, dark crevices and, inside the palace, the women sleep, arms flung over sun-blinded, aching eyes. But even in sleep there is no escape and the heat slips into their dreams and they dream of fires in the barley fields, endless, crackling infernos, and boiling rivers of dead fish. When they wake up they are peevish and disoriented, calling out for sandalwood paste to rub on their burning skin.

The men play aimless games of dice or chess, each move laden with ponderous premonition. They make exhausting attempts to organize evening dances to entertain their raja. Outside, the sun barely moves across the vast swathe of inconsolable sky. Birds drop dead from the trees and old men count their rudraksha beads and dream of rain.

Yuvraj Devavrata, almost a man now, with an achingly soft beard and long brown hair, which he wears loose down his back, is worried about his father. Shantanu pushes away the meal of fried deer meat, rice, and ghee which has been brought in for him, provoking fury and recrimination amongst the palace cooks. Devavrata tells his father of the improvements he made to the palace before the summer, the repairing of the old, crumbling walls and

Ira Mukhoty

the extensions in the main structure. Shantanu listens to his son but doesn't answer, apart from sighing occasionally and calling out irritably for some sugarcane wine. During the evening sabhas, he is petulant with his audience, distracted when listening to complaints about stolen cattle and unpaid debts.

Devavrata has tried to ask his father the reason for his melancholy many times but Shantanu has refused to answer, though often with an ostentatious show of rectitude and waving away his son's anxious concern. One day in June he finally tells Devavrata the reason for his distracted unhappiness. The hunting expedition to the Yamuna forest, the girl with the blue-black skin and laughing eyes, the impossible marriage.

Devavrata listens to him steadily and doesn't show the shock he feels at his father's revelations. This girl his father talks about, a tribal girl from a savage fishing community, the thought that she is to be like a mother to him is abhorrent. The woman she unknowingly seeks to replace is a goddess whose haunting absence will shadow Devavrata all the days of his life.

But Devavrata has been taught by the best munis of the land—spartan men of impeccable ideals and erudition—and he has been taught to be the best of rajas and the best of men. So he steps up to his father, compassion in his eyes, and puts his hand on his shoulder timidly.

'Marry this girl who has stolen your heart, Father. Marry her and bring her here and I will respect her like a mother.'

But Shantanu shakes his head and turns away and will not be induced to speak for a long time. For the truth, he realizes, is much darker and more aberrant. Though the seduction of the dark-skinned river girl is stupefying, he quails at the sacrifice he knows he must ask for. His own weakness and craving fill him with self-loathing but, from the start, he knew that he would succumb.

'She asks for a terrible condition, my son. She asks that any son born to her be raja after me. I cannot bear the thought of denying you kingship, it is your rightful inheritance.'

Devavrata falters at that and turns around to hide his confusion. He opens the door to a hanging birdcage and takes out a small yellow songbird, holding it carefully in the palm of his hand. He can feel the tiny, fluttering heartbeat and the small, spiky talons. He has been brought up to be raja for as long as he can remember, it is all he knows, and cares to know. The certainty of his destiny has anchored him despite the yawning abyss of his mother's absence. He is shocked to realize that his hands are trembling as the ground beneath him slides and his place in the world wavers.

'Do not distress yourself, Father. Her sons can be rajas. I don't want the throne if it is to cost you your heart's desire.'

Shantanu knows it is not yet over and that having repudiated his son, he must now also emasculate him.

'You see, my son, she is not an educated woman like us. She does not understand that our word is our honour. She insists that the only way to ensure you or your sons are not a threat to her offspring is for you to renounce marriage forever.'

Devavrata's grip on the bird tightens spasmodically and he can see the terror in the tiny, opaque eyes. His sorrow and fear drop from him suddenly and are replaced by a rage so crushing it is like the black storms that race over northern Bharat, driven by the hot desert winds of May. He replaces the bird gently in its cage and turns to face his father. Through the cold beam of his anger Devavrata is seeing his father for the first time, the dissolute desire in his eyes and his disintegrating honour. Behind the raja, courtiers and clansmen are standing frozen, appalled at the terrible things the father is asking of his son. One of them, an older clansman with swept-back white hair, steps up and puts his hand on the raja's shoulder. But Shantanu has gone too far now to retract and he shrugs off his uncle's restraining arm. The young prince scrabbles

Ira Mukhoty

around in his heart for a place to lay his rage and he baulks at laying it down at his father's feet. His father and his raja, a sacrosanct thing. So instead, he places that spinning ball of anger beside the fishergirl and there it will radiate its toxic heat and scorch all the women in his life.

'So be it, Father. I vow as I stand here today in front of you, in the palace of my ancestors, that I will never marry.'

There is a collective gasp in the crowd of men at this announcement, of shock and dismay. They rush up to Shantanu to remonstrate, to shake him by the shoulders and rattle the bedevilment out of him. But Shantanu is now in a hurry to be gone from there, to leave behind the polluting smear of shame and dishonour. He rushes away to send his emissaries to the father of the dark-skinned river girl.

Devavrata also stumbles out into the courtyard, lightheaded with sublimated anger. The old clansman goes up to him and takes him in his arms.

'Beta, don't do this to yourself, don't do this to the ancient Kuru race. Your father will get over this senseless infatuation. It is witchery and we will call in a priest to remove the spell that tribal witch has cast.'

But Devavrata pushes his old uncle away gently, folds his hands and bows his head. 'I have given my word, Babaji. The word of a Kshatriya is his life, I cannot take it back. Forgive me.'

The old clansman watches him leave with tears in his eyes while the rest of the courtiers rush about in agitated and aimless confusion.

That night, Devavrata cannot sleep. His wicker bed has been placed on the terraced roof of the palace, under the star-dappled sky. All around him his clansmen toss and turn in the suffocating heat, the air still and choking. Even the rays of the moon scorch his skin and the sky is a mausoleum of dead worlds. Devavrata sees his future stretch out before him, barren and endless. What is to be his place in this world and how will he face his ancestors in the afterlife when he hasn't given them grandsons to walk them into immortality? When he does sleep in short snatches, he dreams of shy, soft-skinned girls and tender baby boys.

He gets up very early, when the dawn is only a premonition on the horizon and quietly walks out of the palace towards the Ganga. He steps into the water which is warm and still, the river dark and narrow before the monsoon rain. Devavrata swims for a long time and the river beguiles and composes him. As he steps out of the river, water running off his long hair in rivulets down his back, he has made up his mind. He turns to salute the rising sun, a sliver of heat at the edge of town. He will tell his father that the promise asked of him is inhuman and counter to dharma. He will tell him that he will be an exemplary son in all ways, for all the days of his life, but that this one thing he cannot do.

As he walks up the baked earth path towards town, he is startled out of his thoughts by a crowd of people lining the dusty road, looking at him with fervid, searching expressions. Devavrata walks up to the people and they all step back to let him pass. He hears them whispering amongst themselves in hushed, awed tones.

'Bheeshma,' they are saying. 'Bheeshma, what a terrible vow he has taken.'

There are ardent young women in the crowd who see the sadness in his eyes and fall into a stupor as he passes them by. Stout merchants with hastily tied turbans, who understand the dense burden of his vow much better than he does, bow down to touch his feet. Desiccated old women, terse and frail, throw freshly gathered jasmine petals on the ground before him.

And so Devavrata walks into Hastinapur and into his future self, reborn yet again from the Ganga and newly baptized as Bheeshma the Terrible, the Solitary, the Renouncer of all Things.

III

The Sisters from Varanasi

In the Kashi Palace

~

In a small, covered veranda in the women's quarters of the palace on the banks of the Ganga on a lustrous early summer's day, the three rajkumaris of the house of Kashi are singing a morning hymn at daybreak.

It is the oldest sister, Amba, who sings the melody while her sisters, Ambika and Ambalika, tap rhythmically on little cymbals and join in the chorus. Amba's voice is strangely full of desolation and heartbreak and, though she sings of the rising sun, it is as though she has a premonition that this is the last day on earth.

By the time she finishes her song, her teacher's eyes, large and kohl-rimmed, are filled with tears. He gets up to bless her, hurriedly wiping his eyes with the ends of his upper garment. Amba bows before him with folded palms, then bends down to touch his feet.

'Guruji, this was our last class. The swayamvar is next week and we will have no more time for our classes. Please give us your blessings and I pray that we have not offended you in any way.'

'Beti, may you bring glory to your husband's house, as you have to your father's. It has been my great privilege to teach you and your sisters. May you be happy in your married life and be blessed with many sons.'

Amba touches her guru's feet one last time and hurries away to her mother's quarters. The two younger girls hurriedly bow before their music teacher and follow their elder sister into the palace.

Amba and the rani are in the narrow, ill-lit corridor that overlooks the men's reception hall. From behind shuttered windows they can observe the movement of the men below while remaining unseen.

There is a controlled clamour in the hall as the men greet each other with self-conscious enthusiasm. The guests for the swayamvar are rajkumars, noblemen, and clan heads from all the major fiefdoms of northern Bharat. They are all on display today and they appraise each other clandestinely, from the lustre of a prince's turban jewels to the casual strength of a courtier's arm clasp. Young servant boys offer sliced fruits and drinks of grape liquor to the men. In the centre of this vortex is Kashiraj himself, host to the princes and father of the brides. A rotund, corpulent man, he looks resplendent today in a dhoti and upper garment of fine dark-blue muslin. His wispy grey hair, usually untrammelled and awry, has been coaxed into a neat bun under a crisp white turban. The hosting of this distinguished and prickly throng is wearying for him. He is more used to the louche company of wandering minstrels, singers, and poets.

The princesses giggle as they watch the men, the exuberance contagious and they feel their hearts beating a little faster. The two younger girls, Ambika and Ambalika, comment furtively on the guests.

'Look, Ambika, wouldn't you like the one whose head is like a drum? You can even continue your music lessons if you marry him.' This about a man who appears to be completely bald beneath his turban and the two girls laugh helplessly, their mirth bubbling between their fingers as they cover their mouths with both palms.

'Hush now, Beti, you will be heard. Have you no shame?' The rani, already frail from the complications of endless pregnancies, has been taxed almost beyond endurance by the organizing of the swayamvar.

'Ma, look, I see the rajkumar of Magadha here already. I think every prince within a hundred kilometres is here, isn't that so?' Amba points out a young man who has just entered the hall with a clutch of clansmen.

'Yes, Beti, they are all here. Your father invited everyone except the clan of the Kurus of Hastinapur. He has heard rumours of the ill-health of that rajkumar. With the older boy already dead, it is said they may be left without any heir soon.'

'Look, Didi, that man standing a bit apart, isn't that Raja Salva?' Ambika's voice is limpid but the look she cuts at her sister is full of mischief. The man she is pointing to is standing next to a pillar, talking to some of the men. He is tall and looks arresting with curling dark hair loose on his shoulders and there is a virile grace in the way he stands with his feet slightly apart, his arm loosely draped around one of the men. There is also a very slight wrinkle of complacency in the weak chin, of benign vanity in the way he occasionally smoothes his thick, black moustache with the back of his hand.

Just then, as if he has sensed the women watching him, Salva looks up at the shuttered enclosure, places his right hand lightly against his heart and bows, the faintest inclination of his head.

Amba quickly steps back from the shutters, scorched, the heat flaring up her face like a burning torch. She has a light, gold-stained complexion and, to her great irritation, she blushes easily.

Ambika and Ambalika are clapping their hands and hopping with excitement, the mannered decorum of brides abandoned in a breath.

'Look, Ma, look. He has signalled to Didi, he knows we are watching!'

'Really, Amba, this is too much. How does this young man have the audacity to behave like this?' The rani is querulous today and has a mind to berate somebody, even her beautiful oldest daughter.

'Ma, you know I have met Raja Salva a number of times at

the musical evenings hosted by Father. Nothing improper has taken place and Father knows of my intention to choose him at the swayamvar.'

'Yes, indeed, your father's musical evenings, where God-knows-what sorts of itinerant mendicants and unsavoury characters are celebrated. Sometimes I think your father is too lenient with you girls, allowing you to interact with all these questionable characters. If the rajas assembled here find out that they are participating in the swayamvar in vain, they will be furious, and will think your father has taken them for fools.'

'Well, Ma, they still have these two shining pearls to compete for.' With the slightest movement of her head, Amba indicates her younger sisters, and conveys a world of derision.

'What are you two doing now, chattering aimlessly like foolish mynahs. Come along and help me finalize your jewellery for the swayamvar.'

Chastened, the girls leave the boisterous posturing of the reception hall and follow their mother through the dark and narrow corridors to the women's quarters.

⏝

The ferocious heat on the day of the swayamvar is a consternation, a premonition on this hot summer day. Without any warning, the balmy spring morning has spiked into an incandescence of light and heat. Despite this, the ancient river city of Varanasi is humming with excitement and anticipation. For weeks now, entertainers, merchants, garland-makers, and labourers have been flowing into the city. The Ganga is full of boats and ships bearing fine cloths, goldsmiths, jewellers, and artisans. The city is blithe and bedecked, coloured pennants and marigold garlands lining all the main streets. In the fenced-off fields, wrestlers, jousters, acrobats, and jugglers entertain the brassy, cheering crowds. The crushed and the dispossessed have assembled, too, waiting patiently for the king's munificence or, occasionally, a rich woman's pity.

In the swayamvar arena, the three princesses are standing on a wooden dais, holding flower garlands. They had woken up before dawn, in preparation for this moment. They have been anointed with oil, and ritually bathed, dressed, and elaborately groomed. Their eyes are lined with kohl, their faces smeared with saffron and decorated with a pattern of delicate white dots. They have prayed before the fire altar of their father's home, before the gentle priest of their childhood, one last time.

Now, they stand before the appraising men, perfectly contained and solitary. Time skids to a halt and they can feel their heart beat in a slow strumming that fills them with ethereal grace. They cannot see the huge, seething mass of men seated in the stands but they see instead the slow, beating wings of a bee. The clink of their gold bangles as their hands tremble is loud in their ears, and the fragrance of the rose and marigold garlands is an overwhelming symphony. The men stare at the women, eyes filled with desire. The women have elaborately coiled hair studded with jewels. They are unattainable and achingly desirable, goddesses waiting to step into their sacred destinies. At last, laboriously, the court herald begins the long and tedious process of announcing each participant, extolling his lineage and clan.

And, so, when the two-horse chariot draws up outside the swayamvar grounds, no one gives it a second glance. A white pennant bearing two green and gold palm trees flutters over the wooden fence. The three sisters do not see the tall, long-haired stranger enter the arena with an easy, confident stride. He is wearing a red dhoti and full armour, a wooden breastplate edged with copper, and is carrying a massive wooden bow. The assembled chieftains notice the stranger only when he is striding up the wooden dais. They think he is a jouster, a performer, rather unexpectedly appearing to entertain them. The sisters see him now, standing before them, with blazing eyes and steel-tipped arrows glinting from his leather quiver. He is a hallucination from their bleakest nightmares, materialized in front of them from the shreds of their collective subconscious. He picks up Ambika and throws her over his shoulder and grabs the wrists of the other two sisters in one hand and drags them out of the swayamvar arena. The girls are screaming now and the men finally get up, startled, as from a trance. They look uncertainly at each other, searching for weapons, but these have all been left in the palace. They stumble, dazed, onto the levelled field. Kashiraj is distraught and uncomprehending, shouting out to the stranger walking off with his daughters.

'Who are you? Who are you?'

By now, the stranger has placed the princesses roughly in his chariot, where they clutch each other, sobbing. He turns back to the assemblage and stands before the foaming crowd.

'I am Devavrata, rajkumar of the Kurus, known in the kingdom as Bheeshma the Terrible. My clan, ancient and prestigious, was not given the honour of an invitation to this swayamvar, so I owe Kashiraj no explanation and his daughters no chivalry. But know this, I take these rajkumaris as brides by force, in front of everyone, as is accepted in the traditions of true Kshatriyas. Anyone wishing to challenge me may do so, I have come prepared for battle.'

Devavrata strings his great bow in one fluid motion and shoots an arrow into the stretched cloth covering the swayamvar hall. The cloth tears apart gently, with a sigh. As Kashiraj and the chieftains search, bewildered, for their weapons through the fluttering ribbons of billowing white cloth, Devavrata jumps back into his chariot in which the princesses are cowering. Scattering flower garlands and water pitchers, the two rust-red horses thunder through the streets of Varanasi. The chariot crosses the town and hurtles through the countryside, with its sparse scrub and creeping forest groves, before the other chieftains have recovered their weapons and mounted their chariots.

In the end, only a handful of chieftains give chase to the swift rust-red horses. The other men make half-hearted attempts to summon their grooms and charioteers and then give up, disconsolate, their impossible quest for the rajkumaris of Kashi ever only a dream.

Devavrata sees the swirl of dust chasing him and turns his chariot around to face the challenging rajas. The horses stop, manes blowing in the wind and hooves drumming gold dust into the air. Devavrata takes aim with his bow and with a few strumming shots hits the wheels of the chasing chariots, sending them all crashing and tumbling onto the red clay.

Devavrata flicks the reins and continues his race towards Hastinapur. He has not gone far from the fallen rajas when he hears a voice cutting through the scouring, pounding wind.

'Stop, stop, you lecherous old man!'

It is Raja Salva and his charioteer, riding a single-horse chariot, built for manoeuvrability and speed. His sparkling, lightning-coloured mare is bubbling and frothing already and will not last long at this speed but, for now, she is the wind, dancing and weaving around Devavrata's heavier, bulkier chariot.

Salva's charioteer, powerful legs flexed to brace himself, whips the horse to a greater fury of speed. 'Take your shot, my raja, you have him in your sights,' teeth bared and whip flying, the charioteer urges Salva.

'Stop!' Salva shouts again, as he finally catches up with Devavrata and thunders alongside him. 'Stop, upon your honour as a Kshatriya, stop and answer for what you have done.'

Devavrata reins in his horses and they stop, steaming in the late afternoon blaze. Devavrata's eyes are opaque with anger and a spasm clenches his jaw.

'I have nothing to explain to you. A Kshatriya has the right to carry away a woman for a bride, if he intends to marry her. I have done nothing contrary to the dharmic laws.'

Salva continues to circle Devavrata's chariot, the mare slowly weaving on dancing, tripping hooves.

'One bride? But you have three, is there no limit to your lust, old man?' Salva snarls, and lets loose a couple of arrows but the arrows thud harmlessly into the wooden sides of the chariot.

Devavrata strings his bow and points his arrow at Salva's chariot. His bow arm moves slowly, following the arc of his moving target. When he releases his arrow, it swooshes through the torpid air, its whisper a deadly promise. Several more follow in a blur and Salva's charioteer looks down in surprise at the three arrows blooming from his chest, sees the glossy, ruby-red blood drip down his thighs and slowly, regretfully, collapses at his post. Somehow his legs remain tangled in the reins and tied to the spinning chariot as his head smashes against the hard earth and stains it with blood and something darker and more sinister, like an unholy anointing.

The rajkumaris scream and Amba grabs her sisters and buries their heads against her breast.

'Sarathi, no!' Salva tries to stop the lurching horse, to untangle his flailing charioteer, when he notices his mare stumble. He jumps off his chariot as his horse takes a few uncertain steps and then crumples suddenly, like a cloth puppet whose distracted puppeteer has walked away. Salva runs to his horse, her smooth silver flanks corrupted by arrows, and gets down on his knees to hold her fierce, heaving head in his arms. The gallant brown eyes seem to look straight at him and he whispers a soothing phrase to calm her boundless animal terror. Salva looks up to see Devavrata nocking a last arrow to his bow and gently places his horse's head on the ground before getting up to stand in front of his dead charioteer and dying horse, his arms hanging down and his bow trailing the ground.

'No, Raja, no! Mercy.' Amba flings herself onto the floor of the chariot and clutches Devavrata's feet with her lac-red hands. 'Spare him, great raja, let him go, I beg of you.'

Devavrata looks down at Amba in surprise. He looks as though he has woken up from a dream, the women forgotten. Amba looks up at him and folds her hands, her vision blurry with tears. She sees his long hair blowing in the hot summer wind and the sweat dripping freely down the tendons of his neck into his armour. A thin line of blood is pearling on his arm from the graze of an arrow. He is beautiful and terrifying, Indra, the god of war himself, glowing in the evening sun.

'Please don't kill him, I beg you.'

Devavrata helps her get up and slings his bow back over his shoulder before taking the reins again, and setting the horses back onto the path to Hastinapur. Amba turns back to look at Salva, standing still next to his gasping horse. There is a dark stain spreading on the ground beside him as the parched earth soaks up the blood—the horse's and the man's. The blood that is spilled this day, on Amba's swayamvar day, is a catalyst, a foreboding, of the cataclysmic events to come. The pillaging of the three sisters and their subsequent treatment is the first truly despicable act. It is the seed cloud that will lead to the hurricane of the war which will end all wars.

Amba strains her eyes to see past the swirling, glittering dust. She sees Salva kneel next to his horse and place one hand searchingly on the horse's shuddering chest. He raises his other hand and Amba sees something glint in the pulsing evening light and, as she watches, Salva plunges a knife with all his strength into the massive, still-beating heart of his horse.

∿

All of Hastinapur is quiet that night under the wide-open sky with its crescent moon flushed red through the dust rolling in from the great western desert. Inside the palace, Amba paces the room she has been given, struggling to crush her panic. She knows that if she ceases her vigil, she will become a spinning inferno of fear and disintegrate into a million shreds of incoherence. Everything in this palace is unfamiliar to her. From the tiny window all she can see is the implacable darkness and she imagines beyond the palace all the uncharted terrors of the forests and their shambling, errant souls. In the palace of Varanasi, the river is a shadow companion at all times, familiar, sacred, and eternal. Even the smells here are different. The smell of the jasmine of her childhood garden replaced by the smell of the guava tree.

Her sisters are no help to her at all. Ambalika lies on a cot, overcome by the two-day journey from Hastinapur, thrashing with fever. Ambika sits next to her, weeping noisily between bouts of sleep, comforted by a retinue of maidservants dispatched by Kashiraj.

Amba goes over the conversation they had with the dowager Rajmata Satyavati of Hastinapur the previous evening. She had walked into their room unannounced when the three girls were still dislocated and dishevelled by their recent, tumultuous arrival in the city. The rani, in contrast, was spare and crisp in her widow's whites, her dark skin sleek and glossy, the air around her tinged with the smell of jasmine. She was followed by a huddle of servants bearing food and clothes and jewellery for the girls. She talked to them kindly enough, bade them a decorous welcome to her palace, but Amba detected the steel in her mellow voice and an implacable will in the way she directed the servants with a single word. The fisherman's daughter has left her past far behind her and rules the kingdom as regent now that Shantanu is dead.

'You will marry my son, the Raja Vichitravirya, tomorrow. Do not be afraid, Daughters, the preparations are all done and you will all be ranis.'

And then she is gone, and Ambalika collapses onto the charpoy, succumbing to the fever.

Now the night is finally done, though day is yet to arrive. Amba has bathed in the dark, pouring jars of water on her head to wash away the dust, sweat, and fear. She has dressed with care and coiled her hair into an elaborate, voluminous bun circled with a string of gold. By the time she is ready, it is dawn and she can hear the strangely sorrowful cry of the koel in the guava trees. Her sisters are finally asleep and she shuts the door gently before stepping out into the courtyard, accompanied by her childhood maid. She asks to be taken to Rajkumar Devavrata and a servant takes them through the somnolent palace to the prince's informal meeting room.

Devavrata has just finished his morning prayers at the fire altar and is discussing repairs to his chariot with his chariot-maker and senani. The purohit is bearing a plate of offerings from the morning prayers. Amba walks into the room and bows deeply to all the men. Devavrata seems surprised and slightly startled to see her but he bows to her graciously and the other men murmur greetings.

'Speak, Rajkumari, do not be afraid, what is on your mind?'

Amba looks up at Devavrata and is shocked at the difference in the man standing before her. He is dressed in a simple white dhoti, like a priest, and his white upper garment is wrapped around his shoulders, hiding his intimidating muscles and his archer's scars. His long hair is loose and dripping wet and there is a daub of ash on his brow. He is austere and unassailable like a holy man. There is no sign this morning of the raging, plundering monster of her swayamvar.

'I seek your forgiveness for appearing before all of you like this but there has been a mistake. I am betrothed to Raja Salva and was to marry him at my swayamvar. This is known to my father, Raja Kashiraj, and was agreeable to him as well. I cannot marry anyone else.'

Amba speaks in a rush, her heart thudding against her ribs and sending her heated blood prickling to her fingertips.

The men look at each other in some dismay. Devavrata is confounded. Amba has spoken in a public assembly, in front of a priest. There can be no convincing her otherwise and he has little option but to acquiesce.

'Very well, Rajkumari. If this is your wish, then you will be sent with a proper escort befitting your status to Raja Salva's home. You may leave at once, if you so desire.'

Amba bows to the men, hands folded, and hurries away.

At Salva's Court

~

Amba waits in the gloomy antechamber of Salva's mansion a long time. She tries to force herself to remain calm but her composure is spiderweb thin and she can feel hysteria bubbling just a breath away.

At last Salva enters the room, alone and, without looking at Amba, goes over to stand near the latticed window. Amba is suddenly breathless, and feels the words turn to dust in her mouth. She takes a step towards him and speaks.

'Raja, it is I, Amba.'

'What are you doing here? Why have you come?'

Amba is certain she must have misunderstood, that Salva has not heard her clearly.

'How can you ask that, Raja? How could I stay away? I explained to Prince Devavrata that I was betrothed to you, that I could accept no other husband in my heart and so he sent me here to you.'

'What betrothal? There was no engagement that I can remember, no spoken understanding with your father, so what are you talking about?'

'Raja, I beg of you, do not tease me in this way, it is cruel.'

Salva's face is fractured by shame and violent self-pity. He steps towards Amba with clenched fists.

'I was humiliated by Devavrata in front of the whole sabha of rajas. My name is mud and people laugh behind my back. Am I nothing that I must accept Devavrata's cast-offs? Go back to him since he won you in front of everyone.'

'This cannot be happening, Raja, you would not say such things to me,' Amba's voice is a whisper, hoarse and uncertain. Her dark eyes fill with hopeless tears.

'I have wanted only you as my husband all these years. You must know this. The gift you sent...'

'Enough! You have said enough! Do not disgrace yourself.'

Salva slams a low wooden stool with his fist and it splinters and scatters like glass.

'You have spent a night under a strange man's roof. How dare you show your face to me? Go back to him, go back to Devavrata, it is the only place for you now.'

Salva storms out of the room as the proud rajkumari of Kashi crumples into the arms of her maid.

At Devavrata's Court

~

The traders, beggars, and messenger boys of Hastinapur stare at the bedraggled procession heading towards the palace. The palanquin bearers stumble with bowed heads, shamed by the rajkumari they can no longer carry and driven to despair by their ceaseless journeys between the two cities. Amba walks in front carelessly, while her maidservant, Jaya, tries to shade her from the intractable sun with a cloth parasol. It is midday and the heat is a drizzling phosphorescence, covering the procession with a prickling, burning blaze. Amba's clothes are heavy with sweat and dust. Her hair tumbles down her back in disordered confusion, the gold hairband lost somewhere along the way. Despite this, the passers-by are beguiled by the beauty of the rajkumari, the milk-like splendour of her complexion and her profile with its fine, shapely nose and curved lips.

Devavrata meets Amba alone, without the distracting protocol of priest or courtier.

'Salva will not have me now. He says I am sullied. I have nowhere to go, you must give me sanctuary.'

She speaks in halting, truncated sentences, unable to truly contemplate what she is saying.

'Certainly, Rajkumari. Your sisters have married Raja Vichitravirya, my half-brother, yesterday. You may marry him and become their co-bride.'

'Raja Vichitravirya! He is a child, and a sickly one at that. I have heard it said he has the deadly coughing sickness. I cannot marry a boy; I am the rajkumari of Kashi. You claimed me as a bride at my swayamvar, it is right that you marry me now.'

'If you have heard rumours about Raja Vichitravirya, then you will have heard about my vow as well. I have taken an oath of brahmacharya and can never marry.'

'Brahmacharya? Then how did you dare come to my swayamvar, unannounced and uninvited, like a thief, and carry me and my sisters away in front of my father and a host of princes? If Raja Vichitravirya wished to marry, he should have had the valour to claim his brides himself. You put your hands upon my body in front of all those assembled men, you must marry me now, on your honour as a Kshatriya.'

Devavrata's voice is suddenly ice and his eyes are impenetrable. He will not show his anger in front of these two women but he withdraws his compassion and his humanity like a cobra that retreats into its coils, merciless and threatening.

'I have not besmirched my Kshatriya honour. I claimed you and your sisters as brides for my brother, not for myself. I offered you a place as rani of Hastinapur. You misunderstood my intentions, that is regrettable. I am sorry, but I can never marry you.'

Amba's eyes slowly fill with tears as she finally understands the magnitude of her loss, the unsoundable abyss of it.

'Raja, I am dispossessed, I have nowhere to go. I beg of you to grant me refuge in your house.'

'If you will not marry Vichitravirya, can you not return to your father's house?'

'I left my father's house a bride, I cannot return unmarried, in this unsanctified wasteland, neither kanya nor devi.'

'Then you have no option. You may seek asylum in the forest, in a holy man's hermitage. You may keep the servants that Raja Kashiraj sent for you.'

'May I at least bid my sisters goodbye before I leave?'

'They are in the married quarters now, quite far from here. It is best you leave immediately.'

Devavrata is now in a hurry to return to the consolation of his armoury and his chariots. He has quelled his guilt and his shame in front of this distraught and broken woman but now the airless room is oppressive. He doesn't want to think about the images Amba has conjured up, his hands on her smooth shoulders or her red-stained palms clasping his feet. Her beauty may be ravaged but it is also overwhelming. He gives rapid instructions to Jaya and then ushers the two women out of the palace.

In the Forest

~

Amba does go to the forest at last, disowned and undone. The meagre retinue wanders from hermitage to hermitage, on rough, overgrown paths where their feet bleed on the fallen thorns of babool trees. In the monsoon season they are assailed and driven to distraction by the insects, the tiny, stinging red ants, the flamboyant tiger beetles, and the winged velvet ants. Their mud huts in the hermitage are flooded and their feet become smooth and plump from being in water for too long. In the winter, the long, frigid nights are terrifying and the frugal meals of barley and peppers demoralizing. Slowly, over the years, the attendants slip away, either quietly at night or brazenly, in a show of bravado and temper. The gold is spent, on avaricious priests and secret jars of barley wine. In the end it is only Jaya who remains with Amba. Steadfast Jaya who was her equal in the classless and timeless games of their childhood.

In her first years in the forest, Amba dissipates her energy along many emotions. Anger towards her father and Devavrata, jealousy towards her sisters, longing and desire also for Salva and the life they will never have together. Slowly, however, she whittles away at her emotions, cleaving all thought and all feeling from her living flesh till all she has left, bleeding in the palm of her hand, is revenge. Revenge on Devavrata becomes the one true and perfect thing in her life. Like a mother tends to her baby, the barren Amba cherishes and nurtures her thoughts of revenge, to the exception of all else.

She forgets to eat, to bathe, and to sleep. Revenge becomes the lucent red heart of the pomegranate seed, the endless night of the black antelope's fur. In her search for revenge she wanders from priest to priest, from soothsayer to tantric sage, but they all fail her. In the end, she delivers herself to Rudra, the great storm god, and asks for his blessing.

'Rudra, give me Bheeshma the Terrible's head in my lap and I will be free. Smear me with his entrails and wash my hair in his blood and I will find peace.'

She dies on a nameless day in summer, a day in which everything is defined by the heat. The colour of the sky is bleached white, the air is pulsing dust and the soul of the day is despair.

Jaya lays the ravaged princess in her lap and weeps over her as she dies, her long hair falling forward and shielding her from the gaze of the priests.

'Do not leave me alone, Rajkumari, do not abandon me now,' she cries.

In her final moment of lucidity, Amba reaches out a searching, wasted hand to wipe away Jaya's tears.

'No more rajkumari, Jaya. Nevermore a girl, or a useless, powerless woman. May Rudra carry me away and drop me back on earth, reborn a man. A warrior, a soldier, or even a farmer. Let me be a man and I will find a way to annihilate him, Bheeshma, that murderer of all my dreams.'

ᶜ

Meanwhile, in Hastinapur, the gentle, complying rajkumaris exchange their brides' dazzling colours for widow's whites in just a few months. They had tried to look after the sickly boy they married but in vain. At night he thrashes on his bed, which has been placed in the courtyard under the open sky so that the healing moonbeams fall on him. He is clammy and cold with sweat, though he raves that he is burning up. His frail body becomes skeletal and he coughs with a relentlessness that dismays his young wives. Finally the rajmata herself takes over the care of her son but by then the white cloth he holds against his mouth is stained crimson with his blood. He dies in his mother's arms, a ghastly and terrifying death, drowning in his own blood while his lungs disintegrate.

The rajmata's grief is ferocious and the two young widows cower in their room, terrified that they will be blamed for their husband's death. For a week, the rajmata is inconsolable and raging, for death has worsted her iron will. Now Hastinapur is without an heir, the ancient Kuru line truncated on her watch. Finally, she rouses herself and calls for a meeting with her advisers and priests.

Rajmata Satyavati steers the discussions about the future of the Kuru kingdom expertly. She allows the advisers and the priests to have their say and, flattered by her deference, they expound at length about the vagaries of fate and the inconstant attention of the gods.

'But the kingdom must have a raja,' Satyavati insists.

The advisers concur and mention the name of various deserving kinsmen, close family and brave men, who would rule the Kuru kingdom well.

But Satyavati has not come so far—from the fetid torpor of her fishing village to the greatest kingdom on earth—to be outdone by a group of indecisive men. She knows that a strong, undisputed heir is indispensable to the survival of the kingdom and she will claw that heir out of thin air if need be. She throws out the word Niyoga into the group, like a coiled scorpion into a pit of mice. The word is potent, challenging, and the men exchange glances and murmured, questioning asides.

'Yes, this can be acceptable, if there is a suitable candidate.'

The men look furtively at Devavrata who is half-brother to the dead boy and who has been regent of Hastinapur all these years, but he shakes his head.

Ira Mukhoty

'I have made a vow.'

This vow is a talisman and an armour, which in time fuses with his very skin so that the vow itself becomes indistinguishable from Bheeshma.

'I have another son,' announces Satyavati, to the consternation and embarrassment of the men. 'I had him long before I met Raja Shantanu,' she continues, calm as a goddess while the men cast illicit glances at her ample curves and the dark slope of her bare back.

'He is a sadhu, a learned and wise man and he will come to us in our hour of need. His name is Vyasa.'

The men nod, the gold of their ear studs glinting in the darkened room.

'Yes,' they say, 'this is acceptable. For the future of the kingdom, let it be done.'

And so Satyavati hurries away to send a messenger to the distant hermitage where she has always kept track of her firstborn son, never knowing when she might need to call on him for help.

And Devavrata remains standing, brittle and silent, the last and only true prince of the Kuru bloodline in the land, gelded by his father's lust and his own pride.

⌐

Rajmata Satyavati summons her daughters-in-law to her chamber on the afternoon of a damp, hopeless monsoon day. There has been a break in the incessant, harrying rain and the sun is shining again. The air is humming and alive with a million short-lived cicadas and croaking frogs. A maidservant sweeps away the water puddles in the courtyard with a reed broom, bent double from the waist as she reaches down.

'Betis, we have thought of a way to secure the future of the kingdom despite Raja Vichitravirya dying before he could have any sons.'

Ambika and Ambalika look at each other dazed, wondering for a moment what magic might be conjured now.

'I have another son, Vyasa, who is a sadhu. He has been summoned to the palace and he will give you both sons. Ambika beti you are the eldest. He will come to you first. Be prepared tonight to receive him in your chambers.'

At this, tears well up in Ambika's eyes and she covers her face in shame and humiliation.

Satyavati quells her impatience and walks up to the sobbing girl and puts an arm on her shoulder.

'Beti, this is also for your own good. Without a son, what are you? A widow, an ill-fated woman with no protector. What will happen to the two of you after I am gone? A Kshatriya widow without an heir is better off dead. At least this way you will be rajmatas too.'

Satyavati is being pragmatic and Ambika recognizes the truth behind the stark words. She wipes her face, now bare of kohl and crimson lac, with the end of her white upper garment and nods wordlessly.

That night, Ambika's maid helps her undress and then leaves her alone in her room. Small diyas flicker on the window ledges and Ambika trembles in dread. Outside the rain slants down, a steady, multi-tonal crashing sound and Ambika feels it is Indra and his hordes summoning the apocalypse.

The door bursts open and a man walks in, wind gusting through the room in an instant. He slams the door shut and latches it securely while Ambika stares at him and starts to cry. Vyasa is stocky and short, with powerful shoulders and long, matted hair. He is dressed in a sadhu's orange robes and wears the holy rudraksha beads around his neck as well as a confusion of amulets and pouches. In the light of the tiny diyas, his eyes seem to blaze crimson and the lines of his face are fierce and bleak.

Ira Mukhoty

His voice though is gentle enough as he approaches the naked, sobbing princess.

'Do not despair, child. I have come to you to do my duty by my mother. I will visit you till you are sure you are with child and then I will never touch you again.'

Vyasa walks up to Ambika and she can smell his ash, sweat, and cardamom odour. His touch is ungentle and brusque, his hands hard and calloused. Ambika bites her lips and averts her face, covering her eyes with her hand in pain and shame. After submitting to Vyasa for several nights, Ambika knows she cannot tolerate another night with him and she pleads with her maid, who has come in on quiet bare feet, to bring her a calming drink of cardamom, ginger, and cinnamon in milk.

'My friend, please take my place with the sadhu tonight. I cannot bear it any more, I will surely die if I have to lie with Vyasa one more night. I beg you, here, take these gold bangles for your troubles.'

The maid is a feisty girl who has had to fend for herself from a very young age. Along with the monsoon wind, the whole palace is sweeping with rumours of the sadhu, of his extreme erudition and yogic power. The maid is a low-caste servant girl, a shadow being. Association with the high-caste, powerful sadhu would certainly be beneficial for her, especially if she were to bear him a son.

She accepts Ambika's proposal and her gold bangles with equanimity and takes the rajkumari's place that night.

Within a year, Ambika, Ambalika, and the maidservant all give birth to sons. Ambika's son, Dritrashtra, is lusty and tempestuous but to Satyavati's furious sorrow, he is born blind. Satyavati knows he will not be deemed fit to be king since a ruler must be whole of body and valorous of temperament. So she waits for Ambalika's baby through the harrowing, splintering winter and, in the spring, Pandu is born. He is pale, certainly, but in all other ways he is fine and strong. The maid's son, Vidura, is the quietest, with large black eyes and umber skin.

The three boys are brought up as brothers, cherished and loved by everyone. Dritrashtra has the unassailable respect due to the firstborn though he understands, with a child's implacable sense of justice, that his blindness will not ever allow him to be king. Vidura's mother is careful to point out to her son the abyss that lies between the rajkumars and himself. Vidura's intelligence is a sparkling, mobile thing and he understands the subtlety of his position early on, and all his life he is able to walk the tightrope between familiarity and respect with grace and elegance.

As for Pandu, he is a charming child, easily brought to tears if he is thwarted in any way. Caught as he is between Dritrashtra's primogeniture and Vidura's casual excellence in all things, he grows up moody and blustery, desperate to prove himself. But for a few years, the children are truly happy in their golden childhood filled with the sharp taste of green mangoes and guavas and blooming flower gardens and anchored by the constant, periodic Vedic rites that validate their place in the world. For a few years, the palace of Hastinapur trips on the sound of their boyish laughter and the old women and their tales of doom and desolation are consigned to the far quarters of the palace. The old women shake their grizzled heads and chew their paan with soft, childlike gums. They mutter to each other or to long departed children, irascible and stinging truths, for they are the only ones to hear, during the cold winter nights when the chilled air carries sounds clearly, the lonely and magnificent lament of the conch of war.

IV

*The Song of the
Peach Blossom*

The Girl from the North

~

The weekly market in the river valley of Taxila is an agitation of sound and colour. There are traders and wanderers from the furthest reaches of the great kingdom of Bharat at this crossroads city at the edge of the world. There are robust, hectoring men selling spices and wool, gold, and perfumes, but also furtive and sly individuals hissing obscure promises of eternal life and enchanting beauty. There is a syncopation of sound, a fracas of different languages whirling and crashing into each other as traders compete to attract the appraising passers-by. The air is charged with the dark haze of expectation, the smell of red-dyed wool blankets and the sandalwood incense which the traders have lit everywhere to keep out the nauseating mineral smell of the butchers' quarters.

Two young women have stopped in the caged bird section of the market. Ignoring the appeals of the sellers of the flashy parakeets and exotic songbirds, they are leaning down instead by the seller of partridges and pheasants. One of the girls, elegant with grey eyes and burnished skin, is holding a common teetar in her hands. She gently holds down the bird's wings with her palm to stop it from flapping and brings it carefully to her face where she can feel the heartbreakingly soft feathers against her cheek. She is amazed by the perfection of the whorls and swirls of chestnut brown against the sandy gold plumage and the gentle, apologetic curve of its short beak.

'Lata, shall we buy this bird as well? Will Ma notice if we bring back another one?'

Her friend is hunched next to her, head covered by a red and blue wool shawl. She reaches out a finger to stroke the hard, inquisitive head and sighs.

'Gauri, I think the rani would not only notice but would probably have it roasted for the raja's dinner.'

The girls are accompanied by three boys laden with wicker baskets containing spices, dried figs, apricots, perfumes, and herbs. The partridge seller is not impressed by these irresolute girls and he looks up with hope as a large man in black robes materializes out of the crowd and thrusts some coins in his direction.

'Partridges, grey and black, and chukar if you have any. I will take them all, and hurry up.'

The partridge seller, short and squat, with tufts of white hair growing out of his ears, is invigorated in an instant. He collects all the startled partridges into one covered basket and hands them to the buyer. The larger man then takes the partridge from Gauri's hands as an afterthought and pushes out through the crowd.

'What are you doing? That bird is mine, give her back to me at once.'

Gauri grabs Lata by the hand and, followed by the boys, shoves through the heaving crowd in the slipstream of the big man. When they reach the edge of the marketplace, they notice the man striding into a field in the distance. In one swooping gesture he removes the cover of the basket and flings the birds skywards, like offering sacrificial oblations to a relentless god.

'What is he doing, Lata? What is he doing to the birds?' Gauri is distressed at the tumbling birds, their scratchy, harsh distress calls as they try to orient themselves and run along the ground on their powerful, stubby legs. Finally, in a whirring of inelegant flight, they strain to gather momentum against the icy air.

'It's a falconry demonstration, Rajkumari, look at all the men watching.'

And Lata is right. Lined up against the edge of the maidan, a group of watchful men in long, dark woollen robes searches the sky intently. Gauri follows their gaze and is startled to see several small, black shapes spinning out of the frigid blue sky. The falcons fold their wings tightly against their streamlined bodies and soundlessly drop to earth at a speed that makes the watchers breathless. Within seconds the falcons are amongst the scattering partridges, the violence of the impact killing the birds instantly. They carry the dead birds like sacred offerings back to the falconers who stand immobile in the middle of the maidan, outstretched arms covered in thick leather gauntlets, like malevolent dolls. There the falconers quickly remove the partridges from the lethal, grasping claws of their killers and cover the searing yellow eyes with a leather hood, the blistering speed and strength momentarily contained.

While the watching men cheer appreciatively and bid for the falcons, Gauri covers her mouth with her hand and struggles to contain her tears. She wonders if in its final moments, the partridge saw for the last time the blue mountains of her birth that circle the city of Taxila in a lover's grasp. Did she see the crystal-clear, burbling water of the Kabul River, the flowering apple trees in the valley and think that she had got away? Or did she hear the deadly rush of air from above and feel her fragile neck snap as the yellow talons sank into it?

Lata takes Gauri by the arm, pulling her away from the crowds.

'Come along, Rajkumari, the rani wanted us back before too long. There have been some important visitors to the palace in the last few days and she says she needs to talk to you.'

⁓

In the large mansion of Raja Saubala of Gandahar, the rani is standing in the courtyard of the stables with her hands on her generous hips, surveying the condition of the newborn calves and their mothers. She turns around when she hears Gauri and Lata approaching and smiles at the girls. The rani is a handsome woman still but her once soaring beauty is now a prosaic thing. Her fine features are smudged by the weight of many pregnancies and her almond milk skin is crimped around her eyes and mouth.

'Beti, there is wonderful news. An emissary has arrived from the city of Hastinapur, in the faraway river plains. He has come with a proposal from the raja himself, for you to be his bride. It is a great honour for all of us.'

'Marriage! But, Ma, the river plains are so far away from home, and it will be peach season in a few months.'

'Peaches? You little fool, this is the most important decision of your life and you are worrying about fruit? You will be rani of the largest mahanagar of this land, can't you see what great fortune you have?'

'But I will know no one there, I know nothing about their customs, how will I manage, Ma?'

The rani knows her daughter's temperament. Despite her clear intelligence she is easily overwhelmed by an emotion that is somewhere between sorrow and pathos and she needs constant guidance to not succumb to the seduction of self-pity. She goes up to Gauri and puts her hands on her shoulders

'Beti, you will not be alone. We are sending Lata with you, I have already spoken to her father. Shakuni will accompany you also and will remain in Hastinapur as long as you need him. Also, all the servant girls and grooms that you may require.'

Gauri looks into her mother's green eyes, at the stippled, multicoloured flecks of her iris that are like the smooth pebbles in the clear waters of the Kabul River.

'So it is already decided? And I am to give up everything I love here? So be it, since you have decided this for me. I have to give up the company of my brothers and sisters and all my childhood friends. I can say goodbye to Pitaji also, since he is raja and must worry about the future of all his children. But, Ma, am I never to see you again either? How will I survive without you?'

The rani has tears in her eyes now and hugs Gauri tightly.

'Beti, it is every girl's destiny to leave her home and her family when she gets married. I did the same when I came to Taxila. But remember this, my child, when you are on your long journey to Hastinapur—for all those long weeks and months, your image will abide in my eyes. When you marry the raja and learn new ways and customs, your memory will haunt my thoughts and long after you have forgotten the sound of my voice and the likeness of my face, caught up in the delight of your children, I will carry you in my heart forever, for a mother's love is infinity itself. I will never see you again, I know, but I will never forsake you.'

The rani holds Gauri's face between her hands and kisses her on her forehead.

And it is true, that in time, there are many things that Gauri will forget. She will stop longing eventually for the heady joy of the peach. She will forget the beauty of her native blue mountains, the rivers and the comfort of her sisters' faces. More sinister yet, she will forget the sound of her own name. But she will always remember this day, standing in the courtyard with her mother under a sweeping blue sky while the deep, husky sound of the cattle lowing is eternal and filled with foreboding, like remorse.

'Ma, there you are, I have been looking for you and Gauri everywhere.'

A tall young man in black woollen robes strides into the courtyard. His dark clothes and his deep-set black eyes give him an air of brooding sobriety but he smiles suddenly when he sees his sister. Gauri runs over to hug him and he is a full head taller than she is.

'Bhai Shakuni, I am so glad that you are to come with me to Hastinapur. I would be lost without you there.'

Shakuni hugs his sister and then turns back to his mother.

'Ma, I am not happy with Father's decision to send Gauri away. I am suspicious of this raja from Hastinapur. Are there no beautiful and virtuous girls left in the plains for him to marry? Why send for a girl from so far away? Also, I hear there is a regent who has been ruling the kingdom for many years. What are his motivations in all this?'

'So many questions, Beta, I am sure all will be cleared up when you reach Hastinapur. Perhaps the raja heard about the great beauty of our Gauri, and also how talented she is in singing and playing the flute.'

The rani is obstinate in her belief in Gauri's good fortune. The alternative, that they are being betrayed in some way, is unthinkable.

Shakuni runs his hand through his thick, curly, shoulder-length hair, and is silent. He is one of five brothers and he is an ambitious young man. He knows that if he stays in Gandahar he will struggle to make a fortune and a name for himself but in faraway Hastinapur, the possibilities are legion.

'Then I will oversee the preparations at once. We should leave as soon as we can, or we will be crossing the desert lands at the hottest time of the year.'

◡

The people of the city of Taxila have lined the streets to watch the Rajkumari Gauri leave for Hastinapur and her future. The magnificence of the caravan that bears her away has never been seen before in their lifetimes, for Raja Saubala, in the face of his fraying hope, has tried to provide in every way against the gauging,

Ira Mukhoty

calculating glances of the clan of Hastinapur.

At the head of the caravan there are glittering horses tripping and shimmying on slim and elegant legs. Then there are the soldiers, sombre but keen, leaving behind daughters and barley fields and sweethearts forever. There are patient cattle and unshorn sheep and dozens of draught animals yoked to wagons and carts carrying gifts as well as all the supplies the procession will need for the way. Jars of water, wood for the bivouacs, rice, barley and wheat, dried figs, apricots from the previous year, and the last of the pomegranates from the winter's harvest. There are servant girls in the retinue, compliant and heartbroken, disposable girls whose destinies will never be recorded and who disappear into the future, shadowy wraiths. There are cooks, priests, physicians and, most crucial of all, a guide. Riding alongside this swaying, lurching caravan in a single-horse chariot is Shakuni. He is wearing a voluminous dark-blue turban and long blue robes and there is a smouldering effervescence in the way he uses his chariot to torment the laggards and the straying cattle.

Gauri and Lata are in the swaying palanquin borne by four straining men in white turbans and loincloths. The girls lean out of the opening at the side, to see the faces of their mothers and sisters for the last time. They are silent as they attempt the impossible task of imprinting on the landscape of their minds the exact shade of blue of the limpid skies and the way their mothers try to smile through their tears. They hear the repeating, heartbeat-like call of the golden eagle. By the time the city of Taxila is a shadow on the horizon, both girls are in tears and they huddle miserably among the warm woollen blankets that smell of home.

The caravan takes the Uttarapatha trade road, away from the highlands of Balkh and the Indus River and heads east towards Magadha. For days they cross the fertile river valleys where the grassland sparkles with springs and waterfalls and streams. They pass the fruit orchards, plum, peach, and pomegranate trees and carefully cultivated vineyards. The air is dense with the fragrance of young fruit blossoms and crushed grass. It is the fragrance of the land itself, the dizzying companion of their childhood, for which the kingdom of Gandahar is named. As they leave the valleys behind and climb the high mountains, the landscape crumbles and scatters into stony and arid hillsides. They stop before nightfall, to set up camp in frigid caves dank with bats. The harried priest quickly performs a puja first, to rid the caves of its icy ghouls, but the usually consoling mantras sound foreign and powerless in these darkening hills. The travellers shiver in the sudden cold of the night, swapping stories about the night ghost, the great snow leopard common to these mountains.

After a few weeks of travel, Gauri and Lata shake off the indolence of loss and are distracted, despite themselves, by the romance of the journey. They come across other travellers, itinerant traders who try to sell them glass beads and ivory bangles, and holy men of every description. They are charmed, also, by all the new things they see along the way. They look out for the furtive but ferocious snow leopard which remains elusive throughout the journey. They console themselves instead with sightings of scampering lizards and swishing snakes warming themselves on the baking rocks. They get out of their stuffy palanquin and walk sometimes besides the slave girls, enjoying the warming sun on their arms. Sometimes they ride in the chariot beside Shakuni and he entertains them with the stories about a hill of gold, and the epic friendship between a raja, Gilgamesh, and a wild creature called Enkidu.

After many weeks of mountain roads, they finally enter the great river plains of northern Bharat. That night the carts are drawn up in several circles like the snug coils of a snake. Camp fires blaze all round the carts and soldiers take it in turns to mount guard. In the centre of the camp, the leader and guide of the caravan, the sarthavaha, is haranguing the travellers.

'Tomorrow we enter the great forests of Bharat. These forests are full of dangers. There are poisonous fruits, animals, and insects everywhere. Never stray from the path and never eat anything unknown. I have known big, strong men fall down dead after eating a tiny poisonous berry.'

The sarthavaha is a sinewy, haunted-looking man with amulets around his neck and arms and an old snake bite on his thigh. He has brought them with impeccable instinct this far and the travellers put their boundless faith in him to take them through the dense forests that lie ahead. At night he lies on his back, muttering to himself while he counts the stars and gets his bearings from the immovable constellations.

The next day, the endless column moves off before daybreak with a grinding of wooden wheels and the soft lowing of cattle, leaving swirling clouds of dust behind. The journey through the forests is slow, beguiling, and endless. They are harassed by the grasping branches and the stinging insects. They get quick, uncertain glimpses of naked tribesmen whose poisonous arrows can drop a grown man in seconds. Who will impale and offer them up as bloody sacrifices to their heathen and ravenous gods. The sarthavaha assures them they are too numerous to be attacked but they are all watchful and tense, fear condensing around them like a fog. They grow quiet and irritable and listen for the quick, hot breath of a tiger or leopard. Occasionally, a soldier gives up his tenuous grasp on reality and runs off laughing into the forest, following his vision of a swaying nymph. Others sicken and die, their guts twisted and scorched by the forbidden berries they could no longer resist.

The river crossings claim yet more lives as the rivers are huge and monstrous, fed by the melting snows. The sarthavaha must choose the best place to ford the rivers and Gauri better understands now his haunted look. As they step into the roiling water, there are always some who no longer have the strength or the desire to fight and are swept away by the cleansing river. The sarthavaha is even more gaunt than before with watchfulness, his muttering now constant and loud. The heat in the plains in summer is greater than anything Gauri has known in all her life. It is an annihilating heat that clears all dreams and all desire. By the time a herald returns to announce that they have entered the Kuru kingdom, Gauri's only thought is that she must escape the blistering light of day.

They enter Hastinapur on a relentless day in May, when the sun has spun the heat into a gossamer-white haze across the sky. The travellers are delirious from the heat and exhaustion and barely notice the fevered activity in the city in anticipation of their arrival. They stumble past the snake charmers and their bamboo baskets hissing with snakes, the sword swallowers and the monkey and mongoose handlers. They barely look at the Ganga, where magnificently decorated sailboats and galleys shimmer on the water. It is only as they enter the great vaulted entrance to Hastinapur that Lata shakes herself from her torpor and forces Gauri to look out of the palanquin.

'Look, Gauri, the raja's great white elephant, like Indra's Airavata himself!'

The royal elephant is a light-grey colour, magnificently decorated with a huge necklace around its neck, bangles around its legs, and a fine striped carpet on its back. The mahout holds the royal standard in one hand and, as the palanquin passes by, the elephant raises its trunk in salute.

Once inside the palace of Hastinapur, Gauri is escorted to her quarters where she collapses in a delirium of exhaustion. For the next few days, she is only dimly aware of her surroundings, of the dark shuttered room she is in and the soft, murmured voices that come and go. She is aware of soft, cool hands on her fevered skin rubbing ointments on her brow and into her hair and of low voices that call to her in words that make no sense.

Ira Mukhoty

Three days later, she wakes up in the morning scoured clean and dry by the fever and filled with lightness. Lata is sleeping on a cot next to her. When she wakes her up, Lata looks away and avoids her gaze.

'What is the matter, Lata? Why do you not speak?'

But Lata still will not answer and instead starts tidying the richly furnished room.

'Lata, speak to me, you are frightening me. What news have you heard of the raja. Is he handsome? Is he kind?'

But Lata's eyes fill with tears now as she shakes out the thin muslin dhotis they have been given by the Rajmata.

'We have been lied to, rajkumari. You have been deceived. It breaks my heart to say this to you, beloved friend, but Rajkumar Dritrashtra, whom you are to marry, has been blind from birth.'

'What do you mean? That cannot be true, you must be mistaken.'

Gauri is cold suddenly, despite the blazing dawn, and she sits back down on the soft cotton covers of the cot.

'Where is Shakuni?' Gauri whispers, but Lata has covered her face with her hands and is sobbing quietly.

As if hearing his sister's whispered plea, Shakuni crashes into the room, pushing aside the guards at Gauri's door. He looks haggard and wasted, bleak lines drawn on his face. He flings his turban onto a low stool and runs his hands through his thick hair before walking up to his sister.

'I see you have heard the news, Gauri. I have been waiting outside your door for three days to warn you. We have been betrayed by this regent, this Pitama as they all call him here. But he is no kindly grandfather, I can assure you. He is a scheming and heartless manipulator, disinherited by his stepmother, who knew no high-born rajkumari from the plains would marry a blind man and so he sent for a girl from the farthest reaches of the kingdom. He gambled that we would not have heard about Dritrashtra's blindness so far away, or that they would only be rumours. And he won.'

'But, Bhai Shakuni, I am not married to him yet. Can we not just go back? Let us go now, right away, before anyone realizes what has happened. Just you, and I, and Lata.'

'What are you talking about? Don't be foolish now, Gauri. Do you not realize how powerful the Kuru clan is? If we were to run away back to Gandahar, they would follow us and they would crush our father's forces in an instant.'

Gauri hangs her head to hide the tears that blur her grey eyes. Shakuni is right in calling her a foolish girl for that is all she is, to dream of a dashing rajkumar waiting for her at the end of the world. Shakuni notices her quiet tears and walks up to her, contrite.

'I am sorry, Gauri, this is in no way your fault; yet you have no choice now but to stay here and go through with the marriage. But I promise you this, I will stay here with you in Hastinapur always. I will look out for you and yours, and I will do everything in my power to protect your place here at the court of the Kurus.'

'But, Bhai, I am to be rani, isn't that so? So my place at the court is assured at least.'

Shakuni takes a step back and glances at Lata, who is listlessly taking out clothes from a large wooden trunk. Lata looks back at Shakuni and shakes her head.

'Dritrashtra cannot be raja, Gauri. He has been deemed unfit because of his blindness. Though he is the oldest, his younger brother, Pandu, has been crowned raja.'

'Unfit? So they would have known this all along, much before the envoy was sent to Gandahar to ask for my hand in marriage. They never intended for me to be rani at all, it was all a fantasy. What is to become of me, Bhai Shakuni?'

Gauri presses her knuckles to the sides of her head, as chaos swirls around her in the gloom of the shuttered room.

'Do not give up hope, Gauri. I have been listening to the rumours that drift through the palace and everything is not quite as it seems. There is animosity between the brothers and factions in court. The iron rule of the Pitama and the Rajmata Satyavati will not last forever. Life is long and full of shadows and the truth is not always what we expect it to be.'

It is late afternoon by the time Gauri is summoned to the rajmata's quarters and the sun has ground the day into ash. A layer of fine dust covers everything in the palace like a spell. Words are weighed down by fine sand and choke in the speakers' throats and bare feet are stained ochre by the red earth. For Gauri, who has known only the cloudless blue summers of Gandahar, the heat is a delirium. All day she has been beleaguered by a multitude of whispering, assessing women. Servant girls bring her dishes of honeyed curd and raw mango chutneys which nauseate her, and melted coconut oil to rub into her hair to soothe her throbbing head. Various women of the household, young wives and elderly aunts, keep clustering at her door to stare at her and comment on her alien grey eyes. They point at her insolently and chatter in fiery animation, criticizing her coarse clothes and her foreign, angular beauty. They keep hissing out a word at her, as if testing a wild animal till Gauri runs towards them in a fury, her humiliated sorrow forgotten.

'Gauri, my name is Gauri. What do you keep calling me? What are you saying?'

But the women run away, tittering with merriment and Gauri is left contemplating the inferno of the day, her anger dissipated.

Two servant girls lead her through narrow corridors to the rajmata's quarters. In the sequestered opulence of the rooms Gauri is assailed by a sensation of ashen starkness as the room appears to be full of women dressed in widows' whites. Trembling with anxiety Gauri stops at the threshold and bows deeply. One of the women calls out to her and Gauri begins to regret her stubborn decision to wear her rougher, coarse-spun clothes from Gandahar. The three women in white are wearing fine muslin dhotis, light as the breeze, and Gauri feels suddenly awkward and uncouth in their presence.

'Come closer, Beti, let me take a good look at you.'

The woman who has spoken to her is voluptuously dark with glossy black hair lit up by a few silver strands. She is introduced to her as the Rajmata Satyavati by a shuffling and bowing manservant. Her widow's whites are irreproachable but her eyes are molten. The other two women, though younger than her, seem crumpled and trifling in comparison. Rajmata Satyavati gently lifts Gauri's chin and looks into her face searchingly and Gauri blushes under the honesty of the scrutiny.

'I see you have not worn the clothes I have sent you, Beti. Never mind, I expect you to be changed by tomorrow. Fine eyes, yes, quite beautiful. You will be a good guide and companion to my grandson. What is it they are all calling you? Yes, Gandhari, the girl from the north.'

Gauri baulks at the stark assessment but finds the words have turned to scratchy dust in her throat in front of this daunting woman. Finally she speaks, and her voice sounds childish and whining to her own ears.

'Rajmata, I was not informed about the condition of Rajkumar Dritrashtra. I did not know that he was blind and I thought that I was to be rani.'

'Are you saying that we lied to you, Beti?' The rajmata's voice is smooth and cold suddenly, all softness disappearing. 'Your father was happy enough to take our gifts and accept our offer and he did not think to ask any questions.'

Gauri looks helplessly at the other two women but the Rajmatas Ambika and Ambalika look away, whether in confusion or complicity, she cannot be sure. Their plump-cheeked beauty was ever only a circumstance of their youth and time has exacted a vengeful price on them. The skin on their face hangs in doleful, apologetic folds and their once slim figures have collapsed into doughy incertitude. Just as Gauri fears she might burst into hysterical sobs, there is a commotion at the door as the manservant announces the entrance of the Rajkumar Dritrashtra.

Gauri is so startled that she forgets her manners and stares unabashedly at the young man who stands uncertainly at the doorway, an older man holding him gently by the elbow. The older man is tall and straight as a palm tree and Gauri knows instinctively that this is the Pitama that Shakuni has spoken of. His long, dark hair is shot through with silver and there is a gauntness about him that speaks of the passing of the years but there is also a sense of implacable strength and virility. He leads Dritrashtra towards the group of women and the rajkumar's steps are faltering and his hands hover in front of him tentatively. He wears an impeccable red dhoti and his necklace and armbands gleam with jewels but Gauri is transfixed by his eyes. They are cloudy and pale and searching, like the sightless worms that twist and snap when dug up from deep within the soil. He moves his head slightly from side to side as if mapping out the contours of the space around him and Gauri is suddenly overwhelmed and repulsed by the sight of his eyes and the thought of his searching hands on her body.

She runs out of the room, pushing past the obsequious manservant, and into the courtyard where startled maids are winnowing rice for the evening meal. In the hot, baked earth of the palace courtyard, Gauri bends over and retches in dry and heaving sobs.

ſ

It has been days since the meeting with the rajmatas and Lata is horrified at the complete disintegration in Gauri's condition. She lies on her bed, sobbing, refusing to eat the dishes of fried deer meat and seasoned rice and shutting her door against the massage girls, the flower girls, and the hair groomers.

'Gauri, rouse yourself, my friend. Do not grieve in this way. All is not lost, you may be happy yet.'

But Gauri turns to face the wall and covers her ears with her hands. Lata sits on the cot next to her and shakes her gently by the shoulders.

'You are a raja's daughter; it is not fitting for you to behave in this way. I have visited the city of Hastinapur and it is a large and prosperous town with more rich traders and people than you will have seen in your whole life. The streets are wide and beautifully clean and they are full of chariots and palanquins with men and women wearing exquisite jewellery. Here, Rajmata Satyavati has sent you these lovely gold bangles.'

But Gauri throws the bangles across the room.

'They just want me to be a slave, Lata. They want me to be Dritrashtra's guide and servant. They were not looking for a woman for him to marry, just a pair of eyes. That is all I am to them and all I ever will be. How can you speak to me of happiness?'

Shakuni walks in and overhears Gauri's last statement. He is the only other person allowed into Gauri's quarters.

'Gauri, you must gather yourself together and get ready for your marriage. I have spent many days listening in on the conversations at court and there is hope for you in the long term. There is considerable doubt over young Pandu's fitness as raja, something to do with an inauspicious birth or a sadhu's curse. He may not be as strong as he appears to be and may not be able to father sons. There are also those who still feel Dritrashtra would make a better raja, blind or not, since he is the first born.'

'But, Bhai Shakuni, I have heard that Pitama has sent envoys to look for a bride for Raja Pandu. Once she arrives, whoever she is, she will be rani and I will be nothing, even though I will be the first bahu of the house.'

'All the more reason, Gauri, to get married quickly and start your married life. With both brothers' fitness in doubt, everyone will be waiting for the birth of a healthy prince. Whoever has a boy first stands a much better chance of becoming rani and then rajmata. This is the only thing for you to remember.'

Gauri is silent at this. So revolted has she been at the duplicity of the Kurus and her visceral abhorrence of Rajkumar Dritrashtra's debility, that she has not been able to see past her marriage. But Shakuni is right. A child, a son, now that is something that she could love. A son who would be hers only, at least for a few years, in this alien and hostile land. But first there is something she must do. Something terrible and irrevocable, to show the rajmatas and the Pitama that she is not nothing, that she was once someone's beloved daughter and a cool and fragrant country's adored princess.

She picks up the bangles from the floor and pushes them onto her slim arms. Then she picks up a long piece of red cloth which she has torn from one of her robes from Gandahar. She ties the cloth like a bandage tightly around her eyes and turns around slowly to face the perplexed Lata.

'Take me to the rajmata, Lata, I am ready now to marry her grandson. But let her see that I will not be his eyes, or his guide, or whatever commodity they have decided I must be. They will not be able to hold my sight against me. I will say I do not wish to experience anything that my husband does not experience and that a good wife must bear her partner's lot equally.'

Lata and Shakuni are appalled, and try to reason with Gauri for a long time but she remains unmoved by all their arguments. In fact Gauri's earlier raucous distress has dissolved completely and she is now strangely calm. In the end, Lata is worn down and she helps Gauri change into the cool, light cotton dhoti and uttaraya that the rajmata has sent for her. Gauri is ready at last to become just Gandhari, the girl from the north. She puts her hand on Lata's shoulder and Lata leads her out into the stark daylight and Gandhari slowly begins walking the seam between lunacy and reason into her future role as matriarch of the Kuru clan.

A Dream of Sons

~

Gandhari wakes up from a familiar, tumbling nightmare, lurching with a shadowy sensation of grief and loss so strong, she has tears in her eyes. She sits up and looks over at Rajkumar Dritrashtra, sleeping next to her. In the pre-dawn gloom, with his long hair loose over his face and his eyes shut, he looks like a very young man, slim and vulnerable, with fine and tender hands that seem to reach for her. But Gandhari guards her heart against wanton feelings of pity or love. Her pared, homespun reasoning is that she will participate in palace life only on her own terms, in as spare a manner as possible. But for now, she needs to deal with the consequences of this recurring nightmare.

Gandhari leaves the room quietly on bare feet and goes to the bathing room where she splashes her face with cold water from an earthenware pot to rid herself of all the possible evil effects of such a calamitous dream. Then she sends Lata to summon her favourite purohit, a young visiting holy man who wandered into Hastinapur one day on scorched feet. Gandhari feels a kinship with this purohit, who is doubly dispossessed, like her, from his family and the land of his birth. He has fierce cheekbones and blazing eyes which are implacable in their ability to draw out all malevolent thoughts and spirits.

He has bathed already, though a vaporous dawn has only now spread over the city, and his wet white dhoti and upper garment cling

117

to his frame. Gandhari sits across from the purohit and allows herself to be mesmerized once again by his unwavering eyes. Gandhari does not as yet wear her blindfold all the time. She wears it only when she must appear in court, or when in the company of the rajmatas, Pitama, and her husband. The utter consternation and dismay of Rajmata Satyavati and Pitama, especially, are a solace to her. Lata has described to her their initial reactions many times, the way Rajmata Satyavati's face crumpled, ageing instantly and irrevocably. Pitama dropped the clay water pot he was holding and the sound of the scattering water was like a benediction.

'You are not the only one who can take on a lifetime vow, old man,' Gandhari thought to herself as she took a few careful steps towards the sound and bent down to touch Pitama's feet.

Now she sits across from the priest and recounts the terrible, choking nightmare.

'It is dark, Babaji, and I feel like I cannot breathe.'

The purohit nods slightly, rudraksha beads slipping through his fingers.

'I try to move but I am held down. Earth, dark and gritty, covers me and gets into my nose and ears. When I open my mouth to scream, my mouth fills with mud and I feel like I am choking.'

The purohit frowns and starts muttering mantras.

'The earth feels alive and full of terrible creatures, enormous worms, scorpions, and snakes, all moving towards me. And it is not just me, my babies are all lined up next to me and I cannot save them from a terrible death.'

Gandhari starts crying softly now, the shadow sadness from the dream like a bruise on her soul.

The purohit puts a soothing hand on her bent head while he chants a series of mantras as the sun finally rises on this cool November morning.

'Beti,' he says finally after a last mantra, 'you are fighting your destiny too much. You must accept your fate even if it appears inscrutable. I will do a special puja for you today and bring you the prasad this evening.'

Gandhari bows low before the purohit and gives him a coin so that he can make the necessary libation of sesame oil and offer gifts to other Brahmins. Then she hurries back to her quarters so that she is bathed and ready in time for the morning fire ritual with Dritrashtra.

Later in the day, once she is finally free from her obligations towards the rajmatas and her husband, Gandhari leaves the palace through a back door. Along with Lata, Gandhari walks to an overgrown field on the outskirts of town where a huge peepul tree reaches brokenly towards the sky. The tree is arrayed in fluttering cloths of orange and red as well as fresh marigold garlands. A woman is carefully sweeping the earth around the tree while another one bows before a small stone altar beside it. This is no ordinary tree but is the main residence of a powerful local yakshi, the great mother goddess both fecund and ravenous. All the women of Hastinapur have visited this tree at some point of their lives. To ask for a good husband or a happy marriage but mostly to ask for a healthy baby. The yakshi is powerful yet contrary, equally capable of granting fertility as she is of devouring unsuspecting children through raging fevers and sudden fits. So the women, when they approach the tree, are careful and circumspect. They bring only the freshest flower garlands and sprinkle the trunk with sugared water, milk, or honey. They smear the tree with coconut and sesame oil and red lac powder. Today, Gandhari places a tiny burning lamp between the large roots and, taking a sip of milk, she circles the tree once, the fingers of her right hand trailing lightly on the massive trunk. Then she carefully spits out the milk onto the tree trunk, her eyes shut, her entire being now vibrating with just one silent desire. A baby.

For it has been six months since her marriage and Gandhari

still hasn't felt any quickening in her belly or any unaccountable craving so typical of a pregnant woman. She knows that everybody is watching her now and her time of grace is fast running out. The women of the house were solicitous at first and subtle in their questions, asking if she craved mango pickle or honey. Now they are shameless in their scrutiny, derisive in their concern. Rajmata Satyavati has taken to questioning her every evening and Gandhari now hurries back to her quarters where she ties on her blindfold and sits in the courtyard in the last of the day's warmth, bracing herself for the rajmata's summons.

'Are you well, Beti?' The rajmata looks haggard these days, her skin no longer gleaming in the flickering light of the diyas.

Gandhari nods, 'Yes, Mataji,' knowing there will be more questions.

'Have you anything to tell us, Beti?' The question is hopeless yet unbearably brittle and Gandhari knows that, next to her, Rajmata Ambika is anxiously kneading her rudraksha beads as she awaits an answer.

'No, Mataji.'

Satyavati sighs and appears to shrivel up a little more. The fabric of her life has been shaped by babies. Either they came too soon, unwanted, or they would not come at all and had to be wrested from a reluctant fate. This girl from the north worries her and she knows the people are saying she has gathered a potent force through her sacrifice. For all the years she has spent negotiating people's frailties and desires, Satyavati knows she was outmanoeuvred by Gandhari's appalling decision to blindfold herself. Now, despite her growing impatience, she reminds herself to treat her bahu gently.

'All right, Beti. Go to your quarters and rest, I will have some special kheer sent to you, it will help in conceiving a child. We will also have a yajna tomorrow. The purohits have promised me that this time they will not fail me.'

And so, Gandhari, led by Lata, goes to Dritrashtra's chambers, where his searching, sensitive hands on the contours of her face still feel like a violation. But she will submit to this and to the unembarrassed ministrations of the purohits and the old women. For she knows now that despite the desperate sacrifice of her sight, this is all that she has been reduced to. She is no longer a raja's daughter or a cherished sister or a sanctified daughter-in-law. She is a womb, a mother in abeyance. And until the day the great mother goddess blesses her womb and allows a child to grow, she is nothing at all. An unstructured and incomplete thing.

An eternity later, when she feels the first slow stain of nausea, Gandhari is filled with a joy that veers rapidly into hysteria. Lata tries to temper her happiness for fear of attracting the ever-spiteful evil spirits but Gandhari will not be contained. She feels the goddess' spirit in her body, in the sudden warmth of her blood and the lustre of her hair. Increasingly, Gandhari prefers to keep her blindfold on at all times, her senses withdrawing from the inconstant world around her to the quickening one within her.

And so when Lata comes running one day in the early spring to tell Gandhari that the envoys have returned and that a new bahu comes to Hastinapur, she doesn't register the urgency of the news at all. She is now a molten, hallowed thing of quick heartbeats, loud, pulsing blood and sudden desires. The constant incantations of the vigilant purohits fill her ears and she is moulded and reshaped in the brazier of their faith.

'Let her come,' she thinks to herself, distracted by her endless hunger. 'Let her try and stake a claim to this kingdom. The firstborn son of the firstborn prince will be mine and I will not allow my sacrifice to have been for nothing.'

bamboo, and plaited leaves, and Dritrashtra sends them constant supplies from Hastinapur, so that they live in relative comfort. He sends them fine-grained rice, honey, and spices but also thick rugs, silk coverings, and steel-tipped arrows. Pandu and his men hunt deer and wild buffaloes and pheasants which are roasted whole on large spits along with carp and trout that are fished from the rivers.

Kunti and Madri's day begins at dawn, with a salutation to the rising sun. Then they help Pandu with the morning sandhyas in the complete concentration that isolation allows; for that moment, they become the flickering flames and the spreading sunlight. After Pandu leaves for the hunt, they have endless household chores to occupy them. They must measure out the rice for the day, complete the ritual of the threshold worship, tend to the creamy white cows which Dritrashtra has sent them, and take stock of the foraged fruits and roots. For Kunti it is a reclaiming of the simple joys of her childhood in Mathura. As winter settles with a sudden shiver, much earlier than it does in the river valley, Kunti decides she could live here forever.

Away from the incessant and glittering gaze of the palace, Kunti feels an oppressive burden lift from her. She tends to Pandu's faltering health with ceaseless care. She crushes fresh roots and leaves herself to prepare his potions according to the physician's instructions and visits the nearby hermitage to consult with their yogis. When his pain is very bad, she gives Pandu the precious soma juice in careful doses that make him sleep and dream of tigers. She explains clearly to Madri all the recommendations of the physician.

'Madri, make sure you are never alone in the raja's company. He must not exert himself until he is strong and well. Do you understand what I am saying?'

The young girl blushes and nods quickly, then pulls her upper garment to cover her face.

V

The Virgin from Mathura

The Road to Hastinapur

~

The wedding procession that leaves the Yadav kingdom on a January morning is frugal and threadbare but the bride in the palanquin is brittle with joy. Kunti has been living a life deferred, waiting for a time when she could leave Kuntibhoja's fiefdom, and all its dark associations forever. At nearly twenty, she is almost too old for a respectable marriage but the groom who rides at the head of the procession in a two-horse chariot is as beautiful as a young god. When Kunti saw him at her swayamvar the day before, resplendent in his red dhoti and gold crown, she lost her heart to him at once, irrevocably and unquestioningly. His pale gold complexion was the colour of freshly churned milk and his fine ornaments appeared to be smelted to his skin. He sat with careless grace on the divan, distracted and restless, but rose with a quick smile when Kunti walked up to him with a marigold garland in her hands.

Kunti's adopted father, Kuntibhoja, had been trying for a good many years to find a groom for Kunti but to her shame and increasing humiliation, no suitable candidate was ever found. Kunti has no dowry, just a few scrawny head of cattle and a trunk of new clothes but no gold, no servants, and no horses. She also realizes now, with regret, that she is not beautiful. She is tall and solidly built with round shoulders and broad hips. She walks with a contrite slouch to hide her height and her broad face, inherited from her tribal mother, though open and warm, is coarse rather than pretty.

Even so, Kuntibhoja is a respected Yadav clan head and an acceptable match would have been found but for the squalid secret that would not remain hidden, even after all these years. Kunti knows that people whisper about her behind her back, and sometimes even, in oblique references, to her face. Lubricious and intolerable half-truths guessed at and adorned.

So when Kunti's adopted mother came rushing in to find her one day when she was helping with the livestock in the stables, she could not imagine that her endless wait was finally over.

'Beti, get ready quickly. We have a very honoured guest visiting us, the Pitama of Hastinapur. He has come with his nephew Raja Pandu, and they are looking for a bride for the raja.'

'Me, Mataji? A raja?'

'Yes, I know, it is quite remarkable good fortune for you, a simple Yadav clanswoman. The raja must need an alliance in these parts but whatever the reason, we must arrange for a swayamvar at once.'

A few cursory and amenable local chieftains were rounded up and an impromptu swayamvar convened, in which Kunti lost her heart and claimed her destiny, however illusory. The haste with which Kuntibhoja offered Kunti to Raja Pandu was indecent but she had overstayed her welcome in his home and he has children of his own approaching marriageable age.

Now Kunti wraps a woollen cloth around her shoulders, shivering as the fog sweeps in from the Yamuna. She does not look back at the large, rambling house which has never felt like home though she has lived in it for more than ten years. She remembers instead the day she was given away by her father, so easily and nonchalantly as if she were a wooden toy or a dish of sweetened milk rather than a substantial child. A day when she was still a cherished child with a name of her own, Pritha. It was a day like any other, in the eternal and unchanging landscape of her childhood, filled with noise and laughter and tears. All of this would be blighted in an instant as, in his large house on the outskirts of Mathura, Shurasena gave away his young daughter to his childless friend in a calamitous and generous act that knocked Pritha right out of the orbit of her life. Perhaps it was his recently abandoned ambulatory and nomadic life that made Shurasena disregard his daughter's need for constancy and home and a mother's love. Certainly the wanton excess of a dozen children when his friend had none at all made the gesture inevitable.

Pritha did not go quietly with Kuntibhoja. She ran through the house, past the stables with her beloved calves, the herb garden, and the armoury till she reached the soot-blackened kitchen area where her mother was boiling rice for the evening meal. She hugged her mother's knees with all her strength and begged her not to send her away. But Pritha's mother, a tribal woman whose endless pregnancies had gouged her out and left her hollowed and parched, shook her head and sighed. She held her daughter by the shoulders and looked at her plain, open face, disfigured now by tears and sorrow.

'Beti, this is not such a terrible thing. Kuntibhoja is a good man and will look after you well. His wife cries day and night for a child and isn't it our duty to share our blessings with them?'

Pritha will always remember the crumbling terror she felt when she realized she had been set aside so easily by her mother. That her love, unquestioned all these years, was a finite and tidy thing which could be folded up and given away. She remembers screaming as she was half dragged, half carried through the house and the distraught faces of her brothers and sisters. She knew, with a child's ferocious certainty, that she would never see them again and that on this watchful, sullen day she had lost everything.

In Kuntibhoja's lonely home, their days were ruled by the purohits. Kuntibhoja's wife, taut and breathless from her childlessness, had the minutiae of her days sanctioned by the local priests and the occasional visiting soothsayer. She was wary of the night, of the scurrilous ghosts and the whispering winds. Pritha was a graceless, awkward child, with large, stumbling feet and long limbs, now carelessly referred to as Kunti, daughter of Kuntibhoja. Kuntibhoja's wife greeted her with suppressed resentment, her presence a constant reminder of her failure as a wife. She was blunt and unequivocal in rejecting Kunti's timid overtures and it soon became clear to the girl why she had been brought to Kuntibhoja's house. She was a borrowed child, an interloper, a child in absentia until the true heir was born. She was there to facilitate the birth of a son by serving the truculent purohits while they navigated the treacherous path to placating the gods.

So Kunti spent the next few years slowly forgetting that she was once the cherished daughter and companionable sister of an exuberant and joyful clan. She never learnt the names of her late-born siblings and she forgot the snuffling, wide-eyed charm of the calves she loved. Instead, she tended to the scraggly priests and their incessant demands. She developed a secret habit of hoarding all the leftover offerings, the laddoos, the ghee, and the honey, which she then ate furtively in the dark of the night. She took some comfort in her abundant thighs and generous arms, the weight a counterpoint to her hopeless feeling of insignificance.

One monsoon, Sadhu Durvasa came by Kuntibhoja's kingdom and agreed to stay awhile in the chieftain's home. He was a sadhu renowned as much for his explosive and unpredictable temper as for his occult powers. Kuntibhoja and his wife spoke to Kunti about the visit of the sadhu.

'Beti, the future of the clan depends on you. If you serve Durvasa well, he will certainly bless this house with a son.' Kuntibhoja spoke to her gently, averting his gaze from her clear, dark eyes in which the sadness was a scalding rebuke.

'Child, do not let vanity or pride prevent you from doing your duty towards the sadhu. You must do whatever he asks of you, no matter how menial.'

Kuntibhoja's wife's directions were stark and merciless.

Kunti had no choice but to obey and she served the tall and gaunt Durvasa with patience and simmering resentment. The sadhu's whims and demands were arbitrary and unsettling. He asked for kheer in the middle of the night and warm water for a bath in the early dawn. He needed a constant supply of freshly plucked tulsi and banana leaves and marigold flowers for his furious and fiery oblations. He had no constancy or routine in his habits, preferring sometimes to pray through the night over the smoky fires while the rain crashed down. His anger was incendiary and his curses abominations. But one day in the midst of the curses, when she felt she could bear no more, Durvasa gave Kunti a gift.

'You have no father anymore, child, you are but a foundling in this house. Learn this mantra I am about to teach you and you will be able to summon a superior being and have sons, as many as you need, to anchor you in this world.' Kunti learnt the mantra and whispered it to herself one day, not thinking it would ever work. But it did and the stranger who walked in with the rising sun that day smiled at her as he caught her hand and dragged her into the hut.

It was a year before Durvasa was ready once again to resume his nomadic wandering. He called Kuntibhoja and his wife before leaving.

'I have been very pleased with the way I was looked after in your house, especially by the child Kunti. She is a true and virtuous kanya, a virgin, in her heart and in her mind. I have taught her some very powerful mantras, which will protect her whenever she recites them. Her selflessness is a tribute to your house and clan. Your house will certainly be blessed with a son, and your clan will endure a hundred years.'

The sadhu's words were indeed prophetic but the first son to be born was to Kunti. Nobody noticed the pregnancy for many months, not even Kunti, who had been so assiduous in her desire to anchor herself to the world with her girth and weight. Finally, one of the old servant women noticed Kunti's swollen belly and ceaseless appetite and after that she was confined to the hut in the mango orchard, recently vacated by Durvasa.

The old woman stayed with her as Kunti dreamt of ripening mangoes and the tiger-claw amulets on her brothers' arms. At last, after two days of expanding, escalating pain, a boy was born, slick and salty with blood. The old woman cleaned the baby and whispered the holy mantras in his ears but Kunti turned away and cried for her mother. For one week, Kunti stayed in the hut, broken by pain and exhaustion. She could not bear to look at the baby, his searching mouth and new, flushed skin. On the eighth day, the old woman returned from the main house, clutching a bundle to her chest.

'Kuntibhoja will not allow him in the house, Beti, it could be inauspicious for the mistress. Such a beautiful baby, it is really a great pity.'

'What shall we do then, Madhu Mai? Am I to be sent away?'

But it was the baby who was to be sent away, floating down the river in a bamboo basket, to take his chances with the tide and the long-nosed gharial. The old woman tucked Kuntibhoja's gifts, golden ear studs and waistband, carefully into the basket and then pushed it gently into the middle of the slow-moving river. Kunti stood by, watching the bobbing, spinning basket in the drizzling sunlight. She was bewildered by her lack of feeling for the baby but had a foreboding, nonetheless, of a monstrous reckoning to come.

Kunti reaches Hastinapur in a fervour of joy and anticipation. She wants to embrace the servant women who garland her as she steps over the threshold of the palace and sing along with the musicians greeting the wedding party. There is the turmoil of newly acquired family members to meet over the next few weeks and a burden of etiquette to remember but Kunti is undaunted. She is finally free from the tyranny of her tainted virtue and her future is sparkling and new as the moon after the deep darkness of amavasya.

Kunti bows low before Rajmata Satyavati, who approves of this young bride's wide, child-bearing hips. Kunti notices and is amazed by Satyavati's diminished but still stormy beauty and is disarmed by Rajmata Ambalika's tiny build. She towers over her mother-in-law when she greets her and Ambalika pulls down Kunti's head with sudden candour to kiss her on her forehead.

'Welcome, Beti. May you have a long and happy life in the Devi's light and may you be blessed with a hundred sons. May you and your husband rule with wisdom over this great kingdom.'

Back in the opulence of the royal quarters, Kunti is still stupefied by the realization that she is rani of this ancient and sprawling mahanagar. The expert hair groomers who have been given to her use their arsenal of oils and combs to tease some weight and volume into her lank hair and they stud the elaborate styles with tiny, glittering gemstones. Her servant girls bring her kohl to outline her far-set eyes with and lac to colour her lips. Her face expertly made-up and decked in all manner of glittering accoutrements, Kunti feels for the first time the intoxicating glamour of beauty. She loses her uncertain slouch and walks tall and true through the palace corridors. She wanders through the outer courts to visit the stables, the elephant stalls, and aviary, and discovers the sheds with the war chariots and the huge royal granaries piled high with rice. Weeks after her arrival, she is still thrilled to be getting lost in the maze of these cool, dark corridors and sudden, blazing courtyards.

In the evenings, tiny clay lamps flicker in the warm night breeze charged with the smell of jasmine and sandalwood incense. There is dancing and singing in the main courtyards. Later at night, Pandu visits her in the royal quarters and Kunti's face is flushed and young and the grape wine is an exhilarating green escape.

An agnistoma is announced, to consecrate the young raja and rani. Priests and workers intersect in the sacrificial arena, measuring out the sacred geometry of the altars and hearths. Huts are installed for the sixteen anointed purohits and planks are dressed for the pressing of the divine, all-conquering soma plant.

On the day of the agnistoma, the sixteen altars are blazing while the purohits sit bare-chested before the fires and pour ghee and camphor into the ravenous flames. Pandu and Kunti sit before the raised main altar and intone the mantras along with the purohits. All around them the fires flare and crackle and the air is dense with smoke and incense. Finally, the golden soma juice, pressed at dawn, is poured into the fires and carries with it to the unpredictable and vengeful gods the binary desires of all the men—a good harvest in the fields and babies in the bellies of their women.

At the end of the agnistoma some of the soma juice is drunk by the raja and rani as they watch the fire burn down to ash. For the next few hours their thoughts swirl and coalesce on the wind and the colours are sparkling stars.

Not long after the agnistoma, Pandu leaves with a small party of soldiers on a tour of the outlying, fractious lands in his kingdom.

The evenings are calmer, the air no longer combusting with Pandu's uncertain energy and Kunti goes often to the large enclosed gardens towards the rear of the palace. This is the domain of the women, with its carefully tended herb garden and flowering shrubs and trees. There are hibiscus shrubs, champa, jasmine, and the fabulous kimsuka whose powdery scarlet flowers make Kunti think of fires on the mountainside.

Ira Mukhoty

Gandhari and her entourage are sitting in the covered pavilions in the centre of the gardens, stringing flower garlands for the evening puja. Kunti walks up to her sister-in-law and bows low before her. Kunti senses that Gandhari bristles over being denied many of the privileges due to the senior wife and is quick to demonstrate her placatory respect.

'Welcome, Rani. I trust you are getting used to the ways of the palace and lack for nothing.'

Gandhari, prompted by Lata and guided by the sound of Kunti's clinking bracelets and the honey-rich smell of the jasmine, maps the contours of the garden in her mind.

Kunti notices Gandhari's swollen belly and satiated indolence and is reminded of the dank and musty hut in the mango orchard.

'Bhagini, you are very kind. Everyone has been so accommodating with me that I have faced no problems at all.'

Lata has already informed Gandhari of Kunti's heavy, graceless limbs and uncertain smile. Serene and replete at last in her pregnancy, Gandhari feels wide and timeless as a river.

'You must be very lonely now that Raja Pandu has gone away. Please come and play dice with me every evening.'

So the two women play dice as the heat rises from the fragrant earth and the air is filled with fluttering yellow butterflies for whom each evening is a lifetime. As dusk descends, translucent lizards come out from the chinks in the stones and fix their fatal gaze on the moths and dragonflies.

As the weeks go by, Kunti is filled with disquiet as she sees Gandhari's body swell though her belly remains taut as a drum. She has seen enough of her mother's endless pregnancies to sense that something is amiss and is not surprised one morning to find the palace filled with the sound of women wailing.

Her servant girls come rushing to her quarters, carrying the morning's garlands, breathless with gossip.

'Rajkumari Gandhari has miscarried! They are saying she gave birth to a misformed lump of flesh, the devil himself.'

'Quiet! Hold your tongue and don't talk rubbish. Anyone can miscarry, it is a terrible thing for Rajkumari Gandhari.'

Kunti tries to contain the women's talk but the palace is molten with blasphemous rumours of black magic and spirits. The young purohit with the blazing eyes is in constant attendance and there is terrifying talk of expiatory rituals over the nameless chimera that Gandhari has birthed.

Pandu returns from his campaigns and life for Kunti continues as before and it is a long while before she meets Gandhari again. She goes one evening to the garden pavilions in the oppressive gloaming of a monsoon day but the friable truce is broken and Gandhari is savage and disarrayed with grief.

'Have you come here to gloat, Rani? Does it give you any pleasure to contemplate my loss?'

Kunti backs away from the snarling woman, startled, but Gandhari cannot stop now.

'One more thing, Rani, isn't it time you had some good fortune to share with everyone? Almost a year since you were married, isn't it so? Surely the Devi has blessed your womb by now. Come, do not be shy.'

Kunti drops the gift of amla and honey syrup she had brought for Gandhari and runs back to her quarters, scattering her retinue behind her. Kunti locks herself in her room and tries to calm down but Gandhari has unerringly drawn out the troubled darkness at the heart of Kunti's life. She is hounded by the covetous rajmatas who constantly enquire about her condition and the appraising Bheeshma who is a silent rebuke whenever she appears before him with her flat belly.

Kunti's isolation in the palace of Hastinapur is complete and dangerous. She has no kinsmen, no allies, and no friends. Her father and her tribe discarded her a long time ago and she knows that no one will take up arms on her behalf. Her only hope against a barren and blighted fate is to bear a healthy son and she is confounded by the polluting blood that stains her dhoti every month. She has no one to talk to about Pandu's nameless pain and his regular use of the soma juice which subdues the pain and gives him visions of conquering glory and invincibility. She cannot tell the rajmatas that Pandu visits her infrequently and often leaves in the early evening to return to the easy bonhomie of his court and that when he does stay with her, he is filled with a blustering breathlessness that terrifies her.

After Gandhari repudiates her, Kunti turns to the gentle and wise Vidura, half-brother and counsellor to Pandu. Vidura is married to Sulabha, a Yadav woman like herself, whose candid simplicity is a sanctuary after the crackling incertitude of palace intrigue. But even Vidura is helpless before Bheeshma's implacable will and a year after Kunti's swayamvar, a new bride for Pandu steps into Hastinapur with red lac on her feet.

The Rajkumari Madri is of such flawless beauty that Kunti cannot even rouse herself to jealousy and must content herself with remorseless heartbreak. Bheeshma has lured the rajkumari away from her brother, the raja of the faraway, sub-Himalayan kingdom of Madra, with gifts of gold, elephants, and jewels for the rumours of Pandu's impotence can no longer be confined to the palace. Kunti sequesters herself in her quarters and girds her heart for a life of loneliness but Pandu comes to seek her out. He has got used to her wise and equable counsel and her unmeasured love and Madri is but a lustrous and vapid child of fifteen who knows nothing of life. Madri disarms Kunti with her wanton disregard for her own beauty and her constant need for the older woman's approval. And so the two women cohabit in increasing incertitude and apprehension, each passing infertile month a blight on their happiness.

The palace, meanwhile, crackles with tensions and intrigue. Factions are formed one day to be broken the next, as rumours of fertility rites and stillbirths drift and weave from Gandhari's quarters to Kunti's. One day, Pandu summons Kunti and Vidura and tells them of his decision to leave the palace to go and live in a forest.

'Vidura, do you remember that physician when we were children? He used to give me herbal drinks and tonics to make me stronger when I was so weak. I would like to consult him before I go.'

'Yes, of course, I remember, Raja. I will send for him at once.'

The physician arrives, gnarled and ancient like a peepul tree, but with a tempered vitality that speaks of discipline and rigour.

'Raja, you were so sickly as a child and so pale. You were slow to grow and the rajmata feared for your life so many times. But my herbs and potions helped you to become strong and your decision to go to the forest now is a wise one. Go with the ranis and I will explain all the strengthening herbs you need to take. I am sure this will lead to the result we are all waiting for.'

So Pandu hands over the reins of governance to Dritrashtra, to rule in his stead during his absence. The brothers hug each other, remembering the chaotic and brash love of their childhood before all feelings got corrupted by their shared and uncertain birthright.

'Look after yourself, Brother, and come back to us healed and with the ranis blessed with sons. I will take care of the kingdom while you are gone, do not worry about anything.'

Dritrashtra holds his brother and his king a long time in his arms, reclaiming for a short while the beloved companion of his childhood games.

'I know Hastinapur is in safe hands with you, Bhai. Vidura will remain with you and will counsel you, as he has done with me all these years. As, of course, our gurus, Bheeshma and Drona, as well.'

Then, Pandu and his wives climb onto the horse-drawn chariot and, followed by their retinue of maids, soldiers, cooks, and hunters, head north towards the Shivalik hills. Pandu turns back to look at the city of elephants, Hastinapur, bleached white and eternal in the light of dawn. He does not know it yet but he will never return to Hastinapur again and the blood that will be spilled over the crown of his birthplace is inconceivable and immeasurable.

Over the next weeks and months, Pandu and his retinue make their slow, meandering way northwards through the fertile twin river valley with its marshlands, and barley and paddy fields, to the Himalayan foothills. They cross dense forests of creeping thorny trees full of peacocks and pheasants and wide rivers filled with sediment and myths. The terrain changes gradually and the blue returns to the sky like a promise remembered. The air is still and clear and charged with the fearsome trumpeting of wild elephants. In the fathomless dark of the night, the howling of the jackals fills the women with a terrible and secret longing.

They set up camp whenever they find a pleasant clearing or a whispering spring but only after it is consecrated by their purohit. Spirits lurk in all manner of places especially in large trees, at crossroads, in caves and rivers. The travellers huddle around the fire altar in the sudden dusk, the purohit a lone sentinel against the terrors of the night.

After many months of travel, Pandu and his wives arrive at Chaitratha forest at the base of the Himalayas. It is a forest of ancient sal trees, chaotic vines, monkeys, and leopards. On the clear horizon are a hundred purple peaks, a constant reminder of Shiva's desolate and sacred home. They decide to stop for the winter in the forest on the shores of the Indradyumna Lake and stay instead for fifteen years. They build simple homes of wood, bamboo, and plaited leaves and Dritrashtra sends them constant supplies from Hastinapur, so that they live in relative comfort. He sends them fine-grained rice, honey, and spices but also thick rugs, silk coverings, and steel-tipped arrows. Pandu and his men hunt deer and wild buffaloes and pheasants which are roasted whole on large spits along with carp and trout that are fished from the rivers.

Kunti and Madri's day begins at dawn, with a salutation to the rising sun. Then they help Pandu with the morning sandhyas in the complete concentration that isolation allows; for that moment, they become the flickering flames and the spreading sunlight. After Pandu leaves for the hunt, they have endless household chores to occupy them. They must measure out the rice for the day, complete the ritual of the threshold worship, tend to the creamy white cows which Dritrashtra has sent them, and take stock of the foraged fruits and roots. For Kunti it is a reclaiming of the simple joys of her childhood in Mathura. As winter settles with a sudden shiver, much earlier than it does in the river valley, Kunti decides she could live here forever.

Away from the incessant and glittering gaze of the palace, Kunti feels an oppressive burden lift from her. She tends to Pandu's faltering health with ceaseless care. She crushes fresh roots and leaves herself to prepare his potions according to the physician's instructions and visits the nearby hermitage to consult with their yogis. When his pain is very bad, she gives Pandu the precious soma juice in careful doses that make him sleep and dream of tigers. She explains clearly to Madri all the recommendations of the physician.

'Madri, make sure you are never alone in the raja's company. He must not exert himself until he is strong and well. Do you understand what I am saying?'

The young girl blushes and nods quickly, then pulls her upper garment to cover her face.

That winter, Pandu and his wives sit by Indradyumna Lake in a swirl of fog and silence and watch, mesmerized, the dainty, staccato steps of mating Siberian cranes.

In the spring, a messenger arrives from Hastinapur palace to announce the confirmed pregnancy of Gandhari.

At once, Pandu becomes clenched and silent and disappears for days on a hunting expedition. When he returns, he sends for Kunti and seeing his fevered anticipation, Kunti waits with dread to hear what he has to say.

'Kunti, you know that Rani Gandhari is pregnant. If she has a son before you do, we will be in no position to return to Hastinapur to claim the crown. You must bear a son as soon as possible.'

'But, Raja, you know that your life is in danger, we cannot risk your health and your life.'

'There is another way, Kunti, but you must listen to me with an open mind. There is a tradition quite prevalent with the northern Kurus, in which a chosen man is allowed to visit the barren wife so that she may have a child. It is called Niyoga.'

But Kunti has raised her hands to her ears and turns away from Pandu in shame and revulsion. Visions of the cold and dark hut in Kuntibhoja's home, where she lay powerless and sobbing, return to nauseate her.

'No, no, Raja. I refuse absolutely. What you ask of me is an abomination and no honourable woman would consent to it.'

'Kunti, please listen to me. That is not true at all. In our ancient texts, it was quite common for our women to have lovers other than their husbands. They were free to roam the world and choose their partners. It is only recently that women are required to stay with their husbands.'

But Kunti refuses to listen any more and runs away to milk the cow for the evening sandhya. Pandu will not try and speak to her about this matter in front of Madri.

But Pandu bides his time and lies in wait for Kunti one day when she is returning from bathing in the river. Madri has been consigned to a small hut as it is her polluting time of the month. Pandu sends away the servant girls accompanying Kunti with a wave of his hand.

Pandu is agitated as he speaks to Kunti now, pacing irresolute circles around her.

'Kunti, this practice has been carried out before, in our very household. The Ranis Ambika and Ambalika too had children through Niyoga with Vyasa. You must know this. It is my wish and my desire that you bear children and, indeed, if you refuse, it is as though you have murdered my unborn sons.'

But Pandu's bluster enrages Kunti. It terrifies her also, as it threatens to split apart her seamless life with its unanswerable past. She can only maintain the lie of her irreproachable virtue by constant denial. She avoids Pandu for many days and is tormented by the decision she needs to make. She wonders also whether this was the actual reason for Pandu's decision to come to the forest. Perhaps he has known all along that it would come to this. How easy it seems for him, the anonymous and magnanimous lending of her womb while she twists and baulks at the thought.

But Kunti also knows that time is no longer on her side and she needs sons now as a bulwark against a life of loneliness and destitution. She needs sons that Pandu can claim as his own since everything Kunti has is his to dispose of as he wishes.

So when Pandu comes up to her one last time with hands folded, a supplicant with tears in his eyes to beg for an heir, her anger disappears and she falls at his feet.

'Forgive me, Raja. It is great adharma for you to have to ask me for something so many times. I only ask that I may choose the father of my sons. A long time ago, Sadhu Durvasa gave me a mantra when I served him well as a girl. It allows me to summon a superior being for this very purpose and I shall bear you a son.'

Pandu is delighted with Kunti's change of heart and makes all the necessary arrangements while Kunti gathers herself in silence to remember that long-ago mantra. The years pass and Kunti gives birth to three strapping boys, Yudhishthir, Bheem, and Arjun. But when Pandu asks her for a fourth son, she refuses. She has done her duty as a wife.

'Enough, Raja, I can do no more. Even the scriptures do not sanction a fourth conception through Niyoga. I have given you three sons to perform your rites and ensure your passage to heaven. You must not ask me for more.'

Meanwhile, Madri, who has been helping Kunti with her babies, is undone by the strength with which they grab her hair and the crushing love she feels at their toothless smiles and she goes to ask Pandu for a child. Pandu speaks to Kunti first, and only when she agrees to it does he sanction the use of the mantra for Madri. When Madri has twin boys, Nakul and Sahadev, Kunti is taken aback and is adamant when Pandu approaches her again.

'I refuse, Raja, I cannot allow Madri to use my mantra again. She tricked me by having two sons in one pregnancy. She may have more sons than me if I allow you to sanction Niyoga through the mantra again.

'I was a fool to allow it the first time, now don't come to me begging for more sons for her.'

Kunti has understood by now the true heft of sons and knows that friendship and sympathy and even love are precarious things easily set aside in the pursuit of the immortality that accompanies sons. So the five boys are brought up in the raucous freedom of the jungle, far from the combustible intimacy of the palace.

The years turn into a decade and still they do not return to Hastinapur. They hear disquieting rumours of Gandhari's magical and multiple pregnancies, a cacophony of sons. Kunti knows that in the palace, the boys will no longer be hers to mould and love but will be handed over to Guru Drona and the Pitama who will make them warriors first and men later. In the forest with the five boisterous boys, she has created the long-ago lost tribe of her childhood and has wrested from her indifferent fate a keystone to hold on to.

Kunti continues to watch over Pandu carefully but she worries about Madri, who has become a beautiful and alluring woman. She notices Pandu following her with his eyes when she goes to bathe in the river and when she sits down with them for the evening sandhya.

One morning, in spring, when the lotuses have begun their long vigil for the summer, Madri comes running out of the forest, dishevelled and distraught. She starts sobbing as soon as she sees Kunti.

'I am sorry, Bhagini, forgive me, I am sorry.'

She is unable to say anything else and Kunti follows her into the forest, icy with fear. When she sees Pandu lying dead under a harsingar tree, she hears a hopeless wailing that stills the song of the koels in the trees and it is the sound of her own weeping—she is crying for the beautiful young man he was and the tortured older one he became. She collapses besides Pandu and holds his head against her breast and kisses the forbidden lips a last time.

'O Madri, how could you. I had warned you against tempting the raja, you knew he was not strong enough to lie with you. I have watched him and guarded him all these years and now you have killed him and made orphans of our children.'

Madri stands forlornly beside the limp body, her tears dried up in the face of Kunti's terrible grief.

'I am sorry, Bhagini,' she whispers, her voice husky. 'I was not able to stop him and I have failed you. I have nothing to live for now, I will sit on the pyre with our husband and be consumed by the flames. You will look after my children as your own for I have seen the love you give them always.'

Pandu is brought back to the camp and the sadhus from the hermitage are summoned immediately to perform the death rites. The first thing they do is to place a few tulsi leaves and a few drops of water in Pandu's mouth. Then they remove all of Pandu's clothes, bathe him, and wrap him in a length of raw, undyed, and uncut cloth. Kunti removes all her jewellery and her bright cotton dhoti and puts on the unbleached white clothes which she will wear for the rest of her life. Madri, sequestered in her hut, puts on her red dhoti shot through with gold and all the jewellery she wore as a bride. The sadhus put a fresh flower garland around Pandu's neck and Kunti twines a holy rudraksha mala around her wrist, the only ornament she can now wear.

Meanwhile, the five boys are in a huddle of confusion and misery. Their mothers are feral and savage in their grief and will not speak to them, so the younger boys cling to Yudhishthir and Bheem. Suddenly, they see Madri come out of her hut, resplendent in her bride's clothes and they rush towards her but she pushes them away. When Kunti sees Madri ready to follow the funereal procession, her eyes fill with tears for the blameless young girl who came to Hastinapur, asking only to be loved. She runs to give her the remainder of the soma juice and forces the liquid past her lips.

'Drink this, Madri, my beloved sister. This is all I can do for you now.'

Kunti hopes that the soma juice will distance Madri from her grief and lessen the pain when the flames singe her living flesh. She watches the sadhus and Yudhishthir carry away Pandu's body on a bier towards the consecrated cremation ground followed by Madri and the other boys. She waits on the threshold of her hut, thrumming with tension and when she hears Madri's screams, she puts her hands to her ears and sobs. The funeral is over quickly, halted early by the sadhus. They bring back the twins who are hysterical with revulsion. They have seen their mother step onto the blazing pyre and hold their dead father's head in her lap. They have seen her twisting and spinning with the flames, a human inferno, and it is a crackling vision of madness and grief that will haunt their dreams for the rest of their days.

The Return to Hastinapur

~

The next morning at dawn, the sombre and macabre procession sets off for Hastinapur. The sadhus have had a long discussion amongst themselves and with Kunti. Her presence in the forest alone, with five small children, is perilous. With no husband to protect her and no father to claim the boys, they are on the verge of a dangerous destitution. These frugal and solitary sadhus have agreed to make an exception to their austerities and accompany Kunti to Hastinapur. They lead the bedraggled procession, their strides brisk and economical after their long years of extreme penance.

For Kunti, this journey to Hastinapur is a bitter travesty of the one she made all those years ago as a bride in a palanquin. She has lost the only man she will love and her future as a widow is uncertain. Her fate, and that of the five boys, depends entirely on the outcome of her arrival at Hastinapur.

It takes the party two weeks to reach the city of elephants and messengers have alerted the residents a while ago. A small group of soldiers is waiting at dawn to escort the visitors to the gates of Hastinapur where a disparate group of tradesmen, curious women, and onlookers is waiting expectantly. Kunti notices that all the members of the royal household are present as well—Bheeshma, Dritrashtra, Vidura, Satyavati, Ambika, Ambalika, and Gandhari.

The eldest sadhu steps forward to speak to the royal family.

'Raja, I have brought back your sister-in-law, Rani Kunti, recently widowed wife of Raja Pandu. He died a short while ago, after living a pious and dharmic life close to our hermitage for many years. These are his five sons, whom I entrust to your care, along with their mother.'

Kunti holds the twins close to her and watches the reaction of the royal household intently. Her whole future depends on this moment. If they disclaim her then she loses everything and faces a life of degradation and poverty. She notices the uncertainty in their eyes. They have not seen her in fifteen years and there is not much left in Kunti of the hopeful bride she was. As for the children, they are a scanty and insignificant lot, dubious pretenders to the throne of Hastinapur.

The sadhu motions to a group standing apart, bearing two biers, and they move forward.

'Here are the bodies of Raja Pandu and Rani Madri, who chose to accompany her husband. We have brought them here so that you may give them fitting funerals, as befits their royal status.'

The sadhus carefully place the biers on the floor and remove the white chador covering the bodies and there is a collective gasp from the townsmen. The restless crowd mutters and ripples forward and a woman in the crowd shrieks. Bheeshma is rigid and bleak with an emotion that Kunti cannot read and fears is intransigence. Dritrashtra and Gandhari, sensing the palpable horror and surprise, try to turn to Vidura for an explanation. But Ambalika is stumbling towards the bier now and crumples onto the bodies. This quiet woman who has lived her life in the shadow of Bheeshma's iron will now slices the clean air with her grief which is a vaulting filament of sound that hushes everyone else.

'My son, my son,' she wails, her long, loose hair covering Pandu's body.

For the bodies on the bier were only partially cremated, the fires carefully stoked and controlled then hastily extinguished before the faces were obscured. The two bodies are shrivelled and blackened and the white bones of their limbs gleam obscenely but their features are recognizable and accusatory. A pile of ash could have been denied, the sadhus and Kunti realized, but not so easily this grisly bride and her once royal groom.

At last Bheeshma steps forward and gently pulls Ambalika away and Kunti realizes that his stillness is an armour and that his grief is lucid and clear.

'Vidura,' he whispers, in a broken voice. 'Go and make all the arrangements for a royal funeral. Our beloved Rajkumar Pandu is come back to us at last and the land of his ancestors will mourn him for the magnificent prince of Hastinapur that he was.'

At this signal from Bheeshma, the people of Hastinapur start wailing and shrieking, tearing at their clothes and hair. All the women let down their long hair in mourning and the sight of the shameless abandonment of these normally decorous women is appalling. Even Satyavati and Ambika and Gandhari tear at their hair and fling aside all their jewellery.

The royal priests bring the sacred fire from the city and build an altar on the banks of the Ganga. The charcoal-black bodies of Pandu and Madri are wrapped in clean clothes, covered in fresh flowers, and smeared with perfume. Then the biers are carried down to the river, followed by the weeping women and men distributing jewellery and garments in honour of the dead. Attendants carry the royal white umbrella and white yak tail fans beside the bodies, reminders of their royal lineage.

On the banks of the eternal river, Yudhishthir and his brothers set fire to the bodies covered in lotuses. Ambalika faints as the flames finally engulf the bodies and the boys are disconsolate and wordless.

Everyone lies down to sleep on the ground that night and no one enters Hastinapur during the twelve days of mourning while the souls of Pandu and Madri scatter slowly into the forgiving sky.

Then, on the twelfth day, a last oblation of food and soma is offered to the dead who are now consigned to Indra. Everyone bathes in the Ganga and puts on new clothes, the old clothes tainted forever by death and so discarded.

As the royal family prepares to return to the city with Kunti and the children, Vyasa steps forward and stops them. He has arrived in Hastinapur during the twelve days of mourning, alert always to the arrival of catastrophic news.

'Mataji,' he tells Satyavati, 'you need not return to Hastinapur now. Having witnessed the funeral of your own grandson, you and Mata Ambika and Ambalika should not return to a life of sorrow and pain. Only old age and death await you now, the time for pleasure and joy is long gone.'

Satyavati is confounded and bewildered and does not understand what Vyasa means.

'But, Son,' she stammers, 'what would you have us do? Three old women like us, where will we go, if not to our home in Hastinapur?'

'You may go to the forest, where there are many hermitages and holy men who will give you shelter. It is time for you to gather yourselves and meditate on death and the afterlife.'

For the first time in her life in Hastinapur, Satyavati is at a loss. She does not know how to sway this hard and forbidding son.

'At least allow my daughters-in-law to remain here. I am old and useless, it is true, and I can manage the hardships of the forest but what will they do? They have never lived outside the confines of a palace their whole lives.'

But Vyasa is already turning away, his fleeting patience spent.

'You will be a comfort to each other and I am sure the rajmatas have no appetite any more for palace life in their bereaved condition.'

Satyavati searches desperately for Bheeshma and for Dritrashtra but they have already gone away. Only Kunti turns around to look at the huddle of women near the river. She is overwhelmed by sadness and pity for them, even the relentless Satyavati. Despite a lifetime of vigilance and ruthless brinkmanship, she is laid low now and discarded like old clothes after a funeral. Kunti knows there is nothing she can do for the women and that her position is still precarious and fragile in the clan of the Kurus, despite Bheeshma's acceptance. So she turns away from the river and the abandoned women and follows the five boys through the high vaulted archway into Hastinapur.

VI

The Scent of the Blue Lotus

The Inferno

~

Years later, when Kunti dreams of the fire, all she will remember is the noise. The crackling, roaring, crepitation of the flames, her desperate and ragged breath and the muffled footsteps of the five boys as they scramble through the tiny, musty underground tunnel. The passage opens into a sugarcane field where the tall, rustling canes give them cover as they run desperately to the edge of the river.

The flames from the burning palace have grown even higher now and they are monstrous as they snap and crash towards the night sky. Kunti turns back for a second to look at the inferno that was her home and she feels the heat from the flames enfold her like the breath of some mythical beast. She turns back towards the boys clustered around her, their faces consumed by their eyes which are dark pools in which a single crimson flame dances.

Kunti pushes the boys roughly towards the small boat that Vidura had promised her she would find by the edge of the river.

'Hurry up, boys, hurry up. We are not safe yet, we have to go as far away from Hastinapur as possible.'

Bheem and Arjun row across the lake while the younger boys cry silent tears of fear and humiliation. They had never quite believed Kunti when she had whispered to them her suspicions about Gandhari's sons. They had all been tempestuous and rowdy playmates these past few years and they hadn't noticed the gradual but corrosive jealousy that had tainted Duryodhan's once generous and volatile love. For them the betrayal is complete and the grief uncontainable.

Kunti turns her back to the flames as the boat slides across the water and stares ahead at the dense black of the forest. When they reach the other side, she doesn't let the boys linger and drags them into the darkness of the jungle. They stumble and run the whole night through the forest, slithering and stumbling over twisting roots. Their clothes are torn to rags and their bare feet bleed darkly into the parched forest floor.

Kunti only allows them to stop in the hour before sunrise, when the koel starts its lonely, husky vigil. They huddle around the massive trunk of a rosewood tree; the five brothers hold their heads in their hands, suffocated by despondency.

But Kunti is thrumming now with exhilaration, relieved beyond measure after these endless months of ferocious and lethal waiting. For years she alone has kept her sons safe in the treacherous court of Hastinapur. Widowed, friendless, and without a single powerful ally or any relative of consequence, she has made sure her sons survived and thrived in the dangerous company of Gandhari's sons. Gandhari's sons, who are legion, while hers are only five. Gandhari's sons who are not really hers at all, but mostly the sons of Dritrashtra and his many concubines. Only a few are actually Gandhari's and yet they are all gathered together in fractious and familiar intimacy under the consanguineous title of Kauravas, heirs of the Kuru race. Under the skilled guidance of the Gurus Drona and Kripa, Kunti's five sons have become expert warriors and shrewd tacticians. Kunti watched over them constantly, while remaining in the shadows of the palace. She baulked sometimes at the complete reversal of her situation when faced with Gandhari, who is replete with the excess of her sons and her role as matriarch. Simmering spats arose between the two women, each one bristling at the thought of slights, real or imagined, in that court where kingship was uncertain and brothers a threat.

Only once in all these years was Kunti blindsided. It was on a spring day, fragrant and still, when an archery tournament was to be held between all the cousins. Amongst the Pandavas it is Arjun, with his clear concentration and fluid limbs who is the best archer by far. To Duryodhan's resentment, Arjun hit all the targets with ease all day and was about to be named the winner when an unknown young man walked into the arena. He was tall with broad, scarred shoulders and a self-conscious nobility which instantly made him the vortex of the jostling and bragging men. He began hitting all the targets with deadly, swooshing arrows and it was then that Kunti noticed the burnished gold waistband and ear studs that glowed warmly against his polished dark skin. She saw the golden orb and the radiating spokes which she had tucked carefully into a floating basket years ago, took a step backwards and fainted into Vidura's arms.

Later, when she was sitting on a wicker bed in the gloom of the evening, Vidura handed her a clay pot of water and she asked him what happened at the tournament.

'His name is Karna,' Vidura told her. 'He is a charioteer's son, much too lowly a person to participate in the tournament, of course, but a fine archer, nevertheless. Duryodhan saw a chance to humiliate Arjun in the contest and consecrated the young man on the spot. He is now Karna, King of Anga, no less, and immensely grateful to Duryodhan for having saved him from ridicule. I am afraid Duryodhan may have gained an extremely powerful and loyal ally today.'

Vidura continued to mutter angrily to himself but Kunti was no longer listening. She was remembering instead a blood-soaked day in Durvasa's hut in which the cloying smell of overripe mangoes had been corrupted by the mineral stench of birth and blood. This tall, striding stranger was her child, whom she floated down a river with his gold waistband emblazoned with the sun. He had survived against all the odds and returned to her, a magnificent warrior drenched in light. For one night, Kunti dreamed of what could have been. She dreamed of claiming this stranger as her own, of holding his oddly familiar face with its high cheekbones and intelligent, haunted eyes in her hands. But by daybreak Kunti had understood that this could never be. She could never do this to Yudhishthir, Pandu's eldest son, and heir to the crown of Hastinapur. All his life she had stoked his dreams of kingship and taught him to rise up to his destiny as a leader of men. She had spent too many years in this febrile court spinning an armour around her five sons out of her meagre widow's tools. It was almost time now for them to step into their destiny and Karna was a sacrifice she would have to make. Now, and forever more, she would relinquish her claim to him and watch him smoulder and glow in another's care.

From that day on, Kunti increased her watchfulness. With Karna by his side, Duryodhan was suddenly untouchable. He was now openly resentful about the Pandavas' claim to the throne and the petty rivalries took on a lethal and malevolent force. When Dritrashtra was reluctantly forced to crown Yudhishthir yuvraj because of the growing popularity of this serious and scholarly young man, Duryodhan's hostility exploded. Kunti saw him flanked by Karna and Shakuni, endlessly murmuring and plotting and her heart became ice.

When Vidura took her aside one day, she was not altogether surprised at the news he brought though it filled her with a blistering fear.

'Duryodhan has lost all semblance of humanity. With Karna and Shakuni to advise him, he has become uncontrollable. My brother Dritrashtra is helpless too, or at least professes to be.'

'What is it, Bhai Vidura, what have you heard?'

'He has ordered his men to build you a large mansion in Varnavrat, which he will make a show of gifting to you and the Pandavas. But his men are packing wax and ghee into the structure of the house and coating it with lacquer, making it highly inflammable. I fear Duryodhan plans to set fire to the place and let you all burn to death in your sleep. Forgive me for being so blunt, but from now on your lives are in danger and you must be constantly on your guard.'

Kunti nodded wordlessly.

'I will have secret tunnels built under the house so that you may escape when the day comes. Tell the boys to prepare themselves for a life of exile in the forest. Tell them to learn the language of the stars and the constellations so that they may make their way even in the blanket of the night. Be prepared, at all times.'

So Kunti herded her sons close to her in the gathering storm of suspicion and distrust and became fraught with watchfulness. She moved into the traitorous house with her sons and threw open the doors to all passing strangers and relatives as is customary Kshatriya hospitality when entering a new house. On the day she saw a poor tribal woman with five children loitering outside the house waiting for alms, Kunti knew it was providence itself that had sent the woman to her.

'Come inside, Sister. Come with your children and eat and drink your fill.'

The tribal woman, with five children to feed, lets down her guard and enters Kunti's house.

She is walking to her death, Kunti thought to herself, such is her fate and that of her children.

The woman and children fell into a stupor that night, satiated by an abundance of food and wine. Kunti decided to pre-empt Duryodhan and instructed her sons to set the house on fire themselves when all the other guests had left. The next morning, when the charred remains of the tribal woman and her children were discovered, it was the Pandavas and Kunti who were mourned and wept for by the people of Hastinapur while Duryodhan exulted in the perfect success of his plan.

The Forest

~

For the next few weeks and months through the interminable summer, Kunti and the Pandavas keep moving through the unknown forests and marshlands northwards and away from Hastinapur. They abandon the last of their fine-spun clothes and learn to wear the coarse, fibrous wraps that they gather from villagers. They wear their long hair in twisted knots on the tops of their heads in the way of wandering mendicants and learn to glean meals from berries and roots. They sleep at night on the hides of animals and forget that they ever slept on soft mattresses of kusa grass and linen covers. They become sparse of speech and angular of limb as all excess is carved out of them. Their boyish muscles slide and bunch under their sun-darkened skin, grow hard and knotted as they become men.

Yudhishthir is initially the most dispirited, having lost the crown of yuvraj. He has a thoughtful, introspective temperament that will shackle all his actions for the rest of his life, and the responsibility of leadership makes him fraught with doubt. The other brothers slope and sidle around him, cutting sharp glances in his direction to gauge his mood. Bheem is bluff and distracted, overcome by an explosive and savage strength which seems to have come upon him suddenly. Arjun is lithe and luminous, coiled and silent, awaiting the call to arms. The youngest boys, Nakul and Sahadev, are little more than adolescents. They are content to be guided by their mother

159

and brothers, secure and apart in the complicit intimacy of twins.

A few days after their escape, sensing the aimlessness of her sons, Kunti sits down in the middle of the day and holds her head in her hands. She realizes that she has to rouse the boys before Bheem is consumed by his simmering anger and Yudhishthir is benumbed irrevocably by gloom. So she holds her head and strikes her brow repeatedly with the heel of her hand.

'Hai! What a wretched woman I am indeed. What a fate worse than death itself has befallen me. O Devi! It would have been better if I had died in those flames after all. What use is survival if this is to be my fate.'

The effect of her words is electric. The boys all look ashamed and Yudhishthir comes running up to put his arm around her shoulders.

'What is it, Ma? Why are you saying such things, what is troubling you so much?'

'Why am I upset, Beta? You are asking me this? Look at me, look at my condition in life now. I have nothing to eat, nowhere to sleep at night, I am dying of thirst and yet my five useless sons ask me why I am unhappy. Five grown sons and yet I am reduced to the condition of the most miserable beggar on earth!'

Yudhishthir steps back as if he has been stung by a cobra. For an instant, he is undone and then he turns to face his brothers.

'Ma is right. For too long we have been oppressed by our own selfish worries. We must look after our mother and provide for her, for we are her home now, her country and her clan. Arjun, take your arrows and bring back something good to eat. Something other than berries and yams. Bheem, bestir yourself, my brother. You are as powerful as the storm winds that bring the monsoon. Go, cut down some trees to build a shelter. Nakul and Sahadev, you have been quiet too long. Use your knowledge of the forest, the leaves and the flowers. Bring back some healing herbs and fresh water from a spring. Hurry now, Brothers, hurry.'

Arjun is gone before Yudhishthir finishes his speech, his arrows a lightning stroke against his dark back. Bheem brandishes his axe with an exuberant roar, swings it around his head once, and strides off to find timber.

Yudhishthir kneels down beside Kunti and begins massaging her scarred and aching feet.

'Forgive me, Ma,' he whispers. 'I have been remiss. What kind of son am I, and what kind of raja would I be if I cannot even take care of my mother.'

Kunti sighs and puts her hands on her son's head.

'You are the best of sons, Beta, and one day you will be the greatest of rajas.'

From that day on, as they travel northwards through Matsya and Panchala and into the seductive enchantment of the lower Himalayan tribal areas, Kunti and the Pandavas never lack for food again. They roast the meat of antelopes and wild goats and learn to fish for trout and mahseer in the sparkling Himalayan rivers. They gather brown, speckled eggs which they boil and eat with rice. They trade meat for cucumbers and brinjals and saffron from golden-skinned girls with flowers in their hair and a song in the patterns on their smooth faces. What they cannot catch or glean or trade they beg for, in the accepted way of travelling holy men, and they are given rose apples and gooseberries, sharp as spring, and grains also, millet and the fragrant, earthy wild rice.

The seasons change and it is winter in the lower Himalayas. The days are saturated with colours and shadows but the nights are frigid and endless. The Pandavas shiver in their ascetic's robes and ask the tribal people for furs. Black antelope skins, leopard and bear pelts, luxuriant and heavy, and smelling of fire and death.

The years pass and the tribal girls with the clinking wooden bracelets and lustrous skin hint at impossible dreams in oblique, flaming glances they exchange with the young men. Arjun is especially popular, with his easy, complicit smile and languid grace but it is Bheem who stumbles upon love first, in an orgy of violence and blood and unexpected tenderness. A tribal girl and her brother come upon the sleeping Pandavas one night when they have strayed further from their hunting grounds than usual. Recognizing them as foreigners, brutish plainsmen who usually have only one objective in mind, plunder and rape, the boy raises his curved dagger and screams at the invaders to wake up and fight. The disoriented Pandavas search confusedly for their weapons but Bheem has already grabbed a heavy, rounded log. He breaks the boy's thighs and smashes his skull, for violence will be his salvation and his path, always. The girl, Hidimbi, holds her brother's broken face in her lap and cries into his bloody hair.

'You have killed him, and he only wanted to protect me. I have no one else to turn to, please allow me to stay here with you because, without my brother, the forest has become alien and lonely.'

So Hidimbi stays with them for a while and she follows Bheem while he forages for wood and food, held fast in the memory of that night set in blood. Bheem is gentle with her, remorse uneasy in his heart. He brings her gifts of wildflowers and small, tart mangoes and her smile is bright and quick. They go away together and build a small hut where they live a life of simple passion that has no need for consecration. Bheem returns occasionally, to visit his brothers, and Kunti does not say anything, but when a son is born to Hidimbi, she knows she must act quickly. There is a pensive distance to Bheem now when he comes to visit and she has seen the unfathomable grace in his eyes when he holds his son, a tiny crumb of humanity, in his warrior's arms.

'Beta, we have been in this place for too long now. We need to keep moving and we cannot take Hidimbi and the baby with us.'

'Ma, Hidimbi would not slow us down, she is a strong woman used to the forest paths.'

'It is not that, my son. We need to remember your destiny and your birthright. You are the rajkumar of Hastinapur and Yudhishthir is yuvraj and you need to reclaim what is rightfully yours. We cannot live the rest of our lives in hiding, living like mendicants and we cannot squander away our alliances. You will all have to marry into families who can support us in our just cause.'

'But what is to happen to Hidimbi, and my son?'

'Hidimbi can return to her tribe, they will not turn her away. And we have acknowledged your son, he will bear his father's name and we will call for him when he is a man.'

Bheem hangs his head but doesn't say anything more. Kunti's implacable will cannot be denied and he won't challenge her on this matter in front of his brothers. The other Pandavas look away, unable to bear the sadness in Bheem's eyes. Their fearless and gallant brother has had to make the first real sacrifice for Yudhishthir's throne and they are restless with the foreboding that there will be many more to come.

'Prepare yourselves to journey tomorrow, my sons. I have heard that Raja Drupad is organizing a great swayamvar for his beautiful daughter and is inviting all the valorous men in the kingdom. Tomorrow we walk to Panchala.'

The Swayamvar

~

The potter is a small, wiry man withered and scorched as if from the fires of his baking kilns. He spends most of his days sitting hunched over his potter's wheel, controlling it expertly with his foot. He appears immobile except for his hands, which spin out sensuous and flowing shapes of pots from a mass of glossy, ochre river mud. At midday, he sits down on his haunches in his courtyard to eat a sparse meal of coarse rice and barley gruel. If the Pandavas are home, they share their alms with him and the meals are rather more appetizing with salted fried vegetables and mango pickles. Usually, though, the Pandavas are scouring the city of Kampilya, begging bowls tied to their dhotis, loping through the roiling crowds.

In the two weeks preceding the swayamvar, Kampilya is brassy with preparations, tumbling with acrobats, wrestlers, and performers. Beside the entrance to the palace, an enclosure bristling with flags has been set up for the wrestling matches which are the most popular entertainment among both aristocrats and commoners. Bheem watches the panting, heaving men, slick with sweat and mud, and clenches his fists in futile empathy. Tambourine players meander through the streets, drumming out excitement and anticipation for the main event. Acrobats and equilibrists balance on fragile shoulders and fraying ropes and defy death for the appreciative, clapping crowds.

Late in the evenings the Pandavas and Kunti gather together in the potter's hut which they have been sharing since they arrived in Kampilya a few weeks ago. The potter is sleeping in the courtyard, surrounded by his terracotta army and dreaming of fire while the Pandavas sit on the earthen floor of the bare hut, eating a scavenged meal off banana leaves.

'This alliance with Raja Drupad is our last chance,' Kunti whispers to her sons, while in the distance the percussion of an erratic drummer competes with the barking of stray dogs.

The Pandavas nod, a flush of moonlight gleaming through the single doorway of the mud hut. They know that Kunti has staked all her hopes on this swayamvar, and that if one of them wins the contest and the rajkumari, then the might of her father's army will march them back to Hastinapur.

'My relatives, the Vrishnis and the Bhojas, have never troubled to look for us or offered to give us sanctuary though they knew that I was all alone in the court of Hastinapur after your father died. We must carve new friendships now, powerful friends to help Yudhishthir claim his crown.'

'But, Ma, why would Raja Drupad want to help us? What interest do they have in the politics of faraway Hastinapur?'

Nakul still struggles sometimes to make sense of their endless wanderings and the duplicity of their cousins. He still longs for the golden and night-black horses that were his passion in Hastinapur. Here in the squalid quarters of the potter's colony, there are no shimmying horses to be seen, only irascible pigs, chickens, and dogs.

'No, Beta, you are right, Raja Drupad cares nothing for us but the kingdom of Panchala is second only to Hastinapur. They are ancient enemies and the Raja has a particular animosity with Guru Drona and will certainly want to help us if it means staking a claim for the throne of Hastinapur. But it is late now, Son, come and lie down next to me. Tomorrow we must wake before dawn.'

Kunti is gentle always with Madri's sons, reminded constantly of her co-wife's beauty when she sees the boys' tender limbs and buttermilk skin. She has never admitted even to herself her complicity in Madri's death but it makes her uneasy and generous around the twins.

Meanwhile, the Pandavas shake out their antelope wraps and lay them down on the ground, wrought together in their sleep by their mother's dream.

It is well before dawn on the day of the swayamvar and in the palace of Kampilya, Draupadi's quarters are already shimmering with the ladies of the house. The married women only, and those with living sons, for widows and bereaved mothers are sequestered away on this auspicious day, their polluting presence a menace and a profanity.

Still heavy with sleep, Draupadi is surrounded by the whispering, jostling women. Her limbs are kneaded and massaged with sandalwood oil and scented lotions till they gleam like warm gold. She is led through the courtyards, stepping over the sleeping musicians, and brought to the water room where the women ritually bathe her, pouring perfumed water onto her head from golden jugs.

At dawn, trumpets and drums awaken everyone, the strident and joyous contralto of the trumpets a counterpoint to the ominous pulse of the drums.

The rest of the palace awakens and soon every quarter is brimming with activity. The cooks in their already steaming rooms stoke their fires and macerate huge mounds of meat for the banquets that will feed the guests and the loiterers all day. In the especially constructed halls of bamboo and cloth canopies, rotund mithai specialists roll out luscious and sticky balls of candied desserts.

There are wine-brewers, butchers, and food dressers, all with their entourages of young helpers and acolytes. Malakars are everywhere, swirling strings of marigold, rose, and jasmine around every pillar and across every awning.

Outside the palace walls a huge field has been enclosed for the swayamvar itself. Its white cloth pavilions glitter in the morning light and the air is expectant with the fragrance of marigold flowers and sandalwood incense. Through the gathering day, the townsfolk will arrive from Hastinapur and beyond, massing around the barriers. Soldiers in resplendent turbans keep order and wrestlers, jugglers, dancers, and musicians entertain the crowds while they wait.

Now in her quarters, Draupadi is getting dressed for her swayamvar. Her hair has been braided with wool tassels and fresh flowers and there is a slim string of gold around her brow. She is wearing a long pleated skirt of white silk, a breastband, and a red wrap around her shoulders. She is wearing a kingdom of gold and precious stones that sparkle on her dark skin like the constellations in the night sky. Her face is ablaze with a pattern of tiny white dots which arch over her brows and cheekbones and there is red paste on her lips and red lac dye on her palms and feet. In her hands she holds a spike of blue lotus flowers, her favourite in the world. The women of the house have been getting increasingly loose with their talk as they finish adjusting the heavy gold waistband around Draupadi's waist. Normally decorous young women and ancient matrons cackle and leer at Draupadi as they sing sly and lubricious songs, clapping their hands and twirling around the room, long skirts swishing.

When she is ready at last, Draupadi walks to the domestic altar one last time in her life, to pray before the familiar, ever-blazing fires of the clan of the Panchalas. Dense and grave with beauty, she bows before each of the women of her house, starting with the oldest first, and asks them for their blessings.

'May the Devi bless you with a handsome husband, Beti. May you hold his love in your heart and may you never have to share his love with anyone else. May you and your husband lead virtuous lives and have many sons.'

While the Brahmins are being fed in the palace halls, in the swayamvar arena the first of the clan heads are arriving with their entourages. Each arrival is greeted with exuberant abandon by trumpeters and drummers while young servant boys walk up and down the seating area, sprinkling sandalwood water on to the ground and lighting incense sticks.

The clan heads all sit separately, on manchas covered with white silk cloths, gaudy as peacocks. Next to them are seated the other Kshatriyas, appraising each other and loudly slapping their thighs and biceps as they greet one another over the clamour of the musicians and the murmuring crowds. They wear linen dhotis dyed indigo or crimson or gold, turbans of twisted cloth and fine leather shoes with thick soles. Brahmins and sadhus are present too, flaming in their red and ochre robes. In the furthest section, massed in genial bonhomie are the ordinary townsfolk, rich merchants, and traders, come to admire the spectacle. The rest of the boisterous crowd, the inconsequential and the uninvited, press against the wooden barriers while the children cluster on trees and scaffolds and rooftops where the coloured flags flutter in the breeze.

Raja Drupad arrives finally, into a swell of sound, like the roar of a river in flood. He greets his guests and takes his seat next to the clan heads and at last Draupadi can enter the arena. She holds a golden jar filled with ghee which she pours into the fire of the altar tended by an ancient priest, white-haired and frail, who utters in a reedy voice the primal salutations of peace to the fire, conduit to the Gods, and to the assembled Brahmins.

'Om Dyau Shanti, Rantariksha Shanti, Prithvi Shanti.'

The trumpets sound one last time and silence floats down onto the crowd, tense and hushed.

Drishtadumna strides into the silence and, standing in front of the clan heads, announces the start of the swayamvar.

'Here is my sister, Rajkumari Draupadi. Whosoever can bend that bow in the centre of the arena, string it, and hit the target, if he is of noble lineage, handsome and strong, can claim Draupadi as a bride.'

Drishtadumna gestures to a huge vat of oil and a massive bow in the centre of the arena. High above the vat, hanging at the end of a long rod, is the target in the shape of a fish. Below the target is a slowly spinning wheel.

'And, remember, you may not look directly at the target, only at its reflection in the oil. And, of course, you must strike the target through the spokes of the spinning wheel. Only the most talented and valorous archer may win my sister.'

All the clan heads and chieftains rise up at this, insolent and brazen with strength and youth. They wave their weapons above them and look at Draupadi, her heartbreaking beauty making them believe the impossible.

Drishtadumna then introduces the various assembled clans to Draupadi—the Yadavs, the Sindhus, the Chedis, the Kosalas, and many more still.

'These brave and worthy rajas are here today for you, beloved sister. You may garland the archer who hits the eye of the fish and become his wife.'

The clan heads jostle each other to be the first to attempt the challenge and there are good-humoured jibes and oblique glances at the dark and magnificent bride. But as the hot afternoon spins into early evening, the laughter and excitement dissipate as few warriors are able even to string the huge bow, much less aim for the target reflected in the slick oil. They walk back to their seats, hanging their heads in shame and thwarted desire. Their feelings of anticipation and hope get corrupted by the impossible challenge of the task and there are angry mutterings against Raja Drupad.

Sitting alone on a simple takht with only her maid Sushila beside her, Draupadi confronts her heart and discovers dread for the first time. She has sat for hours in the swarming heat while the men postured and roared in front of her and she looked only to the silence within her.

I am Veeryashulka, she reminds herself. A bride to be won only by the worthiest and the best of men.

When she realized that she was not going to be choosing her husband herself at the swayamvar, as used to be the custom in the olden days, she asked Drishtadumna to set a task that only a few might accomplish.

'Drishtoo, my brother, set a task for archers, for archery is a noble skill. Make it a difficult task so that the man who succeeds is not only powerful and brave but has grace and a strong mind too.'

Draupadi moulds her destiny in the only way she can, with intelligence and subtlety and also a hard desperation. Now, she looks down at her red-stained palms and the garland of blue lotuses in her lap and listens to the fear in her heart. It will be an inconceivable aberration if no one completes the task and she will have to sit in this hall forever while the lotuses turn to dust and the red lac dye seeps into the blood in her veins.

But, suddenly, there is a commotion in a different quarter of the hall. The crimson tide of sadhus is in an uproar, for the latest challenger has stepped up from amidst their ranks. He is but a young sadhu with matted hair coiled into a topknot and a black deerskin wrapped around his slim hips. He steps into the arena and there are derisive shouts from the startled rajas.

'Sit down, boy, has your fasting gone to your head? This is a tournament for Kshatriyas, not beggarly sadhus!'

The Brahmins are agitated, too, and they shake their rudraksha beads and their deerskins at him and try to hold him back.

'Come back, Beta, if these strong Kshatriyas have not been able to perform this challenge, what do you think you can do?'

But Arjun walks purposefully up to the target and with seamless grace strings the huge bow. While the entire gathering of men watches in a silence that is molten with heat and expectation, Arjun stands with bow pointing up and stares down into the reflection in the oil. His muscles burn and the sweat trickles down his arched back and still he stares at the reflected fish. His heart rate slows down and his breathing stills and finally all he can see in the oil is the eye of the fish. In an invisible blur, he looses his arrow, the crowd gasps, and the eye of the fish is struck.

For an instant there is complete silence and then a discordant caterwauling shreds the air. The chieftains rise up in an explosive emotion that is both despair and rage. They jump down onto the arena, incoherent and savage, and howl like jackals who yearn for the moon. A few of the rajas are jubilant, relieved at last to see the target fall after the hours of grinding futility.

The minute the target falls, Bheem leaps into the arena with a roar to stand beside his brother. He uproots a massive wooden post and swings it around his head like a mace. Yudhishthir and the twins melt into the swirling, seething crowds and return to the potter's hut.

While Bheem and Arjun wait with weapons drawn, the furious chieftains first surround Raja Drupad.

'What kind of swayamvar is this, Raja, where pundits are allowed to participate in archery? And what kind of impossible target did you set? No doubt that scrawny youth used magic of some kind to hit the target.'

But Drupad is stammering and helpless with fear himself. His beloved daughter is standing with a garland in her hands and the chieftains are crashing uselessly around him and the only person who is unruffled is the young priest with the calm eyes standing by the target.

The rajas turn on Arjun and Bheem and a scuffle breaks out while some of the younger pundits also join in the fray on behalf of the brothers with blood-curdling screams. The brothers fight with fluid ease, for they have thought of little else since their arrival in Kampilya, whereas the chieftains are addled, and they have lost the force in their limbs and the precision of their weapons.

A few of the rajas have fallen to the floor, groaning, by the time a man pushes through the crowd to stand beside the brothers. He has skin so dark that his white turban gleams like the moon and he wears a dhoti of yellow silk and a string of marigold flowers around his neck.

'Stop, all of you, great chiefs and rajas. This behaviour does not befit your noble lineages, what is this scrapping and fighting like frustrated children.'

The stranger's voice is strangely melodious and deep, like monsoon rain on parched earth and the men stop, chastised, to listen to him.

'I am Krishna, of the Yadav tribe, and I say that this man has won this bride according to the laws of dharma. All valorous men were invited to this swayamvar, not just Kshatriyas, and there is nothing unjust about his victory. Go home now, my brothers, there is nothing to be gained any more by arguing and fighting.'

And, as if an enchantment has lifted off them, the men fall back, dazed. They gather up their splintered hope and return to their fiefdoms and later, when they are grizzled old men with sparse white hair, they will still sometimes dream of the smoke-skinned girl with slanting eyes and untouchable curves who could have been theirs.

As the men stand back, Sushila leads Draupadi to Arjun and the princess reaches up to place the lotus garland over his bowed head.

Draupadi lifts her gaze for an instant and has a fleeting impression of laughing eyes and shadows before Krishna hurries them all out of the swayamvar arena and into the anonymity of the hustling crowds and the evening gloom.

Draupadi stands apart under a banyan tree while the men talk in hushed urgency.

'I am your cousin Krishna, son of clan chief Vasudeva who is Ma Kunti's brother. I have been looking for you since I heard of the fire at Varnavrat, for there have been rumours about your escape among the tribal people. When I saw the five of you sitting among the sadhus, your bearing and your grace betrayed you and I realized who you were. Forgive me, Bhai Bheem, I was not able to come to your aid earlier.'

Krishna bends down to touch Bheem's feet with folded palms and Bheem raises him and crushes him to his chest.

'Krishna! You came to us at the right time, though I was enjoying teaching all those preening rajas a lesson for the many insults they were throwing at Arjun. Still, a swayamvar is no place for a bloodbath!'

Bheem throws his head back and laughs loudly, startling the passers-by, galvanized by the brawl after months of anonymity.

Meanwhile, Krishna turns to Arjun and puts his hands on his shoulders and smiles. Krishna's smile is like the sun that shines true after a thundercloud and Arjun can't help smiling back.

'Arjun, I have heard so much about your skill as an archer and it is all true. You are possibly the best archer in the kingdom and it is a joy to meet you at last. Now hurry up and take Draupadi back to Ma Kunti quickly, before the rajas find they are in a mood for blood after all. Go now, and we will meet again soon.'

The men embrace quickly and then Krishna returns to the palace. Arjun signals to Draupadi and the three of them disappear into the warren of streets.

As she follows the men through the streets of Kampilya, Draupadi struggles to understand what is happening to her. This day, which had started out in laughter and music and holy rites in the convivial company of the women of her clan, has ended in this moment. In a shameful scurrying through the streets of her kingdom in the company of men in animal skins and begging bowls. She stumbles as she tries to keep up with the brothers and wonders at their striding, loose-limbed pace, very unlike the measured shuffle of sadhus. As for the older sadhu, the one who roared like a lion when he was getting ready to fight in the arena, she has never seen an ascetic whose arms were such a medley of muscles and sinews.

She listens to them talk now as she slides behind them, holding up the hem of her heavy skirt to save it from the cloying dust of the trampled streets.

'Hé Arjun. Did you see that little raja trying to lift the bow? The one who was more like a barking deer than a lion? I thought he might fall over and drown in the vat of oil!'

Bheem laughs uproariously at his own recollection, throwing his arm around his brother's shoulders.

'Yes, and when we started fighting, the rajas from Chedi fell down at the first shove, like babies learning to walk'

'Or like old men who have lost their waking sticks.'

'Or like boys who have drunk too much grape wine'

The brothers continue to laugh as they cross Kampilya but when they reach the outskirts of the town, where the roads disintegrate into rubble and the houses are one-room hovels, they fall silent. The air condenses around Draupadi like a malevolent spirit and she finds she can barely walk any more. The intricate and holy poetry of sandalwood dots on her face has become smeared by the dust of the day and the kumkum in her hair is like a bloodstain. The blooming flower gardens and fruit orchards surrounding Kampilya palace are long gone and so are the prosperous quarters of the merchants with their two-storeyed buildings and latticed windows. They have now crossed over into the watchful territory of the dispossessed. The streets crawl with slinking dogs and hopeless donkeys and the ravaged and broken men returning home are grimy and naked except for the dirty, short dhotis around their waists.

Arjun realizes that Draupadi has stopped and he turns around to encourage her gently.

'We are almost there, Rajkumari. It is not far.'

Draupadi does not answer, for speech itself is fractured now and she does not have the words to explain her panicked sense of deracination to this complete stranger. But in the failing light of godhuli, she has seen the silver scars on the dark skin of his arms like the rice patterns that village women paint on the walls of their mud huts. As the daughter of a raja, she recognizes these scars, for they are the marks of an archer. And Draupadi knows that though he may be wearing deerskin rags and his hair is an abomination of matted coils, this dusky, light-stepping man is a Kshatriya.

Suddenly they are in the potters' quarters and Draupadi is standing in a tiny courtyard, musty with the smell of baking clay. In the evening light the diamonds and gems on her jewellery flicker and sparkle. She is contained and devastatingly beautiful, like a divinity brought to earth.

Arjun steps forward and calls out towards the hut.

'Ma, look what we have brought back today.'

And from within the hut, a woman's voice answers.

'Whatever it is, my son, share it equally among your brothers.'

Arjun turns back in consternation to look at Draupadi, for Kunti's words have carried clearly through the evening air filled with the smoke of the cooking fires. Bheem cuts a sideward glance at Draupadi, his eyes filled with desire and a sudden, startled realization.

Kunti steps out of the hut, followed by Yudhishthir and the

twins. She seems unsure and nervous when she sees Draupadi in the courtyard, but not altogether surprised. It is Bheem who is the first to speak and he is dismayed and angry.

'What have you said, Ma? This is Draupadi, Raja Drupad's daughter and Arjun has won her at the swayamvar. She is not like the alms we bring back, to be shared amongst everyone.'

But Kunti stands in front of Draupadi, shaking her head sadly.

'I didn't realize this is what you were referring to, Arjun. But what I have said cannot be unsaid now, else you make a liar out of me. You must all marry this woman.'

Though she has addressed Arjun, it is Bheem who answers, provoked.

'Ma, what you are saying is unheard of and indecent. We will all be laughed at and derided. Arjun should marry her since he won her. Bhai Yudhishthir, say something to Ma!'

But Yudhishthir is strangely disconcerted and flustered. When he speaks at last, his voice is husky and he is almost stammering.

'I have done everything in my life according to our mother's word. Her wish is sacrosanct and following her command is the same as carrying out Dharma's wish.'

An uneasy silence follows Yudhishthir's words. There is the sound of some drunken shouting in the distance and a baby cries raggedly. In the small courtyard everyone is still and quiet as they gauge the heft of Yudhishthir's words. Arjun, with his subtle and restless intelligence, understands at last the unimaginable truth. He realizes why Yudhishthir left the swayamvar hall so soon after he had won the contest. He knows that Draupadi's flaming beauty has scalded Yudhishthir forever and when he returned to the potter's hut, it was to tell Kunti all that had happened. Kunti would have seen the glittering desire in her son's heart and this charade that they are now all playing is a result of that.

But Bheem is truculent still and not so easily convinced. He throws his wooden post angrily against a corner where it crashes into some clay pots. Kunti walks up to the most volatile of her sons and puts a calming hand on his shoulder.

'Beta, the eldest brother must always marry first. How can Arjun get married before Yudhishthir or you yourself? That would be against all our laws of dharma, you know that. The only way out of this conundrum is for all five of you to take Draupadi as wife.'

Draupadi raises her head at last and looks straight at Arjun. In her kohl-lined, slanting eyes, she wills all the passion and supplication she can gather through her wordless despair. I will marry you, she tells him silently, through eyes filling with tears, though I don't know your clan or your caste, despite the rags and the rudraksha beads and the ash on your forehead. I will marry you, but only you, for you have won me fairly before all. Do not let them parcel me out like a plaything. Stand up for me now and I will follow you forever, even into the furnace of the underworld itself.

Arjun looks at Draupadi and then turns away, shackled by the laws of dharma and hierarchy that his mother has invoked. A single tear slides down Draupadi's cheek and suddenly the weight of this tumultuous day comes rolling over her and she faints gratefully at Kunti's feet.

She wakes up to a darkness so complete it is a blind man's dream. She is lying on the floor on a coarse bed of kusa grass, in a corner of the hut. She can hear the Pandavas and Kunti whispering and the scuffling and shuffling sound of animal hides being flicked out and laid on the floor. The hut is so small that they must all lie packed close to one another like logs laid out for the holy fires. They whisper to each other for a while and she can hear Bheem telling them about the skirmish at the swayamvar and about their cousin, the Yadav, Krishna, who came to their aid. Draupadi strains to hear the quiet modulation of Arjun's voice but he seems silent.

Kunti is silent too as she contemplates the scaffolding of her impossible plan. Arjun has won the contest, as she knew he would, for Drona himself had told her that he was the best archer in the land. Now they have within their grasp the might of Panchala's army itself, for surely Drupad will not forsake his cherished daughter. As for the Pandavas, Draupadi will unite them like nothing else could since the brothers are invincible as the hurricane of war itself when they are together. Each brother has his place in the momentum that is needed to carry Yudhishthir to the throne of Hastinapur and only Draupadi will hold them together now.

At last there is complete silence in the hut except for the sound of the breathing and snoring men. Draupadi lies awake for hours, until she is sure they are all asleep and then she sits up slowly. Her eyes have adjusted to the dark and she carefully takes off her clinking anklets and walks out of the hut. Her head is pounding from her elaborate coiffure with its sharp pins of diamonds and heavy gold chains and she is bewildered at the complete lack of light outside the hut. In her palace there would have been a girl sleeping at her door and a clay lamp flickering throughout the night. In the courtyard of the hut there is only the wispy light of a crescent moon and shadows everywhere. There is the sound of tiny, scampering feet among the piles of rubbish that lie in the mean streets and there is the clicking and whirring of a multitude of insects and creatures for whom the night is a feast.

Draupadi sits down in the courtyard, overcome by a visceral fear of the unknown night. She has nowhere to go to, even if she could summon up the courage to step into the keening darkness and her thoughts are inarticulate ravings. Hunger clutches at her stomach with fierce claws for she has not eaten since the day before and she is rank and sour with sweat and dust.

Draupadi returns to the hut and sits on the kusa grass while she waits for the dawn. As the light spills softly into the room she looks at the sleeping men. Though they are all gaunt from their

Ira Mukhoty

wandering, muscles twist along their arms and backs and they all have archer's scars on their biceps. Whatever else they may be, these men are warriors, all of them, so they are Kshatriyas at least and that is the only solace she has.

Not long after the brothers have woken up, there is a clamour in the narrow, fetid alley outside the potter's hut. Furious dogs are barking incessantly and a commotion of ragged children accompanies a harried emissary into the courtyard.

'King Drupad sends his greetings, and chariots, to accompany Rajkumari Draupadi and her party to the palace for a banquet in their honour.'

The emissary bows before the Pandavas and his turban is a splendid thing in the face of their watchful sobriety.

Draupadi waits with Kunti in the hut while the Pandavas go to the river to bathe. When they return, they have sloughed off their mendicants' disguise and they are reborn like a new dawn. They have washed and cut off their long, matted hair. They have exchanged their animal skins for clean white dhotis and they have given away their rudraksha beads and begging bowls. Before climbing into the chariots, they take the simple weapons they have managed to gather and they appear ready to step into more substantial lives.

When the chariots arrive at Kampilya palace, the men are taken to Raja Drupad's assembly hall while Kunti and Draupadi are taken to separate rooms in the married women's quarters. The minute Kokila Devi walks into her daughter's room, Draupadi throws herself into her arms, sobbing.

'Ma, what has happened to me? Do you know where these men took me yesterday? To the squalid edge of town, where there are no streets and no houses, just hopeless, dark hovels. I was alone and at their mercy. Who are these men?'

Kokila Devi's composure is cracked with worry and she holds her daughter in her arms, like when she was a baby.

'Hush, child, hush. Do not upset yourself like this. You were never forsaken, Beti. Drishtadumna did not let you out of his sight from the moment you garlanded that archer. He followed you all the way to the potter's hut and was able to bring news of you back to the palace early this morning. Your father did not sleep all night, tortured by the thought that some stranger from outside our clans had polluted you with his touch.'

Draupadi is surprised and consoled. The thought of her beloved twin watching over her reduces the desolation and the terror of that night.

'Now go with Sushila and change your clothes and jewellery and I will visit with Ma Kunti meanwhile.'

Draupadi spends a long time in the bathing room, ferociously rubbing the sandalwood paste and kumkum off her face and lets the water run red like blood from the lac dye on her palms and feet. Sushila helps her into a fresh skirt of red silk and the hair groomers twist her hair into an endless braid that hangs heavy down her back, banded with lotus flowers. She eats a meal of honeyed curd and rice in meat broth and is almost lucid by the time Kokila Devi returns to her room.

'Well, Beti, the situation is not as grim as it appears. These men are brothers, Kshatriyas and noblemen. They call themselves the Pandavas and they say they belong to the clan of the Kurus, of Hastinapur. They have been in hiding these past few years as that crown is disputed. Unfortunately, their father died a long time ago so they will need to fight for what they say is rightfully theirs.'

'But, Ma, nobody has heard of these Pandavas before and why have they been disguised as mendicants and pundits, slinking among the lower-caste folk?'

'They have feared for their lives, Beti. They say they are cousins of Rajkumar Duryodhan and that he wishes them dead so that he may rule as uncontested raja.'

Ira Mukhoty

'So they are landless and powerless and yet they seek to marry the rajkumari of Panchala? That is a lofty ambition for men who have fallen so low.'

'Your father tells me that they are not entirely without allies. Krishna, of the Yadav clan, is their relative on Ma Kunti's side and he has sworn to support them in their quest for the crown of the Kurus.'

Draupadi lifts the bamboo shutters aside to look at the tulsi plant in the courtyard. Maidservants swing by on bare feet, carrying heaped trays of flower garlands for the evening sandhya. It seems inconceivable to Draupadi that life goes on like before, after the catastrophe of her swayamvar.

'But, Ma,' she whispers. 'Do you know that their mother wants me to marry all five brothers? That is intolerable and I will not accept it.'

Kokila Devi sighs and sits down on the wicker bed.

'Yes, it is a strange request indeed and yet they are abiding by it quite vehemently, even Ma Kunti. Your father is outraged by this, too, and he is calling for a learned pundit to debate the moral point and to see whether there is any precedent for it.'

Draupadi sinks down onto the floor next to Kokila Devi and lays her head on her mother's knees.

'Ma, it would be shameful for me to marry all five brothers. What would people say of me?'

Drishtadumna walks into the room just then and Draupadi swiftly gets up to embrace him. He is much taller than her now and he kisses her on the top of her glossy head.

'Draupadi, do not be disheartened. I have made enquiries and Krishna of the Vrishni Yadavs is a powerful clan head. It is true that his ancestor Raja Shurasena was removed from the throne of the Yadavs but Krishna has land and riches to the west, in Dwarka. He has solemnly pledged to provide these Pandavas with weapons and horses and soldiers.'

'But, Drishtadumna, I will not marry all five brothers, I refuse to do so.'

Drishtadumna frowns suddenly, arrested in his exuberance.

'Draupadi, the idea is abhorrent to me as well. Pitaji and I both agree that this is unacceptable for a Kshatriya woman but they are immovable on this. Yudhishthir should marry you, as he is the eldest but he goes on insisting that he is bound by his mother's command and they must share you! Now the priest is quoting some ancient and forgotten examples, and claiming that this has happened before and that you are not the first woman to be married to several husbands.'

There is a movement at the door, a sudden glimpse of gold and smoke and Drishtadumna raises a hand in greeting.

'Draupadi, Krishna has asked for an audience with you, to talk to you privately about the Pandavas. Ma and I will go back to the main hall and speak to the priest as well.'

Drishtadumna and Kunti leave Draupadi's quarters and Sushila stands quietly against a wall as Krishna walks into the room. Draupadi recognizes the man who had stopped her swayamvar from escalating into a shameful debacle. He is dressed in a yellow silk dhoti and a slim band of gold circles his brow and holds back his dark hair which falls in uneven curls about his shoulders. His voice is low and gentle and reassuring and Draupadi listens to him despite herself.

'Rajkumari, I understand that this entire situation is very upsetting for you. You have never heard of these brothers before and know nothing about them. Do not be deceived by their appearance yesterday at your swayamvar. I have come to vouch for their lineage and their clan. I can assure you that they are honourable and brave noblemen who will cherish you as the devi that you are.'

Draupadi looks at Krishna from the corner of her eye and she likes the garland of fresh white jasmine flowers that blazes against his bare, dark torso.

'Sakhi, do you mind if I call you my friend, Rajkumari? I feel like I have known you all my life, though we have only just met. There are some people with whom we feel kinship, even though no mortal connection binds us. I feel a special closeness to Arjun as well, though I am equally related to all the Pandavas.'

Draupadi glances up at the mention of Arjun's name, startled. Can this stranger who calls her Sakhi read her heart? She looks up into his face and wonders if she will see the usual blistering desire that flashes in men's eyes when they see her dark beauty but there is only compassion and love in Krishna's eyes and Draupadi is undone suddenly and yearns to give in to the sobs that gather like storm clouds against her heart.

'How can I marry five men, Krishna? If you are my Sakha, then tell me truthfully, what will people call me if I agree to become the wife of five men?'

'Sakhi, you are the devi of prosperity herself, who would dare to besmirch your name? And, moreover, you will be wedded to a just and holy cause, to restore Yudhishthir to the throne of his ancestors and bring back a true and worthy reign.'

And so, all that endless, swirling day, people come and go from Draupadi's room, chastising and arguing and beseeching and all along Draupadi knows that she must succumb. She cannot claim to be unmarried after she was won in front of the entire sabha of noblemen and chieftains. Drupad and Drishtadumna put up a gallant resistance to the suggestion of the five husbands but Kunti and Yudhishthir are adamant.

And so, the next morning, Draupadi enters the assembly hall where the holy fire is burning and a pundit is seated. The Pandavas are already waiting for her and they are magnificent today in billowing linen dhotis and uttarayas of blue and gold. They look up as Draupadi walks to the fire and there is the same scorched and dense desire in their eyes. Only Kunti is outwardly composed, though anxiety glitters in her eyes.

There is an assembly of hastily convened relatives and friends and priests, and Krishna is standing, his smile a sanctuary, next to the Pandavas. The priest intones the mantras and makes the offerings of ghee, milk, fruit, and roasted grain and then Yudhishthir gets up. He takes Draupadi by the hand and leads her around the fire seven times and Draupadi burns suddenly with the realization that with the holy fire as first witness, she is now irrevocably and forever married. She barely hears the vows that the priest makes them repeat as the crackling flames hiss and spit in her ears.

'I promise to cherish you always, and to look after you and provide for you,' Yudhishthir tells her.

Then Bheem leads her around the fire seven times and the black and churning smoke is the breath of the gods.

'I will protect you, and your children, always.'

Then Arjun leads Draupadi around the fire, and her hand trembles in his.

'You have brought sacredness into my life, and have completed me.'

And now Draupadi can hear his soft words and she answers in a whisper.

'I will give you all my love, for as long as I live.'

Then Nakul and Sahadev walk with Draupadi seven times around the fire and by now the hall is acrid and greasy with the billowing smoke and the guests are uneasy, unsettled by the length of the fire ceremony and the excess of grooms. Draupadi listens to the clinking of her anklets and doesn't yet know that her endless journeying with these five men has only just begun.

And, at last, the ceremony is over and everyone gets up in a sudden upheaval of colour and silk and jasmine. The women hustle around Draupadi as she walks up to Kunti and bows down to touch the feet of her mother-in-law.

'May you be blessed, Beti, with the love of your husbands, and may you be rani of the Kuru clan, as is your rightful inheritance now.'

Draupadi stands before Kunti with folded hands and looks steadily into the older woman's eyes. She realizes for the first time that, despite her widow's whites and her unadorned face, Kunti is younger than she had thought.

'Ma Kunti, as Agni is my witness, I have promised to cherish and love and look after your sons for the rest of my life. In return, I ask for only one thing, that no other wife of theirs is allowed into the marital home, ever, and that I alone will be their rani.'

Kunti nods quickly, 'So be it, Beti, I give you my word. I know this arrangement seems unusual and offensive to you but it is also in your best interest. Though Yudhishthir is destined to be raja, our fate is never revealed to us and there is a long and difficult journey ahead of all of you. This way, whosoever of the Pandavas becomes ruler, you will always be rani and there is no uncertainty about your stature.'

Draupadi bows again and then all the women of the royal household of Panchala come up to greet Kunti and introduce themselves to her. And so, by the end of the day, the Pandavas and Kunti have been sublimated from scrappy pretenders into fearsome contenders, with the powerful backing of the kingdom of Panchala and all its allies and the Vrishni Yadavs too.

After the wedding, Drupad and Krishna give the Pandavas sumptuous gifts of war horses, elephants, steel-emblazoned chariots, slave girls, animal furs, silks, and gold. In lieu of their begging bowls and wooden sticks they now have an arsenal and all the gold they will need to see them to Hastinapur. For the next few weeks, the palace is raucous and shrill with activity. The blacksmith's anvil echoes all day long as he hammers and cuts and twists the shape of glowing axes, hammers, knives, and spears from the white-hot furnace. Nakul haunts Kampilya's royal stables, where he is gifted horses decorated with saddle cloths and browbands and plaited tails. Servant girls and boys criss-cross the endless courtyards carrying silk and linen clothes to put in the bride's magnificent trousseau and the goldsmith is overcome by the quantum of gold and stone jewellery that Kokila requires from him.

And yet, during this time, Draupadi herself becomes withdrawn and listless and the Pandavas are sullen and uncertain around each other. Sushila goes to Kokila's quarters one day to tell her of yet another meal of fine-grained rice and marinated pheasant returned untouched. Indra has finally sent the monsoon clouds to northern Bharat after the taut summer and Kokila hurries through courtyards while rain sluices down her bare arms.

Draupadi is lying on a beautifully carved wooden bed and as soon as she sees her mother, she bursts into painful, heaving sobs, covering her eyes with her arm.

'Beti, what is the matter? Has someone criticized you or offended you in some way?'

'Ma, this cannot go on, I cannot live like this. I would rather consign myself to the Devi's eternal care than live one more day like this. The same man is to be a husband one day, a brother-in-law the next, and then a younger brother the third! How can I live with this shame, Ma?'

Kokila steps back, aghast, her hand against her mouth and turns without another word to go and confer with Kunti. The two women speak for a long while in Kunti's simply furnished room while the rain drums a muffled beat on the parched earth and the mynahs sit glumly hunched on the branches of the gulmohar trees. Then they send for the pundit who is old and unworldly but compassionate and who often shakes his head at the intricate web of human lives. Despite all that has been discussed before, he finds the whole situation intolerable, and its implications dangerous.

Brothers as rivals for the same woman, unspeakable jealousies, and sons who will be born to five men, no one sure who the real father is. Finally it is decided and the Pandavas and Draupadi are gathered together to hear the pundit speak.

'It has been decided that Draupadi will live with one husband, for one year, exclusively. At the end of that year, she will undertake a ritual purification by fire after which she will take for husband the second brother. For that one year she will live with only one man, her husband in all matters, and will be treated as a sacred sister-in-law by the other brothers.'

And so Draupadi walks up to Yudhishthir and bows down before him while the other brothers turn away to hide their desolation and go out into the rain to the armoury or the stables to hide from each other the longing they must not name.

In Hastinapur

~

Under a sky chaotic with clouds, in the dawn of a monsoon day, Draupadi leaves Kampilya forever. A special yajna was performed before daybreak to protect the travellers from the terrible dangers of passing through unknown, unconsecrated lands and now they are bathed and anointed and volatile with anticipation.

Draupadi walks out of the sprawling courtyard of the women's quarters, followed by her retinue of maids and friends. She turns back to look up at the shuttered windows on the first floor, where she knows the widows and the unmarried girls are watching and she raises her hand briefly. The previous evening, she had said goodbye to the calves in the stables, the peacocks tethered to the tree in the orchard, the monkeys and the shifty dogs. She gave away her caged birds, her parakeets and songbirds who had listened with dignified and polite attention, head cocked, to all her whispered girlish secrets.

Now as she settles into her palanquin, she is surrounded by a new clan and a web of new relationships. Her own parents and clan, and the love with which she was raised, are to be forsaken, ephemeral guardians of her childhood.

She leans out of the palanquin to look at them, and they are all standing under the vaulted archway leading to the palace. Raja Drupad, Kokila Devi, Drishtadumna and her other brothers with their wives. Suddenly, Draupadi notices a figure a little apart, a tall, haggard woman with sparse white hair. Startled, she recognizes Maatrika Devi, whom she had forgotten about in the events of the past few days. The old woman is wearing a fraying cotton dhoti tied inelegantly high, baring spindly legs, and she is weeping openly, like a child, as she watches Draupadi's palanquin lurch and sway. She throws a handful of roasted grain in Draupadi's direction, a final, lonely benediction.

As the procession slinks through the streets of Kampilya, it is followed by a group of laughing, racing children pulling clattering wooden carts. The boys have shaved heads except for a lock of hair at the crown, and fragile limbs. They pass the vast city granary and the city water tanks, which are overflowing with rainwater. In the prosperous quarters of the rich merchants, the people stand at their doorways or on their balconies, to watch their rajkumari leave. The houses are built of timber and daub and the usually resplendent, powdery white lime plaster is mouldy now with green moss and dark, dank patches. There are birdcages hung from low verandas and, through the open doorways, Draupadi can see patient cows tethered in the inner courtyards.

They pass fruit orchards, bowed by the green weight of late-fruiting mangoes and custard apples and ponds with lotus flowers and a cacophony of slim, brown boys, slick as dolphins. In the poorer quarters, the houses are single rooms made of lime, earth, and cow dung with roofs of plaited leaves. It has been a torrential monsoon this year and the homes are drowning under a mix of creepers and moss and mud.

Soon the party has left the huddle of the town behind and enters the vast swath of countryside to the north of the city. Draupadi is amazed to see the change around her. For ten months of the year this land is an arid mirage, all in ochre and brown with a red haze of dust coming in from the great desert to the west. It is a land of gentle, aimless undulations, crumbling rocks and creeping thorny trees. Now, after the monsoon, Panchala is effusively green. The forests are full of berries—ber, neem, and fig, and their branches hang with flowering creepers, like garlands on a negligent god. Everywhere she looks there is life—tiny, lumbering, metal-bright beetles, disciplined ants, and enormous bees distracted by the fragrance of the star jasmine. They have appeared overnight, as though from the breath of a profligate goddess.

Draupadi leans out of the opening of the palanquin, to fill her heart with these images as a bulwark against lonelier times. She hears the men laughing, as they ride alongside one another in magnificent chariots, gifts from her father. Krishna rides alongside the Pandavas, as he has decided to accompany them to Hastinapur.

She leans back with a sigh and turns to Sushila.

'How carefree they seem, these men, how is it that they can joke and laugh so easily on such a momentous day?'

'Rajkumari, unlike you, they do not have to renounce forever the land of their ancestors and the home of their fathers, their name or their clan. They just absorb women into their own clan, like a river in spate that covers its banks.'

Sushila does not say that she had to leave behind her own husband to accompany Draupadi, and her young son, whose soft brown curls and laughing dark eyes she will never see again. These sacrifices are so pedestrian for a servant girl that it would not do to break one's heart over them.

'And whenever I overhear their talk, they are speaking of weapons, or hunting or battles.' Draupadi is irritable with the stumbling swaying of the palanquin but, just then, Yudhishthir rides up to the women and gives Draupadi a handful of jamun berries.

'We will set up camp at dusk, well before nightfall, for we have many days of travel ahead of us before we reach Hastinapur.'

Draupadi and Sushila share the jamun berries and Draupadi looks out one last time at the low, bruising sky against which a flight of wild geese flashes like lightning, before settling down to an uneasy sleep.

The city of Hastinapur rises up from the choking plains of the river valleys like an impossible dream. The ramparts and turrets flicker white and gold as the rain clouds skid across the sky. Guards at the watchtower have sighted the procession and the sound of trumpets and conch shells blow huskily in the breeze.

Two older men, still and watchful, are standing at the head of a small group of people at the main vaulted entrance. They are both imposing and ferocious, with long white beards stark against their dark skin and long hair pulled back from their guarded faces.

Draupadi looks questioningly at Kunti, who is riding with her in the palanquin. As soon as they crossed over into the Kuru lands, Kunti started instructing Draupadi about the customs of the Kauravas and the people she would be meeting soon.

'Now you are a Kuru bride, Beti, you must forget everything that was close to your heart up till now. Forget your parents and your siblings, your songs and your ancestors. When you participate in the shraddha rites every month, the ancestors you will honour will not be your Panchala family but the Kurus, the Rajas Pandu, Vichitravirya, and Shantanu.'

And to Draupadi this had been more appalling still than the loss of her home and the familiar landscape of her childhood. The fact that her ancestors, three generations of them, had been blown away by the casual sweep of an arbitrary god.

Kunti looks out of the palanquin and then turns to Draupadi.

'They are the Gurus Drona and Kripa, great warriors and honourable men. They taught the Pandavas all they know of warfare and they have always treated them with love and compassion, though they were but orphan sons of a widow woman.'

Draupadi holds back the curtain of the palanquin and watches as the Pandavas and Krishna ride up to the city. They all ride separately in single-horse war chariots reinforced with iron shields and they are sublime and arrogant as young gods.

Kunti looks at her sons too, and remembers the disgrace and terror of their escape from Hastinapur. She remembers also their years of dispirited, shameful hiding in the forest and she cannot believe the fortune they have exacted from their impervious fate.

The Pandavas have arrived at the group of men and they get off their chariots and prostrate themselves in the dust at Drona and Kripa's feet. Draupadi is astounded to see tears in the eyes of the two forbidding men, who lift up the Pandavas and hold them for a long while.

'Beloved sons, you have returned to us at last. We could never believe that you were dead, though everyone thought it was so. All these years we have kept hope alive and have waited for you, and now you have come back to the home of your father.'

Then they all pass under the main archway of the city and into the streets of Hastinapur which have been sprinkled with water and flowers. Roasted paddy is scattered everywhere and there are people lining the streets and cheering, while the drummers lead the procession. There are many women in the crowd too, for the rumours of the bride's beguiling beauty have already reached them and they are eager to see the perfection of her limbs and the splendour of her eyes. They have a darker, more shameful curiosity too, for they have also heard that she is to be shared by five brothers, passed from one to the other like a child's toy.

At last they reach the palace of Hastinapur, and Draupadi and Kunti are helped out of the palanquin. Dritrashtra is standing at the top of the stairs, along with Bheeshma, Duryodhan and his wife, Bhanumati, as well as several other brothers and their wives. Bhanumati and the other wives all walk up to Kunti to touch her feet while Yudhishthir leads Draupadi to the blind raja.

Dritrashtra, Draupadi tells herself, as she bows down before him, remembering Kunti's words. *Uncertain and weak, lost in his love for Duryodhan, and unable to see the spreading stain of violence and jealousy in his son.*

Dritrashtra's searching hands are like the fluttering wings of a dove as he blesses his daughter-in-law and Draupadi wonders if it is infirmity or nervousness that makes him tremble so. His voice also, when he welcomes Yudhishthir, is frail and stammering, as if he had been walking along an abyss and only now contemplated the unimaginable drop.

'Yudhishthir, Beta. How fortunate that you are alive and well. How dearly we have missed you and your brothers all these years.'

And then there is Bheeshma, of the terrible vow. Abandoned by his mother, renounced by his father, and betrayed by his step-mother. A raja in waiting, forever, with no land and no family to call his own. The only real prince of the Kuru bloodline, honourable and inflexible.

But as Draupadi bows before Bheeshma, she is surprised at the gentleness of his touch as he grasps her shoulders to raise her and the softness of his hand which lies in blessing on her head.

'Daughter, jewel of Panchala, welcome to your new home. May you live a virtuous life with your husbands and may you be blessed with many sons.'

Then there is Duryodhan, who comes up to Draupadi now and stands with folded hands before her.

'Welcome, Rajkumari Draupadi. May your grace and beauty bless the clan of Hastinapur for many years. We are indeed proud and honoured to call you our sister.'

Draupadi looks up quickly at Duryodhan. The words are charming and the voice is cultured and smooth but there is a subtle inflection in the timbre of his voice, of irony and sarcasm, and even derision. Draupadi has a glimpse of dark blue robes and jewellery, gold ear studs, a necklace of glinting stones and a heavy gold waistband. She senses in him restless power and uneasy strength but his sudden and glowing beauty is unexpected. His deep-set eyes are direct and arresting and his honey-gold skin gleams. His twisting dark hair hangs halfway down his back and over his shoulders, like a lion's mane. Draupadi frowns and looks away, remembering Kunti's words.

Duryodhan, she had said, holding her head in her hands. *First born and cherished and coveted from the time he drew his first breath, though there were terrible and ominous signs at his birth. The air was full of discordant keening sounds, jackals howling, and donkeys braying, and unnatural, unexplained wailing. But Gandhari and Dritrashtra were besotted and overwhelmed by their son and have always refused to acknowledge his temper, his lust for supremacy and power and, always, his hatred for the Pandavas.*

After greeting the men, Draupadi and Kunti are engulfed by a crowd of women, who take them to Gandhari's quarters. Gandhari is standing, waiting for them in the middle of her room and, when Kunti kneels before her, Gandhari quickly puts her arms around Kunti and puts the taller woman's head on her shoulder.

'Kunti, my dear sister, I am so happy to see you again and to know that you and your sons are alive and well.'

Her words come out in rush, as if she has been holding her breath and meditating on these words for many years. Her relief is guileless and Kunti is smiling now.

'Where have you been all these years and why didn't you come back to us before?'

'Rajmata Gandhari, we have been well enough, and I didn't know what reception my sons would get if we returned to Hastinapur.'

Gandhari looks away, troubled, and rubs her brow as if a pain had come upon her suddenly.

'That house at Varnavrat, the one we gifted you went up in flames. I was always uneasy about it,' she whispers.

'Rajmata, that is all in the past now, let us look to the future, for us and our sons. Let me show you my beautiful new daughter-in-law.'

Ira Mukhoty

Draupadi kneels down at Gandhari's feet and the older woman embraces her warmly. Holding Draupadi's face gently in her hands, she brushes her fingertips carefully over the contours of her face, her arched eyebrows, the inverted lotus-bud shape of her face with a small, pointed chin.

'Yes,' she sighs, 'beautiful indeed. Welcome to Hastinapur, Beti, may you always be happy in your husband's love, and cherished and respected by all.'

Draupadi is astonished at the difference between Gandhari and her dark, flaming son. Where Duryodhan is shifting and restless, Gandhari is calm and still. Duryodhan's beauty is like the sun shining on the warm earth and Gandhari is delicate as the harsingar that only blooms in moonlight. Kunti has told her that Gandhari remains almost exclusively within the palace, in her quarters, or in the main halls. This is her domain and her kingdom, she knows its topography intimately—each step and every surface. But avoiding the more turbulent outdoors means that all the glow has been leached from her and Kunti finds it hard to remember the vibrant, sun-kissed woman she used to be.

Draupadi and Kunti are given Pandu's old quarters, where they settle down with the Pandavas and their retinue. Draupadi is very busy for a while, meeting all the women of the palace and adjusting to the new rhythms of the house. Bhanumati, Duryodhan's bride, is tall and regal with a swaying walk and she brings Draupadi small gifts and they play dice together in the limpid afternoons and go to the flower gardens in the evenings when the sun is an orange stain in the sky.

Then, one day, after a council meeting, Yudhishthir comes to speak to Draupadi:

'The elders have decided to split the kingdom into two, so that I may have my own lands to rule while Dritrashtra retains half the land.'

'But you are the eldest brother, Yudhishthir. Surely this kingdom is yours by right? Why must you share it at all?'

'Raja Dritrashtra was the oldest, too, so some may argue that his son has a greater claim to the kingdom than I do. For the sake of the peace of this clan, so that there is no more jealousy and ill-will, I have agreed to the division of the kingdom. It is Bheeshma's counsel and I find it a wise one.'

What Yudhishthir does not tell Draupadi is that the land that has been conceded to him is Khandavprastha, a desolate little town in the border regions of the kingdom, surrounded by an inhospitable forest. It is an arid land far to the south of the Kuru kingdom—a forgotten place that no one remembers even in their dreams.

Indraprastha

~

The journey to Khandavprastha is precipitous and undignified. Duryodhan has suddenly grown intolerant of the Pandavas' company and Yudhishthir's claim to the crown. The memory of the inferno at Varnavrat flickers between them and the Pandavas turn their backs on the nameless violence in Duryodhan's eyes and the scorn in Karna's arms. And so they leave together, the Pandavas, Krishna, Draupadi, Kunti, and their retinue of soldiers and servants.

After riding for two days, the green pastures of paddy and barley are left behind and they stand at the frontier of a wasteland. Everyone stops and looks in silence at the desolation in front of them—impenetrable scrub and flaking rocks. Only Krishna seems unconcerned, even joyous, as he jumps out of his chariot and stands in front of the disheartened crowd.

'My friends, why do you all look so sad? Were you expecting a ready-built city with streets of gold? This is virgin land and it is yours to shape and mould as you please. Amongst the Vrishni Yadavs it has always been so, we have moved from land to land, building cities and shaping fields. You are Kshatriyas, do not be so easily cast down. Seize this land, my friends, make it yours, and yours only.'

They ride deeper into the wilderness and arrive, finally, at the ruins of Khandavprastha city itself. It is a lonely and bleak place, full of crumbling walls and broken streets inhabited by lizards and snakes, dusty, thorny plants and the aimless ghosts of its past inhabitants. There is stagnant water everywhere, slimy and viscous and fetid with insects.

That night, they light fires in the open and the cooks prepare a dispirited meal. They fall asleep on makeshift beds or in their chariots, and their dreams are filled with icy spirits who wail and drift around them. The next day, they perform a shanti puja for the peace of the wandering souls, taking special care to pray in front of broken-down wells, rivers, old crossroads, and big trees.

The Pandavas are energized suddenly, mesmerized by the vision of a new city built from their dreams, forged in the fire of their effort. Yudhishthir spends freely of the gold he was given by Raja Drupad and Krishna, and sends for artisans and labourers from Hastinapur. They dig wide trenches and build high walls and then the city, milky-white in the autumn light from the lime plaster that freshly coats the walls of the houses, and they call it Indraprastha. Yudhishthir invites rich traders, merchants, and tradesmen from the surrounding towns and villages to live in this city. This city, whose history is yet to be created, with a raja who is young and full of hope and a rani who is as beautiful as the night.

And so the Pandavas move into Indraprastha and resolve to forget Duryodhan's seething jealousy. Yudhishthir and Draupadi live together for this year and Draupadi begins to understand the nuances of her erudite and serious husband. She will come to realize later that he can be fettered by indecision and remorseless philosophical arguments but in this first year, at least, he is magnificent and full of valour.

Yet, in the quietest corner of her heart, Draupadi maintains a distance from Yudhishthir. She is unswerving in all her duties towards him, from the thrice daily sandhyas in which she is his spiritual partner to the last details of housekeeping in which she is meticulous and thorough. But even so, she cannot forget that terrible evening in the courtyard of the potter's house, when Yudhishthir would not look at Arjun and stood by his mother in her strange and cataclysmic decision.

Then one day towards the end of Draupadi's year with Yudhishthir, Arjun walks into the armoury when Yudhishthir is there with his wife. Draupadi is a dark, lithe presence in Yudhishthir's arms and her hair is a wild river down her back. Arjun stares, shocked, for a few seconds, and then turns around without a word and walks out of the armoury.

Later in the day, Yudhishthir goes looking for him and Arjun is hastily putting together some provisions and light weapons for travel.

'Arjun, what are you doing?' Yudhishthir puts his arm on his brother's shoulders, trying to still him.

'Bhai, I am following the terms of our agreement. I came upon you when you were with your wife and now I must be exiled for one year.'

'Arjun, don't be foolish. I release you from the terms of the agreement, you do not need to go anywhere. Please stay here with us.'

'I am sorry, Bhai, but I must go. Sadhu Narad was quite clear about this rule, that there were to be no exceptions.' And before Yudhishthir can say anything further, Arjun jumps onto his chariot and flicks the reins of his stamping horse.

It is true that early in their marriage, the great Sadhu Narad had visited Indraprastha and had had a long discussion with the Pandavas and Draupadi about their complex relationship. To make sure that privacy was ensured and jealousies avoided, he had ruled that any brother who chanced upon Draupadi when she was with her husband would be exiled for a year.

Draupadi is devastated when she hears that Arjun has gone away. His presence at Indraprastha was both a torment and a joy. She watched him surreptitiously, his graceful archer's walk and the way his dark skin glowed in the shadows, like hidden gold. She saw the brothers sometimes when she crossed the sports hall where Bheem tossed his opponents effortlessly to the ground during mock wrestling matches. But when they practised archery, Arjun was the storm god himself and now Indraprastha was godless and dreary.

And then a year has passed and now Bheem is her husband. Bheem of the quick and violent temper and sudden, explosive laughter. But, with Draupadi, Bheem is solicitous and gentle like a mother. He treks for hours in the unnamed forest to bring back the rare wild flowers she has said she likes. A trembling, sunset-coloured fawn also, that he found one day, to keep Draupadi company when he is away. He loves her timidly but entirely, and Draupadi will learn, in time, that he is the only one of the five brothers who will think of her first, always, before duty and before their raja.

And then, at last, it has been almost a year, and there is news of Arjun's return. Sparkling, joyous news which is blighted, suddenly, when Draupadi learns that Arjun has married three women in the past year. Ulupi, a tribal chief's daughter, and Chitrangada of Manipur have remained in their maternal homes, as was her condition, but the third wife is Krishna's own sister, Subhadra, and she rides with Arjun now as he heads for Indraprastha.

Alone in her chamber, Draupadi howls in anguish and heartbreak. And yet she knows she is trapped, for Krishna is their staunchest supporter and most powerful ally, apart from her own father. Krishna, who came to visit her regularly before he left for his own lands the previous year. Krishna, for whom she strings flower garlands herself, rows of hibiscus, and yellow champa, and iridescent shells, for she knows he likes the splendour of many colours against his dark skin, when he glows like a spring day.

So Arjun returns with his new bride, trailing gifts from the wealthy Yadavs of Dwarka. Chariots and elephants as well as an unending herd of cows decorated in silk cloth. And when he goes to greet Draupadi after his return, he is awkward and conciliatory, and shows her the finely crafted hexagonal box he got back for her. But Draupadi turns her back on him, to hide the desolation on her face that she cannot hide.

'Go back quickly to your new bride,' she whispers. 'She must be lonely for your company, now that she is in her new home.'

Arjun walks up to Draupadi, and she can smell the musk fragrance he uses and his presence so close to her is alarming and disquieting.

'Draupadi, you must know that an alliance with Krishna is crucial to us. With Subhadra in our family, the Yadavs will give us their full support, should we ever be challenged again by the Kauravas.'

'Yes, I know, Brother-in-law. It is a wise and pragmatic decision. But must everything in life be governed by politics and clear rationale?'

Arjun looks at the slope of her shoulders and bare back, and the way her dark skin reflects light like polished glass. He is close enough to see the tendrils of hair curling at her neck and the tiny rubies in her ears gleaming like drops of blood.

'You must know what is in my heart, Draupadi, but I am a raja's younger brother and it is my dharma to stand by my brother's decisions. I am sorry for the unhappiness I know it must cause you.'

Arjun walks out of Draupadi's quarters but soon her year with Bheema is over and she sits in front of the fire altar while the pundit chants the mantras which purify and renew her and the holy flames carry away all memory of her previous husbands and she is a bride again.

And that night, when Arjun comes to visit her, there is no need for words and her sighs are the universe and her fragrance of lotus and citrus is the earth itself, dark and warm and eternal.

For that year, Draupadi is happier than she will ever be again in her life. Each day is an endless silence for her to fill with thoughts of Arjun, his easy laugh, and his fierce passion. She carries out her duties towards her mother-in-law and other husbands through an opaque haze, and the past and the future cease to exist.

Krishna and his Yadav relatives come to visit Indraprastha, bringing gifts for Subhadra and Draupadi. The long, hot days of summer are upon them and the young people go to the forest in the still indolence of the evening. Only Arjun and Krishna and their wives and servants, without the constraining presence of the older brothers. They all drink sura and sit in the formless shade of the jamun trees, watch the water egrets, with their brown heads like coconuts and thin yellow legs, walking disjointedly through the marshland like grumpy old men looking for dropped treasure.

One day, Krishna and Arjun disappear for several days and when they return, they smell of fire and slaughter.

'We have cleared the Khandava forest,' Krishna declares. 'When the fire dies down, we will be able to till the land and transform it into fields and pastures for the cows.'

Draupadi is surprised, for the forest was said to belong to the tribal chieftain Taksaka, and a considerable population of Naga tribals lived in the forest.

'What of all those people, did they submit to you?' Draupadi asks Krishna and Arjun.

'We put them to the sword, all of them. We couldn't let any escape alive, otherwise they would have returned to claim the land at a later time. But they are not Kshatriyas, and do not live by our codes so the forest was rightfully ours to claim for our needs.'

Now that it is evening, Draupadi can see the crimson glow of the fire, which rages all night. Draupadi can almost hear screams through the crackling flames and she holds her hands against her ears as she thinks of the animals, the large-eyed deer, the fearless mongoose, and the magnificent peacocks. She thinks of their incomprehensible terror when they realize they cannot outrun the flames. In the morning, a huge plume of black smoke fills the eastern sky, like a maleficent yagna, and for days, ash and cinders fall on the people of Indraprastha like a curse.

And so the forest becomes a smoky, smouldering wasteland, and then a green field of barley, and the years turn into a decade and Indraprastha becomes a kingdom.

Draupadi has five sons over the years, one to each husband. They are the great solace of Kunti's life, each child a precious safeguard against the wilderness of namelessness and destitution. Draupadi has them to cherish for a short time, while they are still organically a part of her, and she ties amulets around their tiny arms to protect them against the evil eye and rubs mustard oil onto their flailing limbs. Soon they must be handed over to the more exacting care of their fathers and teachers for they are warriors' sons and must learn the craft of war. They come to her still, when they get hurt during archery practice or jousting. She summons the physician who carefully applies the big black ants on to the cuts, where they clamp their jaws shut and the physician then quickly twists off the bodies, leaving the suturing jaws in place.

Subhadra gives birth to Abhimanyu, Arjun's son, and there is much celebration and rejoicing in Indraprastha. As Abhimanyu becomes a young boy, Draupadi notices that Arjun takes special care with his archery training, more so than with her own sons, and it is another chafing pain in her heart. But she learns to choose her battles and is intransigent when she needs to be. The Pandavas take other wives, and secure alliances, but the wives all remain sequestered in their maternal homes and are never seen in Indraprastha.

In Indraprastha, Draupadi is incontestably rani. Subhadra has her own quarters where she lives with Arjun and Abhimanyu but the rest of the palace is Draupadi's fiefdom. From the time she gets up, before dawn, when the stars are fading from the sky like a fleeting dream, she is the throbbing heart that directs all their lives. She starts by lighting a little clay lamp in the alcove of Yudhishthir's prayer room so that he can begin his prayers at dawn. While he chants the mantras, she fetches all the things he will need for the morning sandhya, his rudraksha mala, the freshly drawn milk, the kusa grass. When Yudhishthir chants the Gayatri Mantra, she stills her mind, a supreme meditation of silence, to receive the Devi's blissful words.

'Blessed mother, after the ignorance of the night, let me wake into knowledge and light.'

Then Yudhishthir walks to the Yamuna, wearing only a white loincloth, to invoke the blessing of the river while Draupadi hurries away to her quarters, to get ready. Her servant girls have already prepared the paan with cloves and camphor and have lit incense sticks, sandalwood paste ground with petals and leaves and oil, in all the private rooms. While Draupadi gets ready, her clothes are draped over the incense sticks so that they are fumigated with the fragrant smoke and all day she will trail the aroma of lotus and lime.

After her bath, Draupadi uses a paste of honey, fruit pulp, salt, and oil to rub on her gums and teeth. She paints the soles of her feet with diluted red lac, so that her footsteps are a ghostly reminder of her absence. She lines her eyes heavily with kohl and her lips with an orange mineral powder which increases the brilliance of her smile.

The hair groomers then twist and coil her glossy hair into elaborate, plaited buns, studded with shells or pearls or stones. Once she is dressed and has put on her jewellery, she goes to get the younger children ready so that they may greet their fathers.

By the time Yudhishthir returns from the Yamuna, Draupadi is waiting to greet him, and every morning he is startled by her beauty and grace, and it is as if she has been reborn from the fire of his morning prayers.

While the men and the children spend the morning in lessons and weapons practice, Draupadi supervises the midday meal. She is particularly careful with Bheem's preferences, braised goat meat and marinated fish followed by mounds of milk desserts, honey curd, kheer, and bananas cooked in milk. Kunti helps her tend to the fruit and flower garden and there are fruits now all year round. Bananas, mangoes, figs, and all manner of berries.

The afternoons are leisurely and languid and Draupadi plays dice with Yudhishthir or chess with Subhadra or one of the other brothers while the others go hunting or fishing. Then, as the sun loses its ferocity, Draupadi inspects the herb garden, for Nakul will need neem leaves as a disinfectant for his beloved horses and Sahadev favours the kutaja plant with its white flower to treat the cattle when they are ill.

At dusk, Draupadi prepares the evening sandhya and then there are often entertainers, singers, dancers, actors, and poets. There is wine to be served, sugarcane wine or grape wine, and paan after the evening meal, carefully blended by Draupadi's maids.

And so Draupadi learns to pre-empt every husband's needs and she is tireless and unceasing in making their lives seamlessly fulfilled. They learn to count on her for all things, from the triflingly mundane to the all-important yagnas and sacrifices. She becomes the breath of their lives, effortless and essential.

Meanwhile, the Pandavas are busy with the expansion and building of Indraprastha. Their most ambitious project is the building of a magnificent assembly hall, for which they have the expert knowledge and help of an architect from the northern lands, outside the boundaries of Bharat. His name is Maya and he is an immense man with golden limbs the size of tree trunks and his long hair gleams like honey in the sunlight.

Unlike the architects of the river valleys, Maya knows how to work in stone and he knows the secret of brick kilns and coloured tiles. When the hall is completed, it is a thing of intricate beauty and almost magical craftsmanship. The floors are made of smooth blue tiles that look like water and there are shallow water tanks with edges so smooth and water so still that it looks like a polished floor. There are artificial ponds filled with lotuses and lilies made from gold and semi-precious stones and there are real lotus flowers too, so that artifice merges subtly and elegantly into reality and it is like an enchantment. The hall is surrounded by gardens filled with fruit trees and teeming with swans, and peacocks, blackbirds, and ducks, and aquatic plants.

Ten years go by like a dream while they build houses, plant fields and fruit orchards and clear the surrounding scrubland and marshes. Now they have reached the limit of the land they can expand into and Yudhishthir decides to declare a Rajasuya. His four brothers and Krishna ride out of Indraprastha to challenge all the neighbouring chieftains while Yudhishthir remains in Indraprastha to prepare for the sacrifice. The brothers ride for days, asking chieftains and local heads to submit to their rule and accept Yudhishthir as raja, which they all do, without much bloodshed. Only Krishna uses the Rajasuya to confront his old nemesis, Jarasandha, who has been a haranguing thorn in the side of the Yadavs for a long time. With Bheem's help, he defeats Jarasandha and returns, triumphant, to Indraprastha.

While the Pandavas subjugate the neighbouring chieftains, Yudhishthir and Draupadi make the arrangements for the great Rajasuya sacrifice. Countless Brahmins have been invited to Indraprastha and Draupadi oversees the construction of a row of huts to lodge them, each with its own cow, bedding, and food. The Brahmins start arriving, first a few of them and then a raucous, thundering clamour of them. Some are ancient and fragile, with ruined faces and blazing eyes, others are striding and powerful with orange beards and hopelessly matted coir-like hair. They bring their assistants also, young boys with smooth skins and shaved heads. Specially commissioned potters are clustered in a field, baking

Ira Mukhoty

endless clay pots over open-air kilns.

The sacrificial ground itself is carefully measured out and sanctified by the pundits and six fire altars are built to specific patterns with clay bricks. As the pundits gather on the sacrificial ground, immersed in their inner world of private epiphany and breathy chants, the tributes begin to flood into Indraprastha. All the subjugated chieftains send gifts, as do all the relatives by marriage of the Pandavas. The guests come too and many of them have never been to Indraprastha before and they are bewildered by its opulence. Gandhari's father arrives from faraway Gandahar and Raja Drupad as well, along with his sons. The clan of Hastinapur arrives in force, Dritrashtra and all his sons, as well as Bheeshma, Drona, and Kripa. It is a glittering gathering of all the noble Kshatriyas of the land.

The Kauravas are all assigned tasks to help with the Rajasuya ceremony. Bheeshma and Drona oversee the sacrificial rite, Duryodhan collects the tributes from all the chieftains, Dritrashtra's charioteer, Sanjay, welcomes the chieftains and Krishna salutes the Brahmins.

On the day of the sacrifice itself, Yudhishthir wears white clothes, light and voluminous like churned milk and shot through with gold and silver embroidery. The six fires are lit and two dozen priests are chosen to conduct the rites. They pour grain, ghee, butter, sesame, fruit, flowers, and meat into the fire in long, elaborately structured rituals. They chant mantras simultaneously and their voices rise and fall in metred rhythms that thrum with power and beauty. They pray to Agni, Indra, and Varun, and the fires hiss and blaze in echoing answers every time an offering is made.

At the end of the day, Krishna is chosen to be especially honoured because of his role in killing Jarasandha during the Rajasuya. Yudhishthir bows before Krishna and pours water onto his feet and then onto the heads of his wife and brothers. Then, at the very end of the ceremony, the priests sprinkle water on

Yudhishthir and he is crowned emperor, samrat of Indraprastha. Conch shells are blown in celebration and the ceremonial hall is set on fire, carrying away all their mortal dreams and prayers.

The next day, the guests and the Brahmins leave after a final banquet and only Duryodhan and Shakuni remain. Yudhishthir has invited them to stay a few days to visit the city and the palace and also, possibly, to show them that he is no longer the cowering, beggarly orphan boy who arrived on the banks of the Ganga, accompanied by a cohort of silent priests and the half-burned body of his father.

When Duryodhan had stood with folded hands at the entrance of the banquet hall, greeting the guests and accepting the tribute on behalf of Yudhishthir, he had been stunned by the generosity of the gifts. There were jewels and gold and gems, but also gleaming scimitars, deadly battle-axes, finely wrought daggers, and arrows. There were herds of animals, cows, horses, camels and elephants, wool blankets and rare silk drapes. Duryodhan realized that an army's worth of weapons and gold had arrived in Indraprastha in one day and he burned with anger and jealousy.

As for the magnificent ceremonial hall, he is convinced it is bewitched. He stumbles through the hall, mesmerized by the intricate trompe l'oeil and artful blend of reality and illusion. At one point, he walks into a shallow waterbody, mistaking the glass-like surface of the water for polished stone and Draupadi, who is watching from a shuttered balcony, bursts out laughing. Duryodhan looks up instantly, seething with embarrassment. It is intolerable that this woman who is shared between five men, should have the temerity to laugh at him, heir to the Kuru clan.

He leaves for Hastinapur soon after, thoroughly disquieted, and rages, when he is back in his quarters, to Shakuni.

'Uncle, it is appalling that Yudhishthir should be crowned samrat. You know that there can only be one Rajasuya and one samrat per generation so now I will never be able to conduct such a thing myself. And look at all the wealth he has gathered through this pretext!'

Shakuni runs his hands through his thick, curling hair, now streaked with silver.

'And that woman, that Draupadi, who dares to laugh at me! She has debased herself by marrying these five inconsequential brothers and dishonoured the Panchala name. How did she dare humiliate me, a guest and a raja!'

Shakuni walks up to Duryodhan and puts a hand on his shoulder.

'Nephew, calm yourself. I have a plan that will address all your complaints. It has been a long time since your cousins visited Hastinapur. Let us reciprocate their hospitality, and invite them to a game of dice.'

Dice

~

It is a still, vaporous day in the middle of the monsoon season when the Pandavas ride to Hastinapur. The air is bloated with moisture and the clouds are dark and oppressively low in the sky. The marshlands that they cross are reckless with new life and the kingfishers and the egrets are confounded by the sudden excess of dragonflies and beetles and yellow butterflies.

Draupadi rides in the chariot with Yudhishthir and she is happy to be going back to Hastinapur now that their own kingdom has been secured and expanded by the Rajasuya. They were given the dregs of the Kuru kingdom, a husk of land no one wanted and now Yudhishthir is samrat of the twin valleys with enough bounty to last for a generation.

She is still surprised, however, at the alacrity with which Yudhishthir accepted Raja Dritrashtra's invitation to a game of dice, which seems a trifling and preposterous reason for a visit. But Yudhishthir does like gambling above all and he has told her many times that it is a noble pursuit, fit for a raja.

They enter Hastinapur palace and there is a tumult of musicians and dancers waiting to greet them and garland them with fresh jasmine flowers. Gandhari, Bhanumati, and several other daughters-in-law of the clan of Hastinapur are there too, ready to show Draupadi to her quarters in the married women's section but, that very day, Draupadi realizes she is in her monthly cycle. Bitterly

210

disappointed, she informs Bhanumati, who is obliged now to take her to a small, sparsely furnished room, away from the main area of activity.

For the next three days and three nights, Draupadi will have to sequester herself, alone and ignored, while the rest of the household throbs with music, and dance, and excitement. Her polluting presence as a menstruating woman has to be circumscribed and restricted so that no religious ceremony, no entertainment, and no person of importance is tainted by her touch or her gaze.

Draupadi stands in the middle of the small room with its stark furnishing and sighs when she sees all the vials and jars of pastes and cosmetics she had brought with her. She had been so keen to show Bhanumati and the other women all the gifts she had received at the Rajasuya, to appear before them in all her radiance as wife of the samrat of Indraprastha. Instead, she removes all her jewellery, every last gold pin and bracelet, and changes into a single piece of white cloth which she wraps loosely around her waist and then over her breast, and shoulders. She wipes off all the kumkum and kohl from her face, for she may not have a bath, nor use any cosmetics. She unties her hair, which must now hang loose and ungroomed, and she will need to sit out the next three days like a rumpled pariah.

The next morning, Sushila brings food and some gossip about the last evening's festivities. The food is bland—unseasoned rice and plain milk—but the information is piquant.

'There was a delicious and extensive banquet, Rani. All kinds of meats, roasted and fried and cooked with sauces. And so many kinds of desserts, I have never seen such variety in all my life.'

Draupadi nods. The Kauravas are extravagantly hospitable and she knows they would have informed themselves of each guest's preferences.

'And such lively entertainment, I wish you could have seen the magicians, Rani. They cast some manner of spell on everyone and it is said they made a huge tree appear out of nowhere. And what singing and dancing, we could hear it in the servants' quarters too and it continued late into the night!'

What Sushila doesn't say is that the dancers were chosen for their great beauty, as well as their singing, and that they accompanied each Pandava to their chambers. She doesn't say it but Draupadi knows it anyway. It is the mark of Kshatriya hospitality and a prosaic detail of men's lives that need not be spoken about.

'Tonight they will play dice, Rani. They have built a sabha especially for the occasion, with white cloth and colourful banners and Shakuni will play in the place of Duryodhan, for they say he is a talented player.'

And so, that day, Draupadi is alone and she sits in the doorway to her room, her long hair sweeping the floor, and watches the rain fall on the sodden ground. There is a languid peace in this after all, Draupadi realizes—the removal of all combusting expectation and frenetic activity.

But, by the evening, when Sushila comes back with a plate of fried vegetables and barley gruel, the news from the dice hall is worrisome.

'Raja Yudhishthir has lost all his wagers so far, Rani. They say he has lost a lot of jewellery and boxes of gold.'

Draupadi is concerned but not overly so, for such are the fortunes of gambling men. Everything may yet be recovered in one lucky throw of the dice.

It is a while before Draupadi sees anyone again, and this time it is an older servant woman of the Kauravas. She has ostensibly come to collect the food tray but she looks at Draupadi with a strange sideways glance and an insinuating leer in her voice.

'I have bad tidings, Rani. Your raja has lost all of his wealth in the games. His land also, all of it. They are saying you will all be destitute.'

'What? What are you saying, old woman? Send Sushila to me at once.'

The older woman leaves with a mocking bow and a sly smile and Draupadi looks at her leave, furious and uncomprehending.

When she sees Sushila, Draupadi gasps and holds her hand to her mouth for Sushila is crying and has covered her eyes with her uttaraya. The moment she enters Draupadi's room, Sushila falls to the floor sobbing loudly.

'Rani, we are ruined, we are ruined. Raja Yudhishthir has staked, and lost, all his wealth and all his land and all his subjects. He is staking his brothers now, one by one. Indra have pity on us, Rani, we will all be destroyed. The Kaurava rajas are all laughing loudly and spurring on the gambling and Raja Yudhishthir is just not stopping. It is as though he has been possessed by a demon.'

Draupadi cannot believe what Sushila is telling her. She knows Yudhishthir's great vice is gambling, that he can never resist a challenge or a wager but to gamble away all his kingdom, so hard-won? And his adored brothers? That cannot be and she will not believe it.

But there are footsteps now in the corridor, urgent and hurried, and Draupadi is shocked when a manservant appears in front of her.

'You must follow me to the gambling hall, you have been summoned there.'

"What? How dare you speak to me, fool, I am the rani of Indraprastha. I am in no state to appear before a sabha full of men, go away at once.'

But the servant shrugs, insolent and contemptuous.

'Raja Yudhishthir has wagered you, Rani, and lost. He wagered all his brothers, one by one, then himself, and then he staked you as well. Now you have been lost to the Kauravas and they have sent me to fetch you.'

Draupadi holds her head in her hands when she hears this, as there is a sudden, roaring horror within her. She turns her face away, so that this insolent boy may not see the rani of Indraprastha cry for shame and fear. She struggles to control her racing thoughts and then concentrates on the last thing the boy has told her. She turns back to face him and speaks softly.

'Go back to the sabha and ask Raja Yudhishthir this. "Did you lose yourself first, or me?" Go now, and ask him this, exactly as I have said it.'

The boy wants to argue but he sees the formless fury in Draupadi's eyes and turns away without a word.

Draupadi walks the length of her room, her mind a blank wall of fear. She does not understand what is happening and feels that it must be an elaborate, nightmarish charade. Sushila is curled up in the corner of the room, still sobbing.

Suddenly they hear a loud voice shouting down the corridor and the sound of heavy footsteps.

'Where is she, the slave woman? Where is that Draupadi, who is now a slave of the Kauravas?'

When she hears these words, Draupadi backs against the wall of her room, her lips trembling as she struggles to control her tears.

Dusshasan, Duryodhan's brother, strides into her room, his jewellery gleaming with unexpected opulence in the stark room. He walks up to Draupadi and grabs her white robe and starts pulling her out of the room.

'Stop, what are you doing? Where are you taking me?' Draupadi is sobbing now as she stumbles behind Dusshasan. Her bare breasts are exposed as Dusshasan has pulled the robe so roughly that it has fallen off her shoulders. With desperate strength, Draupadi pulls back the end of her robe and wraps it tightly around herself, and bows before Dusshasan.

'I beg of you, please come to your senses. What you are doing is against all Kshatriya rules of conduct. Where are you taking me like this?'

'There are no rules for slaves, though, and that is what you are. You have been wagered and lost by your husband and now you must appear before the Kauravas in the sabha.'

'I am in my monthly cycle,' she whispers. 'I am in a single cloth, my hair is undone and there is blood on my robe. You cannot make me appear before a crowd of men, you cannot.'

'I care nothing at all about your confinement or your cycle. You will come with me now.'

Dusshasan grabs Draupadi's wrist roughly and pulls her to the gambling hall while she screams and pleads with him.

When they arrive at the gambling hall, Dusshasan shoves her into the middle of the sabha where she stands, sobbing, her hands covering her face. Through her grief and her despair, she hears the strange taunts, which seem disconnected to her, as if she were just an actor in an absurd, appalling play.

'Daasi,' they are saying, 'slave girl, come here, daasi, and stand before us.'

Dusshasan grabs her wrist again, provoked by the taunting voices.

'Come on, daasi, I will take you to the slave quarters where you belong.'

Draupadi pulls away her hand and stands, panting for breath, in front of all these men. She is wearing the same crumpled and stained robe from the day before since she may not change or bathe for three days. Her hair is in obscene disarray about her shoulders and she has not been seen by a man in this state since she became a woman, all those years ago.

She looks up from the corner of her eyes to look at her five husbands, and when she sees them, she is filled with despair, for she knows they cannot save her now. They are sitting on low stools, hanging their heads, and clad only in their dhotis. All their jewellery, their uttarayas and turbans are lying in disordered heaps around them. To see them reduced to beggars, in this company of Kshatriyas, shocks her to speech.

'I need to ask this assembly a question. Who did Raja Yudhishthir first wager, himself, or me? If he wagered himself and then lost, he was no longer in a position to wager me, since as a slave he owns nothing and has no wife.'

There are further shouts and taunts at this point, but no one answers her directly. The older men, Drona, Kripa, Bheeshma, and Dritrashtra, stand silently, dismayed.

Finally, Bheeshma speaks up, in a faltering voice, but only to dissimulate and equivocate.

'It is a difficult question you have raised, a nuanced question. The ways of dharma are not always easy to understand. I cannot answer your question.'

And then the men start shouting again, scandalous and immoral taunts.

'Whore!' they shout. 'Daasi, you are nothing but a fallen woman with no rights and no say of your own.'

'Sahadev!' Bheem shouts suddenly, enraged and helpless and unable to contain himself any longer. 'Bring me some fire that I may burn Yudhishthir's hands, for those are the hands that staked and lost Draupadi.'

But Arjun turns to Bheem at once and puts a hand on his shoulder.

'Control yourself, Bhai. Raja Yudhishthir is our older brother and our guru. We can never go against his will. That is our highest dharma.'

The other brothers nod silently at this and Draupadi is heartbroken and dismayed at their adherence to that one law that binds them all together. These five husbands, whose uncertain destiny she has faithfully followed, whom she has loved and cared for as best she could, for them she is such a cursory bond. She is angry, at last, and it is a liberating and empowering thing

'What is this respect for tradition and culture you speak of, Husband? What kind of tradition says you must not speak ill of your elders, but you can accept the humiliation and torture of your wife?'

And a voice speaks out at last and it is Duryodhan's young brother, Vikarna.

'What is going on in this sabha is evil. Draupadi was wagered after Yudhishthir lost himself so what right did he have to wager her? Moreover, she is the wife of the other brothers too so he could not legally stake her once he had become a slave himself.'

'Sit down, Vikarna, you are a child in this assembly of men. Draupadi is a whore because she sleeps with five men. She is unchaste and deserves to be treated as a slave and a whore.'

This time it was Karna who spoke, in his deep, resonating voice and Draupadi's anger grows in layers, like an unfurling lotus bud.

'She is a whore, I say, and she has no claims to modesty at all. Dusshasan, pull away the cloth she is wearing.'

Dusshasan laughs and walks towards Draupadi and starts pulling at the end of her robe.

Bheem gets up from his seat, unable to contain himself.

'As I stand before my elders in this hall, in the presence of all my ancestors, I vow to kill this man in battle and to drink the blood from his chest for he is a sinner and a coward.'

Draupadi snatches her robe away from Dusshasan and cries tears of rage and impotence.

'Is this the way to treat a woman? Any woman? Much less the daughter-in-law of Raja Dritrashtra and the granddaughter-in-law of Bheeshma. For any woman to be dragged by her hair into an assembly of men, where she is mistreated and humiliated, is this dharma? And you call yourselves Kshatriyas?'

Draupadi is a torrent of rage now, like the Yamuna in flood, and her anger carries her beyond the confines of this gambling hall and into the wider world where she is sure of her honour and her name.

'I am Draupadi, daughter of a raja and sister of a yuvraj, wife to five warriors, and rani of Indraprastha.'

But the men ignore her words and Karna speaks up again.

'Draupadi, the Pandavas are no longer your husbands. You belong to the Kauravas now. Go to the slave quarters and choose one of the Kauravas as your new husband.'

Duryodhan laughs loudly at this, throwing back his head, his tawny hair blazing around him. Then he leans forward to look Draupadi straight in the eyes and slowly pulls up a corner of his dhoti so that his left thigh is exposed.

'Come,' he says softly to Draupadi, slapping his bare thigh loudly, 'come and sit on my thigh, beautiful daasi.'

'I will break your thigh, Duryodhan. I say this in front of all my ancestors and my elders in this hall and the gods in their heaven. I will break your thigh, I swear it, and if I do not, may I be denied immortality after my death, when my bones are ground to dust.'

It is Bheem again, tempestuous and volatile Bheem, who is the only one of the brothers who allows his passion to rule his heart.

Dusshasan laughs and grabs Draupadi by the hair but she spins around and pulls her hair away from him. She holds her hair in her own hands now and spits venom at Dusshasan.

'My hair, which has been sullied by this beast, shall remain as it is now, untied and unwashed, till the day I can wash it in his blood. I swear this, by everything that I hold sacred, that I will wash my hair in the blood from his heart, and only then will I know peace.'

There is ominous silence after this, as the men contemplate these scandalous words. She has spoken of blood lust and vengeance, and they are uncomfortably reminded of her bleeding state in front of them, polluting and dangerous and calamitous.

Vidura stands up finally to say that he could not accept that Draupadi was won, but no one answers him, caught in the impasse

Ira Mukhoty

of their conflicting desires.

Arjun speaks softly, almost to himself, to ask whose master is he, whose own self is vanquished? He is talking about Yudhishthir but seems apologetic and unsure, loath as always to contradict his older brother.

In the grating silence, a distant howl of a jackal is heard, a lonely and bloodcurdling lament, and soon there is a discordant chorus of howls and no one in the hall can ignore this terrible omen of bad luck.

Dritrashtra gets up, Gandhari at his side, and stumbles towards Draupadi. He is clammy with sweat in the turbid air, leaning heavily on Sanjay. Dritrashtra knows the power of a virtuous woman's curse, and he is terrified for the life of his sons.

'Daughter, forgive me, forgive my sons, please, for the humiliation they have caused you. Do not curse them, Beti, ask me for anything and it is yours. You have proved yourself to be a true and valorous daughter of this house.'

'If you wish to give me something, Father, please free Raja Yudhishthir from slavery. I would not have my sons have a slave for a father.'

'Done. But ask for something else, Daughter.'

'Then let my other husbands be free as well, and be given back their weapons and their chariots.'

'Done. And I return to them all their wealth. They may return to Indraprastha with all that they came with. But ask for something else, Beti.'

'No, Raja, nothing more. With my husbands free, and armed with their weapons, I do not need anything else.'

Draupadi folds her hands and bows before Dritrashtra and follows her husbands out of the hall.

And so the Pandavas and Draupadi return to Indraprastha, in silence and shame. And when another invitation to play dice arrives, in which the loser must give up his kingdom and go into exile for thirteen years, they return to Hastinapur, inexorably drawn to the torment of their fate.

And again, in silence and in shame, Yudhishthir loses.

The Pandavas leave for exile and Indraprastha is abandoned. Over the years, the disheartened citizens, bereft of their raja and his wealth, leave Indraprastha and the city is reclaimed by the voracious peepul trees and the rambling ghosts. Indraprastha becomes a ruin, over the ruins of Khandavprastha, and the Pandavas never return.

VII

Conversations in Exile

Twelve Years

~

Draupadi is sitting on her haunches, cooling a huge mound of steaming rice with a flag-shaped bamboo fan. Her hair is twisted into a rough, loose braid over her shoulder and her face is a slur of sweat and dust. The clamorous crows compete with the bleating of the tethered goats and the air is heavy and turbid with smoke and heat. It is midday and the visiting scholars and pundits are settling down in the shade of the massive neem tree, waiting for their meal. Draupadi hears a sudden commotion in the courtyard and sighs, there will not be enough rice for everyone if there are more guests today.

'I came as soon as I could, as soon as I heard what had happened. Forgive me, Raja Yudhishthir, for not having come sooner.'

The voice is deep, melodious, and familiar. Draupadi drops the bamboo fan and rushes to the courtyard where she sees Krishna, surrounded by the Pandavas. They are slapping him on the back joyously and clasping him to their chests. She goes back into the house to quickly prepare the madhuyana, the ritual drink of sugar, ghee, curd, honey, and herbs, which Yudhishthir presents to Krishna and which he drinks in three mouthfuls.

As soon as Krishna sees Draupadi, he goes up to her and folds his hands.

'Sakhi, I am so sorry to see you in this condition. I couldn't come any sooner for news of your exile reached me very late. Forgive me.'

223

Krishna's voice is gentle and full of compassion and suddenly Draupadi is overcome by the anger and the humiliation that has been roaring inside her and scorching her thoughts these past few months.

'Oh, Krishna, do you know how they treated me? Those vile Kauravas? They dragged me into the assembly full of men when I was wearing just a single, dirty cloth. And they laughed at me, Krishna…. They laughed at me and called me a whore.'

And Draupadi covers her face and sobs as the Pandavas silently look out of the doorway and at the dogs, who gather companionably in the courtyard at mealtimes.

Krishna lets Draupadi cry for a long time, and then he gently makes her sit on a bare bamboo divan.

Draupadi looks up at Krishna, her lashes wet with tears.

'How could they treat me so? I am the daughter of a raja, I am the wife of the Pandavas, and still they were able to humiliate and torment me. I despise my husbands' strength, Krishna, they were not able to protect me when I needed them most. What good was Bheem's strength and Arjun's skill? I curse their strength and their valour.'

'Sakhi, the insults of the Kauravas will be paid for, many times over, do not trouble yourself in this way.'

'You call me Sakhi, Krishna? Where were you when I needed you? No, I have no husbands, no sons, and no brothers. Even you, Krishna, you are not really mine at all.'

'Sakhi, I promise you revenge. All those who have insulted you, and reviled you will die, I swear it. The holy mountains may shatter, dear friend, and the heavens themselves may collapse but my promise will stand and you will see your enemies killed.'

At last Draupadi calms down, and wipes away her tears with the end of her uttaraya. Krishna is the first to offer her revenge, unconditional, violent, and slaughterous revenge. He is the first to truly understand her desire to see blood spilled for what she has gone through, and to promise her redemption. The Pandavas are more circumspect when she rails against her fate. They sublimate their shame about her humiliation into their righteous penance in the forest. For them, the rigours of forest life are trifling, this deracination a natural state, since they have spent so much of their lives in exile already.

'And now we must live like cast-outs, no better than beggars, for thirteen years! But Krishna, Arjun is the best archer in the land. Should he not go and fight Duryodhan and show him we are not his slaves?'

'That would be a mistake, Draupadi. Karna would defend Duryodhan and he would kill Arjun, without a doubt. He is a magnificent warrior, no matter that he sides with a fiend like Duryodhan. The Pandavas are weak at the moment, Sakhi, they must gather their strength and bide their time.'

So Draupadi gets up, momentarily reassured, helping the serving girls to dish out the cooled rice to all the scholars and priests in the courtyard. There is fried boar also, for Bheem goes hunting every day, though there is no time for the basting and the marinating in lemon and tamarind that they would have done in Indraprastha. The meat is tough and fibrous and Draupadi gives her share away to the grateful dogs.

Then, in the afternoons, there are long discussions with the visiting sadhus, on morality, philosophy, and dharma. Draupadi listens for a while, leaning against the side of the hut, while the maids scour the pots with ash and paddy husk. But soon she will need to prepare for the evening sandhya, for Yudhishthir is rigorous in the observance of all the rites. The Brahmins are fed again, as are the insects and the birds. And then the Pandavas may eat after the guests have all been served, and, at the very end, it is Draupadi's turn. She eats her meal sitting on the floor, off a fresh banana leaf which is green as spring. And, through the entire, bustling day, Draupadi stokes her hate like a brazier and the litany of Kaurava names is a holy meditation: Duryodhan, Dusshasan, Karna.

Upon Krishna's suggestion, it is decided that they must start arming themselves against an inevitable battle and Arjun is delegated to go to the Himalayas and collect all the weapons he can. He is impatient to be gone and is careless about hiding it.

'You take our hearts with you, Partha,' Draupadi whispers, her eyes dark with the tears she will shed when he is gone.

Arjun touches her smooth cheek lightly with his fingers and then turns away, and it seems to Draupadi that all her life, he returns to her only to leave again.

Krishna leaves soon after.

'Suffering is essential, my dear Draupadi. It is the great guru of our life and teaches us all we need to know. Unhappiness, like happiness, is ephemeral. Do not allow either to rule your heart.'

And he smiles as he says this, a blazing, delighted smile like a child who has seen his mother after a long day. As if what he has said isn't the most haunting and exhilarating thing that Draupadi has heard in all her life.

And so, a year goes by.

⁂

In the dusk of a winter's evening, the Pandavas and Draupadi are gathered around the campfire, silent in the contemplation of their rambling, deafening thoughts. They are wrapped in coarse blankets against the icy wind and around them the night falls all at once, like a sigh.

It is Draupadi who speaks first, exasperated as always when the brothers give in to gloom and despondency.

'To think that Duryodhan is enjoying all the luxuries of kingship in Hastinapur. At this very moment, he will be getting ready for the evening entertainment; he will be wearing a beautiful silk dhoti and gold jewellery and he will sleep tonight on a carved wooden bed covered with a soft mattress. And you, poor raja, though you were anointed with sandalwood and crowned samrat, here you are tonight covered in mud and rags.'

The brothers shift uncomfortably and continue to stare into the flames.

'How is it that you are not consumed by vigorous and righteous passion? Look at your brothers, idling away their youth in futile dissipation and endless ritual.'

'Draupadi, you need to control your anger. We all do. At the moment, my dharma is forgiveness and in this I believe I am a better man than Duryodhan.'

'Indeed, Husband, and I think that you are foolishly deluded in believing this. The only focus of your thoughts and actions now should be to reclaim what is rightfully yours. To walk again in prosperity and in wealth as is your absolute right as a king and Kshatriya.'

When Yudhishthir does not reply, Draupadi exhales loudly and wraps the blanket around her head.

'It seems that you are unmoved by our suffering, your brothers' and mine. I fear you care more for the idea of dharma than our mortal condition. And what has dharma given you? You have done everything that the scriptures say you must do. You have performed the sacrifices and fed the Brahmins and still you have nothing but misery where Duryodhan luxuriates in prosperity. Where is the justice in this, Husband, where is your just retribution? God is like a puppeteer, playing with us like a child with his toys. I see no justice in God's plan and, truly, I pity you for being so weak for in this system, you might as well be powerful and grab what is yours.'

It is Bheem who answers finally, provoked by this vision of a swaggering Duryodhan.

'I think Draupadi is right. Where has the path of righteousness got us, Bhai? I say we have done our time in exile and should go back now to fight for what is ours. We are Kshatriyas, not Brahmins to be spending all our time in rituals.'

'Control yourself, Bheem. I have given my word as a Kshatriya that I will undertake thirteen years in exile and I will stand by that pledge. Draupadi, you are a learned woman and know the shastras but you are indulging in needless arguments and giving in to doubt. That is the path to madness and degradation.

'I believe I will get what is due to me if I stay true to my dharma. The path to the gods is hidden and mysterious but we must keep our faith in our dharma and our destiny.'

Draupadi wraps her arms around her knees and looks up at the sprinkling of stars through the haze of the smoke.

'Perhaps you are right, Husband, and we cannot know all the ways of the gods. But I do know that in the matters of kingship and politics, self-assertion is essential and you cannot leave everything to fate.'

Then she lays her head on her knees and silence returns to the group.

And so, the years go by.

Draupadi and Satyabhama walk up to the pond on the outskirts of the small village close to the Pandavas' hermitage. There are lotus flowers in the pond, floating incongruously alongside the glossy, black buffaloes who are wallowing in the cool water, their long-lashed eyes shut against the warming spring sunshine. Hunched white egrets sit on the unmindful buffaloes, occasionally catching the skidding pond skaters in their blunt, orange beaks.

Draupadi leans against the trunk of a kimsuka tree, the fragrant and cool breeze a lonely, sensual pleasure. The crimson, beak-shaped kimsuka flowers collide against the pristine blue of the March sky, and for a few precious weeks, the leaching heat is held at bay.

Satyabhama, Krishna's wife, sits by the pond and unties a cloth bag containing a snack of salted puffed rice which the two women share. With the Pandavas and Krishna away for a few days on a hunting trip, it is a rare moment of untainted tranquillity and Satyabhama carries on with a conversation they had started at the hermitage.

'But with five husbands, Draupadi, how do you manage every day? How do you keep them all happy and content, secure in your love and yet uncorrupted by jealousy? I find it hard just with the one husband!'

Draupadi laughs aloud, startling a scampering striped squirrel carrying away a stolen meal of rice grains.

'Yes, but my Sakha Krishna is different. He is all men in one. Serious and playful, mysterious and pragmatic all at once. And yet, Satyabhama, you are his favourite.'

And it is true, that though Krishna has many wives and concubines, it is only Satyabhama who accompanies him when he leaves Dwarka. This Yadav woman, daughter of the treasurer of Dwarka, is a tempestuous storm of a girl and Krishna keeps her close to him while his more pliant wives stay at home.

'It is not the same with the Pandavas. Their motivations and desires are easier to understand.'

Just then, a group of village women come up to the pond, clay pots against their hips and Draupadi falls silent while they fill their pots with water. They have red hibiscus flowers tucked into their tightly braided hair and their shell and wood bracelets clink against their pots. They cast slanting glances at the dark woman with the illicit, loose hair and swing their long braids over their shoulders in virtuous disapproval. Once their pots are full, they balance them carefully on their heads and walk back home on sashaying hips and straight backs.

'I have nothing to distract me from my duty towards my husbands now, Satyabhama. My sons have all been sent to my father in Panchala and Ma Kunti stayed back in Hastinapur, as she is too old to accompany us.'

Satyabhama thinks she hears the breath of a sob in Draupadi's voice but she can't be sure. Draupadi hardly ever speaks of her children, as if they are an indulgence she must always deny herself.

'So all day long I serve my husbands. I anticipate their wishes before their desire has even taken form in their hearts so that they are never dissatisfied or unhappy. For Yudhishthir I make sure our hospitality is unwavering so that the Brahmins and the scholars bless him with their presence. Bheem loves to feel needed so I make impossible requests of him and he never fails me. As for the twins, Ma Kunti was always careful with them so I pamper them as best I can and they are grateful and gentle, and bashful still, after all these years.'

'You have not mentioned one husband, Draupadi. Krishna's great friend, Arjun.'

And now Draupadi does sigh and there is a subtle change in the slope of her shoulders and she is irresolute and uncertain suddenly.

'Arjun, yes, he is different,' Draupadi whispers.

'Whatever I do, it seems he is always waiting to leave, listening to an inner voice that calls him away. And when he returns, I come to life again and everything in between is just a suspension of time.

'I watch him when he is with Krishna, their easy friendship and careless loyalty, and my love seems insubstantial compared to theirs.'

Draupadi looks away quickly from the intolerable pity in Satyabhama's eyes.

'I have tried anger and tears and threats but he only smiles or gives me gifts to make up for his indiscretions.'

'But no matter, my aim is always to keep them focused on their destiny as Kshatriyas and rajas. My virtue is faultless, Satyabhama, and my conduct is immaculate and I will not falter now in my path. I keep my hair untied so that each time they see me, they see their own shame and degradation. Each time I walk pass them, unadorned and in rags, they remember the battle that lies ahead.'

Satyabhama nods, she has heard Krishna say this before.

But what Draupadi does not tell Satyabhama is that she sequesters herself at night, every night, and through all these lonely years of exile. Her long, loose hair reminds the Pandavas of her polluted state, which is not yet purified while Dusshasan lives and, as a polluted woman, she will not lie with them any more. There will be no babies born in these fragrant and tumbling forests. Never again will Draupadi feel the life grow within her, feel her bones grow heavy and molten and the blood run slow and meandering through her veins. The Pandavas do not say anything, daunted by the accusation in her eyes, and the silence of her wrists when she doles out the rice, when there is no gold to lie against her dark skin.

'You will be avenged, Draupadi. You have heard the Kaurava women laugh, and you will see their tears one day.'

Satyabhama looks at Draupadi and understands that no explanation is needed for the Pandavas' devotion to their wife. Even in a simple cotton dhoti with no jewellery and with her hair cascading down her back, Draupadi is the most alluring woman she has ever seen. Her dark skin flickers with light like the pebbles on a shallow riverbed lit by sunlight and her eyes are bruising promises.

Draupadi looks up at a flock of cranes flying by, taking away their ancestors' spirits to the other world once again.

And so, twelve years go by.

The Court of the Fish Clan

~

The Pandavas wait till dusk in the forest before they can complete their final, macabre task. They are weighed down by all their weapons, their bows, arrows, daggers, and swords and, besides, Bheem is carrying over his shoulder the stolen corpse of an old woman.

As the shadows lengthen into the night, the Pandavas hurry to a large, spreading shami tree that grows at the edge of a cemetery. They hide all their weapons in the hollow bark of the tree and Bheem ties the corpse of the woman to the branches, leaving the arms to hang down like a ghastly puppet.

Breathless with revulsion, they rush back to Draupadi who is waiting by the smoking campfire in the forest. Yudhishthir wipes the moisture off his forehead and settles down next to her.

'We will tell the villagers that we have left the body of our old mother on the shami tree, according to our tribal customs. That will deter anyone from getting too close to the tree and discovering our weapons. That, and the foul smell of that decaying body. What a bleak and lugubrious place it is.'

The Pandavas settle down around the fire, silent and uneasy. They have spent twelve years in exile in the forest and they are as flinty and craggy as the lifelong sadhus whose paths they have crossed. Their beards lend a fierce uniformity to their faces and Yudhishthir's long hair is now streaked with grey. They are sun-

232

darkened and spare, with new strength and old scars. They now have to spend only one more year in exile but it will be the hardest, for they must remain hidden and disguised, with no trace of the samrat of Indraprastha and his brothers and wife. For this they have chosen a relatively small and obscure town to the southwest of Hastinapur, the fiefdom of a local chieftain and cattle-herder, Viratnagar.

'Bhai Yudhishthir, I don't like to think of you serving another raja, you are the samrat of Indraprastha and our raja and guru. It is humiliating and degrading for you.'

Draupadi is not surprised that Arjun worries about Yudhishthir's comfort before hers. Now, after all these years, she knows that for Arjun, his older brother's honour is their collective honour and he walks lightly the shifting line between his duty and his passion.

'I will not go as a courtier to Virat's city, Arjun. I will go as a Brahmin, as an expert in casting dice. I know enough of the Vedas to convince Virat and my honour will be safe. What worries me is how Bheem will hide his strength and his anger. He is as strong as a bull, and always raring for a fight and the people of Viratnagar will never have seen anyone like him.'

Bheem is leaning against a tree, arms behind his head, getting ready to sleep. He smiles at Yudhishthir and looks down at his lethal muscles in surprise.

'No one will notice my strength, Bhai Yudhishthir, for I will be hiding in the kitchens.' Bheem laughs appreciatively, untroubled by their bleak surroundings and well pleased with his stratagem.

'I have haunted the kitchens of Hastinapur often enough as a boy growing up and I know all the sauces and spices the cooks use. I know how to braise fish, and baste meat, and slice vegetables and Virat will need to know nothing more.'

'Bheem, that is an excellent idea, you will be safe in the kitchens and well hidden from all. Nakul and Sahadev, naturally you will go as horsemen and cattle experts. Keep your beards untrimmed and your hair matted and no one will notice your good looks and noble bearing.'

The twins nod, satisfied that they will be in the stables together, and with their beloved animals.

'Now, Arjun, what about you? Your skill is archery but if you go disguised as an archery instructor to teach Virat's sons you will be betrayed as a Kshatriya at once by your technique and expertise.'

'I have been thinking about that, Bhai Yudhishthir. And I have thought of a disguise so removed from what I am that no one will imagine I am a Kshatriya, and a raja's brother. I will go as a eunuch, to instruct Virat's daughters in the art of singing and dancing.'

There is a shocked silence at this suggestion, but Arjun is undeterred.

'It is the only way I will remain hidden, in a disguise so outlandish that no one would think to question me. Raja Chitrangada taught me many folk songs when I travelled in his kingdom and I think I will manage well enough. I will have to wear bangles and armbands to disguise my archer's scars and my hair is so long anyway, Draupadi will show me how to braid it.'

Arjun smiles at Draupadi but she looks away from him, frowning. This disguise means that Arjun will be accepted into the inner sanctum of the unmarried girls' quarters and Draupadi is furious at the thought. But before she can resolve to think of an objection, Yudhishthir is talking about her.

'Raja Drupad entrusted you to my care, Draupadi. I made a vow to him with the sacred fires as my witness to look after you like a rani. I hate to think of you serving another woman.'

Draupadi shrugs, still angry at Arjun.

'I will not go as a slave girl or a maid. I will go as a sairandhri, an expert in beauty and cosmetics. Do not worry yourself about me, Raja, I will make myself indispensable to this rani, whoever she is.'

Over the next few days, the three oldest Pandavas infiltrate the city of Viratnagar and the court of the raja and, at last, it is Draupadi's turn and she is standing at the entrance of the capital city of the fish clan, flanked by Nakul and Sahadev.

After their years in the forest, in solitude, or in the eccentric company of holy men, Viratnagar is riotous and overwhelming. Along the main avenue, the wood and clay daub buildings hustle claustrophobically together and the streets are dizzying with crowds. The trio walk slowly down the street, stepping clear of the gutter that froths with scummy water, bewildered by the sudden shouts and near collisions. There are sun-darkened peasants, with narrow hips and short dhotis tucked in between their scrawny legs, hurrying along the street. Groups of young men, urbane in dyed robes and sleek moustaches, stand under the banyan trees and argue noisily, spitting emphatic streams of paan against the tree trunks. Occasionally, a palanquin clears a way through the crowd, its bearers shouting out a warning at the passers-by. There are also itinerant entertainers with trained monkeys dressed in a bride's red skirts or snake charmers with coir baskets hiding their slithering cobras. People lean out of their windows or balconies, behind latticed screens, to watch the crowds go by or to shout out to the passing trinket sellers and hawkers. Leading away from the main avenue are smaller, meaner gullies with wretched children and rooting pigs and this is where the dispossessed live, the sweepers and the scavengers and the great, heaving unseen.

At the very end of the avenue is the residence of the raja. It is just a large mansion, not a palace at all, as the Matsya clan consists only of a humble collection of straggling villages surrounding the small town and the twins know it will not be very long before a stranger is noticed. They leave Draupadi standing alone in front of the mansion while they watch from the shadows of a nearby lane and, soon enough, a messenger presents himself before Draupadi and summons her into the rani's presence.

Sudeshna, the chief wife of the Raja of Viratnagar, is an insipid, capricious woman with worried eyes and fine hands. She inspects Draupadi unashamedly, puzzled by the trace of hauteur despite the worn and simple clothes. Draupadi has twisted her hair into a headcloth so that she no longer flaunts her untied hair but nothing can hide her lustrous, night-sky skin and her quiet poise.

'Who are you? Why have you come here to Viratnagar? You are not a regular servant woman, I can see. Your clothes are frayed and old but they are of a fine quality and you do not have the cowed look of the girls who serve.'

'I am Malini, a sairandhri, expert in the art of cosmetics, toiletry and garland-making. I have served the Ranis Draupadi and Subhadra, who looked after me well so I am not as wretched as the serving girls can be. I offer you my services if you would like to use them. I know the secret of many Ayurvedic cosmetics and am also an expert in elaborate hairstyles.'

Sudeshna stands in front of Draupadi, irresolute. She looks down at the wooden box at Draupadi's feet and imagines all the unguents and powders in it and bites her lips in frustration.

'I would very much like to keep you here, Malini. The beauty of the ranis you mention is known even to us and I should be grateful for your help. But I have a problem, the raja is a lusty man with a fondness for beautiful girls and I would not be comfortable having you around him.'

Sudeshna frowns at Draupadi, conflicted, but Draupadi snaps her head up at this and holds up the palm of one hand.

'Five husbands, Rani, I have five powerful Gandharva husbands who have sworn to protect my honour with their lives. I fear no man and I promise you I will be safe from your husband's unwanted attentions.'

Sudeshna still has her doubts and she is shocked at Draupadi's outspokenness but the seduction of the wooden box is irresistible. And so Draupadi is given a small room at the end of the flower garden and she spends her days pounding herbs and crushing leaves for the rani's cosmetics. She makes face packs with crushed lentils and honey and the rejuvenation powder which Maatrika Devi had taught her. She puts fragrant sticks of cinnamon in the rani's clothing to keep out the moths and to perfume her clothes. She massages ghee and coconut oil into the rani's lifeless hair and makes it gleam.

The months pass and Draupadi struggles to maintain a suitably subservient deference in the face of the rani's wandering moods. Sudeshna is brittle and volatile because of the raja's straying attention and some days she locks herself up in her room and pushes Draupadi away if she tries to calm her down. Then Draupadi goes looking for one of her husbands, Nakul and Sahadev in the stables or Bheem in the kitchen, and whispers her bitterness and frustration to them. They are always gentle and sympathetic with her but it galls her to find them content with their tasks, remote in the tranquil anonymity of their lives.

'Remember why we are here,' she hisses in a hoarse whisper. You are biding your time till you can reclaim your kingdom. This is not what you are, you are Kshatriyas and brothers of a raja and this work defiles and degrades you.'

And they look at her with the accusing eyes of children.

Sudeshna summons her one day, on a stormy evening bloated and heavy with the promise of rain.

'Take this jar of wine to my brother, Malini. He has expressly asked for you. It is an honour that he has noticed you at all.'

Sudeshna does not look at Draupadi as she says this, she is feeding her caged partridge which she then places in the moonlight.

Draupadi is uneasy. The rani's brother is a lecherous, vain man with large, staring eyes and a rough manner.

'Rani, I don't think it would be proper of me to go at this time of the night. Please send someone else.'

'Are you refusing my brother's express request, Malini? I assure you it is perfectly safe for you to go, I give you my word.'

Draupadi takes the jar of wine and leaves the room silently, with a sickening premonition of inevitability. When she reaches Kichaka's room it is as she had feared. He is waiting for her alone in his room in the flickering light of the clay lamps and he grabs her waist as soon as she enters. Draupadi's reaction is violent and instantaneous. She pushes Kichaka with all her strength and he stumbles, confused and already drunk. The jar breaks and the wine spills onto the smooth earth floor and while Kichaka struggles to stand up, roaring, Draupadi is out of the door and running through the night.

Draupadi runs to the only person she knows who will respond to her outrage. Bheem is sleeping on the floor of the kitchen and Draupadi lies down next to him, crying softly. Bheem wakes up in the dark, startled to find his wife in his arms and disoriented by the smell of lotus flowers and wine.

'Draupadi! What is the matter, why are you here? And why are you crying?'

Bheem gently holds his wife's face in his hands, feeling the moisture of her tears.

'Can you really wonder that I am unhappy, Husband? Because of that great gambler I am reduced to this, to a serving girl tending to another woman's needs. All day long I must scurry around for her, carrying water for her bath and enduring the cruel remarks of the other servant girls.'

Bheem runs his hands through his dishevelled hair and clenches his fists helplessly.

'All this while my five brave husbands live like mice, hiding behind their disguises, going against all Kshatriya morality.'

'I am sorry, Draupadi. I hate not being able to protect you from this disgraceful year of servitude after all you have endured with us in the forest.'

'Of all my husbands, you are the bravest and the strongest, Bheem. I have seen you wrestle with wild animals in the jungle, and subdue them with your bare hands while I thought I would faint from fear.'

'What would you have me do, Draupadi? Just say the word, and I will do it.'

'Look at my hands now, Husband. Chapped and dry from pounding herbs and powders all day long for that woman and once I was the rani of Indraprastha.'

Draupadi runs the tips of her fingers over Bheem's face so that he can feel how rough they are now and Bheem holds her hands in his and crumples and cries tears of shame and anger.

'There is one thing you can do for me, Husband,' Draupadi whispers. 'That vile and corrupt man, Kichaka, tried to force himself on me this evening. He is always following me around and makes lecherous and offensive remarks when the rani can't hear him. I am scared of him, Bheem, next time I might not be able to save myself from his attacks.'

Bheem gets up without a word and crashes out of the kitchen and the next morning, a sobbing and hysterical servant girl discovers Kichaka's bloodied and broken body in his room.

There are screams and raging accusations by Sudeshna but Draupadi is only a woman and she holds her palms out and shrugs, barely hiding her smiling contempt.

⟡

The mood in the clan of the Matsyas is volatile and then there are rumours of cattle raiders preparing to attack the raja's herds of cows while he is away from his capital. The young rajkumar, Uttar, is unprepared and uncertain and cannot gather his scattering courage to counter the raiders. But the thirteenth year of exile is over at last and Uttar finds help walking up to him from the unlikeliest quarter, a eunuch from the inner sanctum of the unmarried women's quarters.

Arjun walks up to Uttar, tearing off his bangles and his armbands and ripping away his head veil, shrugging off this paraphernalia easily and painlessly like a snake sheds its skin. He puts his arm around the irresolute and shocked young rajkumar and smiles at him as he loosens his long hair from its braids.

'Do not be afraid, Rajkumar, I will help you chase away these cowardly cattle thieves. Prepare your chariot and wait for me, I will bring back my weapons and be your sarathi for the battle.'

And so when Raja Virat returns to his city, he finds the samrat of Indraprastha living in his court and he is appalled to realize he owes a troubled gratitude to a eunuch who has transformed into a warrior.

As he looks at Arjun, boisterous and familiar among the war chariots and the rearing horses, Virat is horrified at himself, to have thought that this agile, blistering archer was ever anything but a lethal Kshatriya. For a year he has been given unfettered access to the unmarried girls of the house and now Virat's usual indolent and lascivious dissipation is burnt away by his shame.

'Arjun, you must marry my daughter, Uttara. No other chieftain will marry her once it is known a Kshatriya visited her in her quarters. She will be cast out and her honour will be mud and she is just a blameless child of fifteen.'

Virat is hoarse with urgency, ruined by the thought of handing his beloved daughter over to the man who betrayed his trust. But he has no option and he must act quickly before news of this tragic farce spreads throughout Matsya.

'I cannot marry her, Raja, she is like a child to me. But my son Abhimanyu is a brave warrior of sixteen and Uttara may marry him.'

So the wedding is quickly arranged, and Abhimanyu,

Ira Mukhoty

accompanied by his mother, Subhadra, is brought from Dwarka and marries the gentle and tentative Uttara. The wedding is attended by Raja Drupad and Rajkumar Drishtadumna but Draupadi is solitary and forlorn despite the presence of her father and brother. Arjun has chosen Subhadra's son for this marriage with a rajkumari while her own firstborn son by Yudhishthir is much older and yet unmarried. She is humiliated and choking with bitterness to think that while the Pandavas used the old laws to bring about the charade of her marriage to the five of them, they have discarded those laws when it suited them. So the youngest brother has married first while her sons wait patiently for their uncertain destiny. The heartbreak and betrayal for Draupadi is multiple and subtle and it is Krishna's nephew who is chosen and she knows with an aching certainty that Krishna must have had a hand in this decision too. That for all the times he has professed to love her as a sakhi, he has chosen his lineage and bloodline when it mattered the most.

Watching Abhimanyu circle the sacred fire with Uttara, Draupadi wonders for the first time whether Arjun chose to infiltrate the women's quarters as a eunuch for this express purpose, to compromise Uttara, and to secure an alliance for himself and his son. But this is the corrosive path to madness and Draupadi wills herself to instead concentrate on the sacred flames and remember her long-ago oath for blood and revenge.

The War Council

~

Soon after the marriage of Abhimanyu, a gathering of rajas is convened at Virat's court. Raja Drupad, watchful and ferocious with old age and sensing a final reckoning with his old enemy, Drona, is present as the doyen of the group. Krishna is there, too, accompanied by his remote brother, Balaram. The Pandavas send for their sons in Dwarka and Krishna's son Pradyumna returns with them. Virat is now an ally too, through the coercive marriage of Uttara and it is a war council, even though the Pandavas are reluctant to call it so.

'The Kauravas are my brothers. Perhaps they will return Indraprastha to me, now that I have fulfilled all the conditions of my exile.'

Yudhishthir is wistful and evasive, even to himself. He will not contemplate the dharmic horror of war with his cousins, not when he has performed all the penance that was asked of him. He is a handsome, brooding man now where once he was an awkward and uncertain youth. What he doesn't know is that in these thirteen years, Indraprastha has been reclaimed by the god of unseen time and the coloured tiles in the sabha are splintered and broken and a giant peepul tree grows out of the crumbling ruin that was once the raja's quarter.

Krishna crosses his arms and looks at Yudhishthir, and his thoughts are bloodier.

'Let us send a messenger first to Hastinapur, to ascertain what the Kauravas intend to do and whether they are willing to return his kingdom to Yudhishthir.'

Balaram, standing apart from the group, is unconsciously distancing himself from the gathering momentum of the discussion.

'Yudhishthir lost his kingdom through sheer folly,' he snaps, impatient with the Pandavas' equivocation. 'He has no option now but to be conciliatory with the Kauravas, and accept whatever they decree.'

Raja Drupad has seen the wasteland of his dreams and he understands the consequences of his black yagnas that invoked vengeance.

'Let us send messages to all our allies to prepare for war and, meanwhile, we will send a Brahmin to Raja Dritrashtra in Hastinapur to find out what their intentions are.'

While the messengers are sent out, the war council, as well as Draupadi and Subhadra, move to Upaplavya, a small town outside of Viratnagar where all the allies are to gather.

A few days after the Brahmin is sent to Hastinapur, Dritrashtra's charioteer, Sanjay, arrives in Upaplavya, and his message is provocative.

'Raja Dritrashtra sends me to say he is very sorry for all the hardships you have been through, but these thirteen years were the result of your own madness during gambling. Now what happens ahead depends on you, but you should choose the peaceful way for what would be the point of a war in which so many would die.'

Krishna answers for Yudhishthir, and he is reasonable and pacifying.

'The Pandavas ask only for justice. Give them back what is theirs.'

Sanjay returns to Hastinapur and consternation and doubt settle into Upaplavya.

'Perhaps we should settle for peace, at any cost,' Yudhishthir repeats endlessly.

'We should avoid war; how can we fight our own brothers?' Bheem and Arjun agree.

'Peace is cetainly preferable to war; let us try to convince the Kauravas,' Krishna adds.

Only Draupadi is clear in her certainty and her anger.

'How can you talk about conciliation with an evil person? To negotiate with evil is adharma and it is your right as Kshatriyas to fight for what is yours when you have been wronged.'

But the Pandavas and Krishna look at her as if she is a vision from a bleak nightmare and they return to their discussions without answering her. They will settle for peace, and a humble, quiet life, and Draupadi's anger will be sacrificed in a breath. Draupadi rails alone, or at a terrified Subhadra, and despairs that she cannot fight in their place. She would throw away her breastband and strap a quiver across her chest and take Arjun's great wooden bow if she could. She would watch the Kurus' warm blood run into the cool and hungry earth and she would know that justice had been done.

At last it is decided that Krishna will be sent to Hastinapur with an offer of peace. The Pandavas have asked for five towns, one for each brother, and Indraprastha is forgotten.

Draupadi goes to meet Krishna before he leaves and she holds out her untied hair which coils over her shoulder.

'Remember my vow, Sakha, when you speak to those despicable men who humiliated me. Do not forget what they did to me and what I have sworn to do. That I will only tie my hair again when I have consecrated it with the blood of Dusshasan.'

Krishna nods, and he knows in his heart it will come to this.

'I go to seek peace, because it is right to avoid bloodshed if possible, but I know there will be war in the end.'

'You are bound to protect me, Sakha, for you call me your

friend. But if you will not help me and if my husbands will not fight, then I will ask my old father, my brothers, and my sons to fight for me and avenge my great humiliation.'

And at that moment Draupadi is careless and indiscreet with the heft of the men in her life and she is foolishly reassured by this abundance.

'Dritrashtra's sons will be dead on the ground before this is over, Draupadi; you will have your vengeance.'

And so on a monsoon morning, dark as the night, as if it were the end of all days on earth, Krishna leaves alone for Hastinapur. The Pandavas and their allies watch him leave as they guard their hopes and dream of war.

The Two Queens

~

The city of elephants is now dark under the burdened monsoon sky and Kunti walks out of her stark quarters into a cool wind whispering of rain. No one pays any attention to Kunti as she walks by, hunched in her widow's whites and prayer beads. Kunti is unaffected by the disregard, for she has lived like a fleeting spectre these past thirteen years with Vidura and Sulabha in their modest home at the very edge of Hastinapur palace. She has wrapped her life tightly around herself like a warm blanket in winter till it has condensed into a dense and dark thing. Kunti knows she is a constant, aching reminder to Dritrashtra and the other gurus of the scandalous banishment of her absent sons and that is all the acknowledgement she desires. She knows this, and for the sake of her sons she has borne these years of petty humiliations and endless servitude that is her lot as a widow living on the mercy of others.

Now she stops for a while next to the cattle sheds, where the warm bovine smell rises up like a blessing, and she looks at the sky and the skidding clouds. It has been thirteen years now since she last saw her sons, when they left Hastinapur in shame and sorrow, dressed in rags and smeared in ash. Thirteen years that have settled in the lines of her face and the shapeless, soft spread of her belly. Kunti crosses the courtyards into the women's quarters of the palace and stops at last at the threshold of Gandhari's room, for her weekly game of pacheesi with the rani.

'Come in, Sister, come in. I have been expecting you for the past half-hour.'

Gandhari is sitting on a low bamboo stool next to a small table on which the game of pacheesi is already unfolded and ready. She turns her blindfolded face towards Kunti and smiles.

'You are wondering how I know it is you? Forgive my bluntness, Sister, but you are bigger than most of the other women in the palace, and your footsteps are heavier and unmistakable.'

Kunti sighs and looks down at her wide, splayed feet, bare on the cool, beaten earth floor, and the generous spread of her hips and thighs. In defiance of her increasing irrelevance, her body has grown larger and heavier with the years. She has pains in her knees now, her hips are stiff and her back bent, and she imagines the grinding of her bones and sinews under all the weight.

She walks into the room and bows down before Gandhari before sitting at the small table across from her.

'Let us begin, Sister. Raja Dritrashtra is sleeping after his midday meal and we have at least an hour undisturbed before he wakes up.'

So the two women play pacheesi as the sky grows heavier and presses down on the palace, and the cowrie shells clink as they throw them onto the cruciform cloth. The small wooden windows are open, to let in the watery light and the slippery wind and Kunti marvels at how Gandhari lightly touches the thrown cowrie shells to count her points.

'So the thirteen years are over, Kunti, and your sons have completed the terms of their banishment.' Gandhari's voice is soft and her head is bent towards the board.

Kunti breathes out suddenly and nods, forgetting that Gandhari cannot see her.

'Yes,' she says. As if she didn't know, as if she hasn't been counting each year, each month, and every last minute and collecting them like pebbles in the empty expanse of her lap.

'Your sons sent a Brahmin to Hastinapur a few days ago, to ask for the return of Indraprastha to them, and half of the kingdom. I was in court at the time, next to Raja Dritrashtra.'

Gandhari speaks evenly, as if discussing a remedy for toothache.

'The Gurus Drona and Bheeshma wanted to return their kingdom to your sons but Duryodhan would not listen to their proposal at all and he sent back the Brahmin very curtly.'

Kunti nods again, somehow she has always known that Indraprastha was an illusion, born of Khandava's fire and returned now to dust.

Just then there is a darkening of the already faint light and Bhanumati is at the door, holding a tray with two clay pots of flavoured buttermilk. Duryodhan's chief queen is still slim and statuesque after all these years, with quiet grace in the movements of her bronze limbs.

She places the pots next to the seated women and bends low to touch Gandhari's feet and then Kunti's. Kunti stands to embrace the younger woman. She has always been very fond of Bhanumati and her equable poise. But what can she bless her with and what will be the implications of her blessing with the future unfurling like a bloodied river at their feet?

'May your sons live long and virtuous lives, Beti.'

Bhanumati bows to acknowledge the blessing.

'You were speaking of my husband when I walked in, Rajmata.'

'Yes, we were, Beti. I was telling Ma Kunti that he will not listen to reason where the Pandavas are concerned and has refused to return Indraprastha to them.'

Bhanumati wraps her uttaraya tightly around her shoulders, chilled suddenly by a hissing gust of air and a premonition that sits like ice in her belly.

'Raja Duryodhan is my husband and my king,' she whispers. 'It is my duty to follow him in all things and he is the god of my days. It is not for me to question his decisions, Ma.'

The older women watch her as she bows and walks out of the door on light and silent feet.

'Bhanu is a loyal wife to my son, and that is how it should be, Sister. But I know that Duryodhan is wrong to be so intractable and confrontational with his brothers.'

Gandhari rubs the bandages across her eyes lightly, as if overcome by a vision too painful to tolerate.

'After the Brahmin had gone back, your nephew, Krishna, the Yadav, came next to the court, two days ago, with a new proposal.'

'Yes, he is staying with me in Vidura's home. I cooked some long-grained rice flavoured with ghee for his evening meal. Luckily, we had some meat left over from the last hunt and I cooked it with tamarind. And curd, of course, it is his favourite dish.'

Kunti talks of the prosaic details of rice and meat so that she doesn't blurt out the intolerable truth about her fear and hope when she saw Krishna after these long years. Her tears, held in for so many years, soaked Krishna's uttaraya as he held her while she cried against his breast. His face, tired and compassionate, which she held in her hands while she searched in his eyes for some shadow of her sons.

Gandhari sighs as she leans her forehead against the heel of her palm.

'Krishna said that the Pandavas ask only for five villages, now. Just five villages, and they will give up Indraprastha and Hastinapur forever. And Duryodhan laughed at him and vowed that he would not give them even five pinpoints of land.'

Now, Gandhari rocks her head from side to side against her palm and her voice is a hoarse rasp.

'Why is he like this, Kunti? Why will he not listen to the advice of his gurus and his elders? Why is he not willing to be generous and large-hearted, when he is in a position of strength? He is pushing the Pandavas to war, for he leaves them no option but to fight for what is rightfully theirs. And blood will be shed, Kunti, our sons' blood, and our brothers' and our fathers' too.'

Kunti stares at Gandhari's face and sees the tears stain the white muslin of her bandage. She glances at the delicate pallor of Gandhari's skin, her fragile wrists, and her fine hands.

'What tortures me, Kunti, is that perhaps it is my fault. I was too consumed by the righteousness of my sacrifice to be an exacting and careful mother. I was so unsure of my own worth I couldn't show him where he strayed from the true path. I forgave him all his cruelties and his violence, and now he is savage with power and greed and it is all because of me.'

Kunti reaches out to hold Gandhari's soft hand in her own rugged ones.

'Don't say that, Rani. You are his mother; what could you do but love him, especially after all the prayers it took before Rudra blessed you with a son. Raja Dritrashtra, perhaps, should have been firmer with his sons.'

'Raja Dritrashtra is a weak and vacillating man, Sister, let us be honest now in these dark days. He is foolish and vain and it pleases him to have his son Raja of Hastinapur at the expense of the Pandavas. We will be led to ruin and to slaughter.'

Both women are quiet for a while, swept up in the whirling current of their thoughts. Despite Kunti's reassurance, Gandhari continues to blame herself for her son's arrogance and vows now to do all she can to set things right. When the time comes for war, which it will now imminently, Duryodhan will stand before her, resplendent and blazing in his steel armour and marigold garland and he will bow down, his unbound hair flaring down his back, and he will ask for her blessings before he steps onto his war chariot. Her blessings, which have been formed at the altar of her sacrifice, will make him immortal and unconquerable. And Gandhari will place her soft palms on her son's head and say, may the righteous side win. And there will be doubt, fatal and insidious, for the first time in Duryodhan's eyes as he kneels down to touch his forehead to his mother's feet.

Finally, it is Kunti who speaks first, almost despite herself, as if what she is about to say will seal this conversation and will lead them to a new world, with new rules and uncertain destinies.

'I have sent back a message to my sons, Rani Gandhari. I told Krishna to instruct them that they must fight for what is theirs, to gather their strength and declare war if that is the only path left for them.'

What Kunti has told Krishna is much more stark and terrible, but Gandhari does not need to know this. Kunti has meditated on these words for the past thirteen years and they are the song to which the seasons change and the holy fires burn. Each word has been wrought until it is flaming and branded on her heart and there is nothing more to say.

'Krishna, tell my sons this:

"They are Kshatriyas and were cleaved from Brahma's chest to live and die by the sword and in this lies their dharma and their salvation. Yudhishthir goes straight to hell, if he perseveres in the path of the ascetics and the Brahmins, instead of claiming his destiny and his inheritance as a warrior. I will condemn and disown him if he forgets his righteous indignation and crawls like a worm in front of evil. May they blaze up, even if only for an instant, in a fearsome and all-consuming raging fire rather than smoulder for an eternity in a choking smoke. May they claim their glory on the battlefields, as Kshatriyas, so that the world remembers their valour and honour till the end of time. There is no other reason for them to go on living as they are, shirking their duty and begging for scraps. Better for them to be dead, than to live this life of destitution."

'May they rise up, Krishna, in rage, passion and strength. May they fight as men and die as immortals.'

Kunti does not say all this to Gandhari but there is one thing she feels she must say. The rain has started falling on the courtyard, splashing fat drops that gather momentum like keening grief.

'Rani Gandhari, nothing that befell my sons hurts me as much as the humiliation that my noble and blameless daughter-in-law, Draupadi, endured in the gambling hall.'

At these words, Gandhari flinches as though she has been struck.

'The shame of Draupadi's treatment burns in me today, as it did all those years ago, Kunti. I fear for my sons, in this life and the next, for the disgrace of their behaviour demands a bloody price.'

She gets up slowly, as if she has suddenly grown very old. With one hand, she carefully sweeps the cowrie shells onto the floor, like discarded breadcrumbs.

'So it will be war then, Sister. And we will meet now only on the other side of the battlefield, where we will count our glorious dead.'

The two women embrace each other, their bodies taut with unspoken fear, and Kunti walks out of Gandhari's room into the driving rain. By the time she reaches her own quarters, she is soaked to the skin but she accepts the rain like an absolution, for she has one more deed to do before the cleansing war. Earlier in the day, before Krishna left for Upaplavya, he took Kunti aside and spoke softly so that only she could hear what he was saying, for what he was saying was treacherous and profane.

'You must go to Karna, Ma Kunti, and tell him of his true birth. Tell him that you are his mother, just as you are the mother of the Pandavas.'

Kunti looked at Krishna, appalled, her skin prickling with shame.

'Karna is a fearsome and magnificent warrior, Ma, and I fear for the lives of the Pandavas if he remains by Duryodhan's side.'

'But he has hated us all these years, Krishna, he will not accept the Pandavas as his brothers,' Kunti stammered with dismay.

'No, he will never accept the Pandavas, or indeed betray Duryodhan for he is a man of honour above all else. But it will weaken him, this forbidden knowledge, at least enough for Arjun to have a chance at defeating him.'

So Kunti stands now in the scouring rain and knows it will be a long night ahead of scorching doubt.

At midday, she goes out to the Ganga where she finds Karna, praying to the sun god at the river's edge. Kunti stands under a tree, watching Karna as he cups the holy river's water and pours it over himself and stands with bowed head in the lustrous monsoon light. He looks lonely and vulnerable and Kunti clenches her palms against her thighs for it is a primaeval treason that she must now do.

Karna turns around from the river and notices Kunti and he walks up to her with a warm smile, his long hair dripping down his back. He is wearing only a short white dhoti and his powerful thighs and shoulders flex as he bows before her but his smile is unexpectedly tender and his voice is as warm as the river.

'Ma Kunti, why did you trouble yourself to come all the way here? You should have sent for me if you needed something and I would have come to you.'

Kunti looks up at her formidable warrior son and her heart quails at the words she is about to say, which will undo him. But she gathers her resolve and knows that there are many types of sacrifices that she has made along the true path and the sacrifice of Karna is perhaps the most heartbreaking one of all.

'You are my son, Karna, my firstborn son, born to me before I married Raja Pandu and you are the elder brother to the Pandavas. You are a Kshatriya, Beta, a warrior by birth.'

Karna is silent for a while, his eyes are haunted amber pools and when he speaks, his low voice is like the distant rumble of thunder.

'My mother? Where were you for all these years, Ma Kunti, when I howled for a place in this shifting world. A Kshatriya? How can I call myself one, when I have never received any of the rites and the consecration of a true Kshatriya? Even a hated enemy could not have undone me the way you did by abandoning me. Now my son has married into the Suta clan too, and this is my clan till I die. People would laugh at me and call me a coward if I ran to Arjun now at this unseemly hour. Duryodhan gave me a refuge, a name and my honour, and whatever I achieve in life and in battle, I will lay down at his feet.'

Kunti has helpless tears in her eyes, of shame and pity, and she covers her betraying face with her hand.

Karna's tone softens, and he promises her only one thing, before he turns away and heads towards the war council.

'I promise to kill only Arjun. Only he is my equal in war and I will spare the others, as they are not fit to fight me. Whatever happens, Ma Kunti, and whichever one of us survives, you will still have five sons at the end of the war.'

VIII

Legion

Kurukshetra

~

Summoned by the breathless messengers, allies converge at Upaplavya and soon the small town is clamorous with soldiers from all over the kingdom. The Matsyas, the Chedis, the Bhojas, and many more still—there are volatile warriors and stamping horses in the narrow gullies and the barren fields. The Pandavas soon decide to set up battle stations on the edge of Kurukshetra, the great battlefield outside Hastinapur. Within days, rumours of immortality begin to spread for those who die on this dusty plain.

On a monsoon day, the army of the Pandavas moves out of Upaplavya, in effervescence and cacophony like a wedding party. At the battle camp, they dig a defensive moat and post soldiers all around the periphery. Tents are strung together and storehouses are built for arms and weapons. Makeshift kitchens are set up to feed the endless hordes, and physicians and veterinarians wait patiently and they are the only ones who know to dread the coming days.

On the far side of the field, the Kauravas set up their own camp and for a while there is a joyous carelessness to the preparations and thoughts of death and defeat are put aside, like stones dropped into a well, their fall muffled and absorbed by the murky water. The land itself is prolific with life. The rain-sodden earth is dotted with tiny saplings, tightly furled leaves green as hope.

At last it is the day of battle and the Pandavas and Krishna climb onto their war chariots. They are grave and dense with armour and have scimitars tied to belts around their waist and whimsical and fragrant marigold garlands around their necks. They have been blessed by the holy fire and they are marked by Vishnu's red tilak on the forehead. The war chariots are reinforced with shields and each chariot bears a banner with a warrior's emblem. In the scrum of battle, the disorientation of war, these banners will help the soldiers decide whether they must die or flee, converge or fall back. Yudhishthir's banner is a golden moon circled with the planets and Bheem has a silver lion with crystal eyes. All five brothers are aligned now next to each other, banners fluttering and war horses dancing. The foot soldiers stream out behind them endlessly, holding bows and arrows, clubs of wood and iron, and flashing swords.

Silence falls at last and time crunches up in that moment into a single, eternal instant and into that silence, Krishna lifts up his conch shell and blows its breathy, oceanic roar into the still and waiting air. Then Yudhishthir lifts his conch shell and then Bheem and all the Pandavas and soon the silence is shredded and vibrating with the chilling and resonating call to arms of the holy shankha. On the far side of the field, Duryodhan is sitting on the splendid grey war elephant of Hastinapur and he blows a corresponding challenge into his conch shell and then the drums of war begin to beat, a slow, rhythmic cadence that liberates the soldiers from their fears of mortality and they run screaming through the soft grass of Kurukshetra.

All day long and into the next few days, the battle rages. Each new day, the soldiers gather their chaotic courage anew and rekindle the fire of their rage so that they become slivers of pure passion and die perfect deaths on this battlefield far from the paddy fields and palm trees of their birth. The fighting is so intense and unending, the faces so disfigured by blood, that confused and crazed soldiers kill their brothers and their allies and the banners lie trampled in the glossy mud.

After a few days of battle, Draupadi, Subhadra, and Uttara, unable to bear the irrelevant waiting in Upaplavya, shift their quarters to the war camp. Draupadi is shocked to see the change in the Pandavas who are now brutal and savage with bloodlust.

'I did not want to fight, Draupadi,' Arjun tells her the first evening he sees her in the camp after that week of battle.

'I saw my brothers, my gurus, and my ancestors lined up in front of me and my heart quailed and I put down my bow, overcome by revulsion at the thought of fighting my own kin. What desires could I possibly cherish of owning the earth for which I must commit these heinous, fratricidal acts?'

Draupadi knows how terrible it must have been for Arjun to contemplate killing his own gurus, whom he reveres as much as he does the fire-born Agni.

'But Krishna spoke to me then. He is my charioteer for the battle, as you know, and he spoke to me and his words filled me with peace and quietude.'

'What did he say, Husband? You must have told him you feared the consequences of the blood on your hands of your own brothers and gurus.'

Arjun shakes his head as if trying to dislodge an errant thought from his brain. He washes his hands and face in the clay basin of clean water that Draupadi has brought for him and the water runs red with blood.

'He said I had nothing to fear. That no evil consequences from killing my own gurus could befall me if I trusted in him completely. That I should carry out my Kshatriya duty dispassionately, with no attachment to the rewards of my actions.'

Draupadi helps Arjun remove his armour which has buckled against his body where the blows have struck hard and Draupadi flinches when she sees the livid bruises on his chest and sides.

'And then, when I asked him to show me who he really was,

since I have felt for some time that he is not quite an ordinary mortal like you or I, he smiled and for a fraction of time that smile seemed to fill the whole sky. I don't know how to explain it but it was as if the whole battlefield fell away, the soldiers disappeared, the sound of the shankhas and drums became very muffled and distant. And for that instant, there was only Krishna, as if Krishna became all of the universe, the past and the future, and all things, kings and beggars, dissolved into him.'

Arjun sighs and sits down to a simple meal of rice and meat in broth, brought in from the churning kitchens.

'All I know is that Krishna gave me the courage to pick up my bow again, and to aim it at my beloved gurus with peace in my heart and he has saved me from my own capricious resolve.'

Draupadi nods and picks up the basin and leaves the tent to throw out the dirty, bloody water.

Outside the tent, Draupadi notices Krishna talking to a group of soldiers. In the commotion of distraught faces, some shamed by hopelessness and gloom, others gleaming with an unnatural and febrile excitement, Krishna remains equable and joyous. Draupadi is struck by the thought that though Krishna lives each moment more fully than any one else, he retains a core of laughter, as if he knows this is all a game, a deadly game but a game nonetheless.

Meanwhile, the horrors of the war keep piling up like corpses and the mud outside the surgeons' tents is slippery with blood and the cries of the wounded haunt the dreams of the sleeping soldiers and in the dawn they are exhausted by the vigil that death keeps for them.

On the ninth day of the war, death strikes closer, within the charmed circle of the Pandavas themselves.

'Iravan is dead,' Bheem says quietly to Draupadi that evening, his eyes dark shadows of pity, and Draupadi spares a fleeting thought for Ulupi, the faraway Naga girl who has paid with the life of her son for her few days of bliss with Arjun.

And then the following day, the returning soldiers are broken but jubilant, and incredulous too.

'Bheeshma is dead, Bheeshma is dead,' they say to each other as if repetition of this unseemly and terrifying possibility will make it fact.

The Pandavas, too, are exhausted and Arjun is silent as he crashes through the camp looking for clean water to bathe in.

Later that evening, after the soldiers have settled down to whimpering sleep and the wood fires flicker irresolutely in the bloodied dusk, Draupadi goes to Bheem.

'We knew we had to kill Bheeshma,' Bheem whispers, 'if ever we were to win this battle. He was commander-in-chief of the Kaurava army and he mobilized and galvanized the soldiers like no one else. He fought like a lion, Draupadi, despite his old age. He seemed to be in all places at once, his chariot with its palm tree banner moving like lightning across the field. Our soldiers just dropped their weapons and starting fleeing, disgracefully and hopelessly.'

Bheem holds his head in his hands, still assailed by the sight of Bheeshma, his long white hair flying like the furious wind, his eyes the god of death himself.

'Finally, it was Arjun, with your brother Shikhandi as charioteer, who was able to slay Bheeshma after doing battle with him all day long.'

Draupadi marvels at Shikhandi, the gentle, pliant playmate of her childhood, now a warrior with extraordinary fluidity and skill as a charioteer. But Shikhandi was always apart, his misleading strength when he played with his sisters a counterpoint to his dancing grace when learning the martial arts with his gurus. But he put aside his childhood skirts and glass bangles when ordered by his father to wear the sword and bow of the warrior and this slow-smiling chimera sibling stepped quietly into the destiny forged for him.

'You remember how Bheeshma was often uncomfortable in your presence, Draupadi? He seemed uneasy sometimes in the company of women.'

Draupadi does remember how wary Bheeshma always appeared to her, his natural reserve exacerbated when women were around. In the days before their banishment, when she haunted Hastinapur with her hair undone, he seemed to flinch each time he saw her unbound hair with all its connotations of impurity and pollution and blood.

'So I think he was unsettled when he saw Shikhandi and even this slight hint of a forbidden feminine presence on the battlefield unnerved him,' Bheem adds with the candour that is so typical of him.

'But it took all day and many arrows, Draupadi, before he was killed and when at last he dropped his bow and tumbled off his chariot, his body was covered in arrows and blood stained his white dhoti red. We were all silent for a while, we could not quite believe he was dead, and then one soldier started cheering, and then the others all joined in and somehow it seemed a desecration that we should celebrate the death of that fearless old warrior.'

But desecration or not, Bheeshma is dead at last. His long guardianship of the throne of Hastinapur is over and somewhere in the ether Amba is smiling.

Then, Bheem walks up to Draupadi and gently lifts her chin and his battle-scarred hands are rough against her smooth skin. His skin smells of smoke and blood and crushed marigolds.

'I have not forgotten my promise to you, beloved wife. Now that Bheeshma has been removed, the Kaurava army will crumble and you will wash your hair in Dusshasan's blood.'

*

Ira Mukhoty

Meanwhile, in the palace of Hastinapur, Gandhari lives a fraught existence, where hope and fear both are constantly thwarted by their distance from the battlefield, half a day's ride away. Every bit of information brought back from Kurukshetra is awaited with unbearable expectation and, at the same time, everyone is suspicious of each last bit of rumour, its veracity and precision, and Dritrashtra squabbles like a child with Gandhari, harried by the unendurable wait.

In the women's quarters, the countless daughters-in-law lead lives of isolated marginality. Only Gandhari is privy to all the updates from the battlefield as she waits with Dritrashtra in the raja's council hall for Sanjay to bring back news of the Kaurava warriors. Gandhari then makes her way back to the rani's quarters, where Bhanumati is ragged with waiting. She sits all day next to the fire altar, chanting mantras of protection and when she sees Gandhari approaching, her voice is hoarse with anxiety.

'What news of my husband, Rajmata?'

And everyday Gandhari is able to reassure her with a light hand on her shoulder.

The other women are largely unaware of the true nature of the battle. Some live in a charmed delusion that their husbands have gone on a hunting party and the disjointed news that they hear makes them confused and they grow irritable and blame it on the heat. But some are widows now, and do not know it yet, and for a few blessed hours they put kumkum in their hair and red lac on their lips and avoid the stony stare of the messenger boys.

One day, Gandhari returns from the council hall and her hands shake as she stands in front of Bhanumati, who asks her the same, tired question like a mantra.

'Your husband lives, Bhanumati.'

'But?'

Gandhari winnows her words with care and pity.

'But your son, Lakshman, is dead, beloved Bahu. He died a warrior's perfect death on the battlefield and he has joined his ancestors in the glorious afterlife.'

And Bhanumati leans back her head against the wall of the courtyard and screams at the grave sky, undone by this attack she had not guarded against.

But death in Kurukshetra is partial to none and later that same evening Arjun stumbles back to the camp and his lean face is haggard with grief and his steps are uncertain, as if he has lost his way.

Subhadra stands in front of him, pale in the uncertain evening light and Arjun holds her hands in his own.

'Forgive me, Subhadra, I could not save him. Our son is dead, Abhimanyu is dead. They trapped and outnumbered him and I could do nothing to stop them.'

Draupadi watches quietly as Subhadra cries in Arjun's arms and then she walks up to them to gently pull away the sobbing woman and Arjun looks at her with opaque and unseeing eyes. Suddenly the rage and the grief bubble out of him and he lurches back towards the sombre soldiers.

'I will kill them all,' he rages, 'I will kill every last cowardly Kaurava who taunted my son and cut him down when he was on the ground and unarmed and all alone against so many of them. I vow, I vow, as I stand on this blood-soaked ground that I will kill them all.'

And Arjun picks up his shattered weapons and his brothers crowd around him to contain his grief and finally it is Krishna who puts his arm around him and leads him away. He must temper his vows along with his grief for each oath is tabled and will be accounted for and he must not be too profligate in his rage.

But the carnage continues and the next day it is Bheem's tiny forest boy, Hidimbi's son, grown now into a mighty warrior, who is killed by Karna. The Kauravas die too, a cohort of them, and the number of widows in Hastinapur is legion.

After Bheeshma is killed, Drona is made commander-in-chief of the Kaurava army and he comes looking now for his old childhood friend and adversary, Drupad. Draupadi's old father has a chance now to avenge his honour but the memory of that ancient defeat makes his arm tremble and his aim is skewed and Drona shows no mercy when he sees the despairing fear in Drupad's eyes. Drona also kills Virat that same day and in her lonely tent which she shares with a weeping Subhadra, Uttara tries to gauge the extent of her bereavement. She has lost her husband and has become a widow before she really knew what it was to be a wife and now her father is dead and at the age of fifteen, she faces a lifetime of dependency and uncertainty. But she does have a secret consolation, and she holds it close to her and it is all that anchors her now to this traitorous world.

But Raja Drupad's death does not go unavenged very long, for the very next day Drishtadumna, Draupadi's twin brother, remembering perhaps the black yagna that preceded his birth, kills Drona in battle and all those childhood summers practising archery in the nacreous dawn are reborn in the moment of Drona's death.

In Hastinapur, Dritrashtra is felled by the news of Drona's death.

'Drona, my formidable old friend, you have abandoned me to my wretched old age while you go to your glorious rest,' he sobs.

But on day sixteen of the battle, when the physicians have stopped tending to the wounded, overcome finally by the shattered limbs and crushed entrails, Bheem returns to the camp shouting for Draupadi.

'Draupadi, where are you, come quickly. Draupadi, your humiliation is avenged at last.'

Draupadi comes running out of the tent when she hears Bheem and she gasps when she sees him. There is a strange patina on him, a dripping, glossy thing and she realizes he is covered in blood. He is holding out his cupped hands towards her and she sees, with horror and dread, that there is more blood in his hands.

'I have killed Dusshasan, Draupadi, I ripped his chest and tore out his heart. That fiend who defiled you is dead and I have brought you his blood so that you may anoint your hair and redeem your vow.'

And before Draupadi can react to his words, Bheem smears the blood from his cupped palms onto Draupadi's bent head and she can feel the warm blood pearl down her face and it is as if she is crying tears of blood. Bheem crushes Draupadi to his chest and they are bleak with blood like a newly birthed, malevolent creature.

The killing is relentless now and Karna is slain by Arjun and there is dismay in the Kaurava camp. Shakuni is killed soon after and Duryodhan is suddenly bereft of his staunchest supporters. The great tribe of the Kaurava brothers is decimated and the earth of Kurukshetra is saturated with their crimson blood. So, at last, when Bheem stands in front of him with his twirling mace, Duryodhan contemplates his death for the first time since the battle began. He looks around at the destruction that surrounds him in the trampled mud. His beloved gurus, his brothers, and his great friend Karna and he understands that this is as flawless a time and place to die as any.

The sound of the crashing maces is terrifying and Krishna and the watching Pandavas clench their teeth and steady their hearts against the sound that courses through their blood. But Bheem is indefatigable and at last Duryodhan is lying on the clammy, squelching mud and his thighs are broken and his thoughts are a seething mass of red pain.

The Pandavas gather around the fallen Duryodhan and his gaze goes from one brother to the other and suddenly, calamitously, he laughs, blood bubbling through his lips.

'So you will be raja now at last, Yudhishthir, after all these years. But raja over what, and whom? There is no one left to rule over, to share the spoils of war. All our beloved elders and gurus are dead, our children and our brothers too. The palace is full of grieving widows and your kingdom will be one of tears and sorrow. I have lived all my life as a raja, in the greatest mahanagar on earth, while you have crawled all your life on your belly like a beggar. Which one of us is really the winner, Yudhishthir?'

Duryodhan's voice is raspy with pain and blood but his face is strangely peaceful now, his eyes lucid and clear.

'I am happy to die here, today, surrounded by my brothers and gurus. I am a Kshatriya and there is no better death for me than to die on this glorious battlefield.'

And as the sombre Pandavas contain their spilling emotions, Duryodhan looks past them at the layered sky and the tumultuous clouds are reflected one last time in his golden eyes.

The Pandavas return to camp and the war is finally over. The surviving soldiers and chieftains rouse themselves to celebrate the end of the bloodiest battle they have ever known, and, in Hastinapur, Bhanumati is taking off her golden bangles and wiping the red kumkum off her brow forever. Dritrashtra is beyond consolation, the army of his sons is dead and Gandhari retires to her quarters to survey her fraying heart. In Vidura's quarters, Kunti's thoughts are a long exhalation at last, though she is ashamed to feel so much joy when the palace is haunted by the wails of all the widows.

There is ragged jubilation in the Pandava camp that night but at last the few remaining soldiers fall asleep too and only Krishna is awake in the cavernous night. His informants from Hastinapur have news of treacherous vengeance and he goes stealthily to the tent where the Pandavas are sleeping. He wakes up the brothers and the three women and they stumble and slip through the gory churned field of Kurukshetra to the abandoned camp of the Kauravas. In the splintering dawn they watch uncomprehendingly as a crescent of fire appears over the opposite camp. They look at Krishna questioningly but his eyes are as unreadable as a winter's day.

What they do find out, from a running, gasping soldier garrulous with fear, is inconceivable.

'Everyone is dead, slaughtered,' he stammers, his hair singed and his skin smelling of smoke.

'Drona's son ambushed the Pandava camp and murdered the warriors as they slept. Your sons are all dead,' he adds, looking at Draupadi, blunt with fear. 'Your brothers, too, Rajkumars Drishtadumna and Shikhandi and all the others. Strangled in their sleep. Then they set fire to the camp and the remaining soldiers burned to death, or were cut down by Drona's son and his accomplices as they tried to run.'

Draupadi looks at Krishna and there is time for the crackle of only one lucid thought before the darkness of grief billows through her.

Meanwhile, in Hastinapur, Dritrashtra cannot bear to remain in the palace where the echoing corridors remind him that he is now disinherited.

'Gandhari, come, let us go and pray at the sacred river for the peace of all our dead sons, there is nothing left for us here now. Summon Sister Kunti also, let us all go together.'

So Gandhari sends for Kunti, who has remained sequestered throughout the battle in Vidura's quarters. She lifts up the ravaged Bhanumati, and sends emissaries through the city to the mansions where the countless Kaurava women are taking off their gold waistbands and anklets and dropping them onto the floor like scattered dreams.

And so Dritrashtra, Gandhari, and Kunti walk out of Hastinapur palace trailing a lamentation of women in white like the vortex of a storm. The appalled merchants and tradesmen in Hastinapur watch these distraught women stumble by, their hair untied and their grief uncovered, and they are shamed by the extravagance of their mourning. Many of the women do not know the magnitude of the carnage, the extent of their destitution. They live meagre lives outside the palace and it is only now, when they see their weeping sisters, that they begin to weave together the threads of the story.

Outside Hastinapur, the ragged gathering crowds into horse-drawn chariots and heads for the Ganga. On the way they come upon three panting men, squalid and pungent with grime and smoke and blood.

'Raja Dritrashtra, it is I, Ashwatthama, Drona's son,' one of the men stops Dritrashtra's chariot and shouts despairingly at him.

'Your sons fought like lions and all kinds of foul methods were used to kill them. My father is dead,' he adds suddenly, his breath frayed with sobs and fear.

'But I avenged your sons, Raja, I avenged Duryodhan's death. I have killed all the Pandavas' sons and their remaining allies and set fire to their camp. Now we must run away and hide for the Pandavas will be looking to massacre us.'

And the men disappear into the swaying kans grass and the chariots carry on to the river. When they arrive at the Ganga, the exhausted women walk up to the river and offer prayers of peace for the souls of their dead husbands and sons. The swirling water is warm and hurrying and the egrets look on dispassionately as the women pour water gratefully over their swollen faces.

By noon the sun is ferocious, the air steaming and spangled with light and even the shadows are molten. The women sit under the neem trees, half asleep in the torpor of the afternoon when they notice a small group of people approaching in the distance.

It is the Pandavas, along with Krishna and Draupadi, who have heard of Dritrashtra's flight from Hastinapur and have come to meet them at the river.

Dritrashtra and Gandhari stand together to wait for the party and their emotions furl and collide in them for it is not only the killers of their sons and grandsons who are approaching, the creators of a hundred widows, but the victorious new kings and they hold their future in their hands.

Gandhari tries to still her pounding heart which makes her fingers tingle and her head throb and she is only dimly aware of Dritrashtra saying something and then Bheem is standing in front of her and she is gasping with sorrow and fury.

'Please forgive me,' Bheem is saying, to her consternation and surprise. 'I killed your sons, and my own brothers, and we were children together once and had the same gurus and teachers. They fought like true Kshatriya warriors, Ma Gandhari, and I killed them for I feared for my life and I was full of terror in the scrum of battle. Duryodhan was invincible and it took all our might and effort to slay him.'

Gandhari wavers, made speechless by Bheem's candid and manly admission. She is consoled also to hear that Duryodhan died a warrior's death and that no son of hers was betrayed by cowardice in battle.

'But remember, Ma, if we used all the means at our disposal, and sometimes it seemed unfair, it was because Duryodhan was duplicitous when Yudhishthir lost his kingdom at dice. We knew then, and we know now, that those dice were loaded and that Yudhishthir's kingdom was stolen from him.'

Gandhari knows there is some truth in what Bheem is saying and she has always wished that Indraprastha had been returned peacefully to the Pandavas. But the savagery of her sons' deaths confuses her and she comes back to the one image that continues to horrify her.

'But my son Dusshasan. They say you tore out his heart and drank his blood like some inhuman monster from the netherworld. How could you do such a thing to your brother, Bheem?'

'Ma, I swear to you I did no such thing. Yes, I killed Dusshasan, as I had vowed I would. I ripped open his chest and took his blood in my hands for Draupadi. You were there, in the sabha, when she said she would never know peace till she had washed her hair in his blood and I only helped her fulfil her oath. Dusshasan behaved like a brute and a beast. He humiliated Draupadi in front of all those men and he deserved to die.'

Bheem is suddenly querulous at the thought of Dusshasan's broken body and scrappy about the blame he is willing to accept.

'All their lives, your sons behaved deceitfully and constantly tried to deprive us of what was rightfully ours. Why did you never try to contain them and show them the path of true dharma? Now we are standing here covered in their blood and the blame is not all mine, it is not all mine, it is yours too.'

Gandhari crumbles then, always aware of her own yawning fault in failing to control Duryodhan's crazed arrogance. She starts sobbing then, and her tone becomes piteous.

'Dritrashtra had a hundred sons, and you killed them all. Could you not have spared one at least, for his old age?'

And Gandhari is amazed to realize that this is what hurts her most now, that pity for Dritrashtra has replaced her grief and her rage. She always knew, in the quiet wilderness of her heart, that Duryodhan was fighting an unholy cause and death was the only possible outcome for him. But Dritrashtra's sorrow over the death of all his sons has shaken Gandhari and, after all these years of guarding her heart, she is absolved now by the pity that overwhelms her.

But her question is only for the heartless wind, which sweeps it away into the clouds and now Yudhishthir is in front of her and his voice is low and quivering with apprehension.

'It is I, Yudhishthir. Curse me, Ma Gandhari, for I deserve it. I am the cause of all the destruction and the killing so curse me now.'

And Yudhishthir's words make all the Pandavas feel like burglars and profiteers and they are uneasy and ashamed.

But Gandhari and Dritrashtra have no choice now but to bless the Pandavas and their hands tremble as they lay them on the Pandavas' heads, stained with the blood of the Kauravas.

Kunti finally steps forward and gazes at her sons, whom she has not seen for more than a decade. The Pandavas are bemused by the bent, sagging old woman who stands in place of their eternal mother. They did not remember her being quite so diminished and her hands on their faces feel clammy and unfamiliar. Kunti herself is shocked at the grey in Yudhishthir's hair and the dark shadows on Arjun's face.

But Yudhishthir brings Draupadi to Kunti and she sobs gratefully into the older woman's arms.

'My sons are dead, Ma Kunti. All my sons are dead. They were murdered in their sleep and they did not die Kshatriya deaths and there is no one now to avenge them. They were unmarried and there will be no wife, no son, ever, to honour their memory but I must swallow my sorrow for my husband is raja now and I am told there must be an end to the killing.'

Kunti leads Draupadi to Gandhari and it is a consolation to talk of dead sons to a woman who understands her pain.

'You are right, Daughter, nothing is as terrible as the loss of a child. To have no child left, not even one, to cherish and to love and to see us to our death, is to make a mockery of a mother's heart.'

And it is a strange comfort to hear Gandhari's words and Draupadi lays down her aching head in the older woman's lap.

But the heaving mass of widows has grown irritable with uncertainty and exhaustion and they all decide then to walk to Kurukshetra, to see the unmentionable truth themselves.

Long before they reach Kurukshetra, they see a dark smudge spiralling in the dappled evening sky and it is a deadly swirl of vultures funnelling over the battlefield on the warm thermals. As they get closer, the air is charged with a smell so fetid and overpowering that they must tie cloths over their faces and take shuddering, retching breaths. And then, as they near Kurukshetra, there are the wails and the screams from the abyss of hell itself. Dying soldiers and wounded horses writhe in the sticky red clay like insects in a jar of honey. The dead lie where they have fallen, bristling with arrows. Dark shapes, hunched and aberrant, slide and slope among the bodies and for a soaring instant, the widows imagine it is the souls of the dead painfully extricating themselves from the corpses. But then one of the women screams as she realizes what it is and realization dawns shockingly on all the others and they run into the field, crying and flapping their hands uselessly at the dark shapes. Vultures, their beaks glutted with glistening entrails, have settled in droves among the corpses, competing with the wild dogs, who snarl and snap at each other in their frenzy, and snuffling boars, murderous incisors shining in the lowering light.

The women slip and fall on the festering bodies, crazed and shouting out the names of their husbands and sons, looking for a sign that they can recognize in all the gore and blood of the disfigured dead. Suddenly, there is a wail, louder than the others, as Bhanumati recognizes Duryodhan. His legs are broken and he is covered in bruises but his face is miraculously untouched and Bhanumati falls on the mud beside him and gently gathers his ferocious head in her arms. His tilak is smeared now but it is still bright red, as if he has walked away from the holy fire only minutes ago and the marigold garland around his neck is only slightly withered. Bhanumati's grief is an arc of pain that vaults over Kurukshetra and the other widows are sobered into silence for a while. A widow leads Gandhari over to Bhanumati and both women weep over his stilled, once raging heart.

The women have fanned out now all over the field like ghosts, savage with grief and horror. They search desperately for a familiar armour or armband and sometimes an irrational resemblance to a beloved face is enough and they claim an abandoned body for their own.

Uttara is there, too, holding Subhadra by the hand and looking for Abhimanyu. When she finds him at last, she sighs as if in contentment and sits down gratefully beside him. She murmurs sweetly to her dead husband, stroking his unmarked brow with gentle fingers and at last Subhadra is sobbing as she pulls her away forcibly for Abhimanyu is foul with decay and his eyes are red wounds where the voracious birds have pecked them away.

Gandhari is overcome by the magnitude of the sorrow of her daughters-in-law and the unpardonable excess of the massacre. She finds Krishna standing quietly at the edge of the field and she can no longer contain her bitterness.

'Look at all these wailing widows, Krishna, who will console them now? Look at these proud warriors and brave husbands. See how death has levelled them all, where are the laughing, virile men of yesterday? Look at these women, since I cannot, Krishna, and mark each one in your heart for I will not allow them to be forgotten. These women have never known sorrow before, or hardship. They are gentle, cultured women who were cherished by their families and given to Hastinapur so that we may have them as goddesses in our homes. Now look at them, their clothes spattered in mud and blood, brazen in their sorrow and shameless in their bereavement.'

Krishna stands silently in front of Gandhari, allowing her to express her unfathomable pain.

'And these men, Krishna, all these men, generations of Kuru men dead on this field. Honourable Kshatriya men who led dharmic lives. Now the shrieking of these vile vultures and scavenging dogs is to be their last song on this earth.

'Could you not have stopped this war, Krishna, you who were privileged and had access to both the Pandava and Kaurava clans? Could you not have brokered peace between these brothers and avoided all this bloodshed? I think you could, and I blame you for these sobbing women and dead men. Just as you stood by and watched these brothers kill each other, so too will your own kinsmen slaughter each other and you will be the cause. I curse you, Krishna, and your clan, and the women of your clan will shed tears just as these women here are crying inconsolably.'

Krishna flinches at these words, which are harsh and ominous with the weight of Gandhari's righteous sacrifices.

'Ma Gandhari, surely you must accept part of the blame, too. You were present in the sabha when Draupadi was shamefully humiliated and you didn't stop your sons. Nor did you reason with Duryodhan and make him share the kingdom with the Pandavas, as he should have. Their claim was legitimate and justified. As for my clan, well my kinsmen are indeed capable of killing each other, since I don't think anyone else can.'

Then Krishna's voice becomes gentler.

'You are a Kshatrani, Ma Gandhari, your sons were ever born to die, for a Kshatriya's honour is to be found only on the battlefield.'

Then Krishna turns away and walks towards Yudhishthir and Gandhari is left alone, and the droning flies swarm over the corpses and around her face like a noxious smoke.

Dritrashtra is standing next to Yudhishthir, a trembling hand on his shoulder, and he points around at the carnage he cannot see.

'What about all the bodies, Yudhishthir, how will we conduct appropriate rites for all these dead warriors? I cannot just leave my sons to the scavengers, their souls abandoned.'

'We will hold the rites for all the fallen warriors right here. Let us collect all the wood we can find and we can have mass funeral pyres for the different clans.' And this macabre task is Yudhishthir's first duty as raja.

So the wood is hewn from the broken chariots and lances, and arranged into huge pyres. The men bind their faces with white cloths and lift up the rotting corpses whose skin slips off like old moults. The vultures flap huge, furious wings and the seething flies lift off from the eyes and mouths of the bodies, leaving grievous absences. The bodies are placed onto the pyres, and there is an attempt to sort them by clan but the work is hazardous and uncertain. Hasty priests throw incense and some cursory libations into the pyres and then the fires are lit. All through that evening, as the wind picks up and twists the flames in all directions, the huge fires burn. There are pyres for the Kurus, the Matsyas, the Panchalas, and the Gandharas and most of these clans are decimated to the last grandson.

Draupadi is standing a little apart watching the pyres burn and Uttara is standing next to her, leaning into Draupadi. She looks up and sees the familiar yellow dhoti of Krishna on the far side of the pyres and the thought that had been careening inside her clicks into place. Krishna sees her looking at him and Draupadi nods slightly at him and then looks back at the pyres, for she has understood a small, insidious truth. She remembers their precipitous flight from the camp in the middle of the night while her sons and brothers were left behind to be murdered in their sleep. There is no Vrishni pyre at this mass funeral and while all the major clans of the river valleys are laid low, Krishna's clansmen are unscathed. Moreover, the only heir with a claim to the throne of Hastinapur to have survived is the secret that Uttara hides in her frail body. So Krishna's nephew is dead but through his hastily arranged marriage to Uttara, the clan of the Vrishnis finally has a claim to kingship and the eternal kingmakers will at last be rajas.

As the fires start to burn low, the crowd slowly begins to move irresolutely away from the field of war, out into the polished darkness. Yudhishthir looks around Kurukshetra one last time and is surprised to see Kunti stumbling through the mounds of churned mud and unclaimed bodies.

'What is it, Ma, what are you looking for in this terrible place?'

And Kunti looks up at her son, a stranger almost in his battle scars, and whispers at last her uncontainable secret.

'I am looking for Karna. He is your brother, my eldest son, born to me before I married your father. I thought we should give him a Kshatriya's funeral since I could not give him anything else all his life.'

Yudhishthir listens to Kunti in horror, and searches her face for signs of madness. Perhaps, he thinks, the horrors of the war have driven her to insanity but her eyes are bleak and calm.

'A brother? I had an elder brother all this time and you never told me? With Karna by our side, the world would have been ours to take and now we have killed him? How could you keep this a secret all my life?'

And Yudhishthir grabs his mother by the shoulders and Kunti shuts her eyes in shame, for this is the first time he has laid his hands on her in anger. But Yudhishthir spins around and starts shouting out for his brothers, stepping over the dead soldiers.

'Where is Karna, where is my brother?' he wails aloud and once the other Pandavas are told the truth they search the field desperately with him. At last Karna is found, identified only by his shield with the embossed sun, and Yudhishthir lifts his cold and broken body into his arms and carries him towards the pyres. He pushes away the soldiers when they try and help him and he calls out for the pundits to come back.

A new pyre is lit and the exhausted pundits return to chant the death mantras and their voices rise over the crackling flames.

From darkness lead us to light

From death lead us to immortality

And the Pandavas stand in front of the pyre with folded hands and reply.

Om shanti, shanti, shanti.

The Ganga

~

The Pandavas return to Hastinapur as conquerors and the tradesmen and the beggars silently watch the haggard procession walk by. They bring back Dritrashtra, Gandhari, Kunti, and all the widows and the palace becomes a place of hushed silences and inconvenient tears. Colour itself is banished and the exquisite and adorned rajkumaris of yesterday are transformed into wild-haired wraiths. All the valorous young men are gone, too, dead on the battlefield, and there will be no more large-eyed, lisping babies and swift children. Yudhishthir is benumbed by doubt and despair and secretly believes that Duryodhan was right, that this kingdom of ashes is a curse and a burden.

Dritrashtra grieves interminably for his sons and Gandhari feels their presence in the shadows of the peepul trees. They must hold their sorrow close, however, furled and dense in their hearts for it would not do to parade it too openly in front of the Pandavas who are impatient now with talk of the Kauravas. Dritrashtra would like to leave Hastinapur but Yudhishthir will not hear of it.

'Pitaji, Ma Gandhari, you must stay here with us and lend us your wisdom and your experience in ruling this kingdom.'

Yudhishthir's words are kind, but his eyes are distant and Bheem smirks openly and slaps his biceps loudly as if remembering the last hours of Duryodhan and Dusshasan. Convention does not allow Yudhishthir to let the old people go and forces them all into a

278

squalid and shearing intimacy that wears them out.

Kunti returns to her old quarters in Vidura's house and the Pandavas are annoyed and want her to assume her status as rajmata. But Kunti knows that reality has been altered by her revelation about Karna and her relationship with her sons will never again be what it once was. She can see it in the Pandavas' eyes, which flick away when they see her, in their sudden need to be gone when she walks into a room. She is hurt, at first, then uncomprehending, as the rift becomes an abyss and Vidura is the only person she can talk to.

'What else could I have done, Vidura? Should I have told my sons earlier? But Pandu died so soon and I was a widow and how could I claim Karna when I had no one to protect him?'

And Vidura is always sympathetic.

'You did the only thing you could, Kunti. You did it for your sons and for their legacy.'

But it is hard for Kunti when even Nakul and Sahadev do not come to enquire about her and the shadows now remind her of Karna, lustrous in the noon sun, accusing her of denying him his Kshatriya birthright. Her days and her nights are haunted by her sons, dead and alive, and they are all bitter and remote.

So for fifteen years the older people live lives of appeasement and dissimulation and then, at last, Dritrashtra feels he can do this no more. He overhears Bheem one day, laughing loudly at his recollection of the war, the way in which he tore open Dusshasan's chest, and Dritrashtra knows it is better to die than to stay in the palace any longer.

'Yudhishthir, Son, we are old now and do not have long in this world. We have decided to end our lives in a hermitage in the forest, in prayers, meditating on the afterlife as is customary for those at our stage of life. Please give us permission to leave.'

And Yudhishthir sends an entourage with them, cooks and attendants and priests, and it is a relief to see them leave with their unspoken accusations and frail voices. But he is surprised to see Kunti stand up to join them at dawn, after the holy rites have been said.

'Ma, why are you leaving? Your place is here in the palace, with your sons and your family.'

'Beta, I was rani once, when your father was raja. I lived a life replete with great yagnas, and celebrations and joy. I do not need, so late in life, to partake of your kingly honours.'

And Kunti leaves, too, leading Gandhari by the hand while Vidura helps Dritrashtra, and the horse-drawn chariots disappear into the rising sun.

Meanwhile, in the palace, Uttara gives birth to a son, Parikshit, a few months after the war. This child becomes the fierce centre in the eddying currents of her life. He saves her sanity, and gives her a fragment of joy, which will be sufficient for her, and she puts aside all other expectations from life. Subhadra and Draupadi take him in their arms, breathing in his snuffling breath of almonds and milk.

In Hastinapur, as of a common accord, Draupadi remains the wife of Yudhishthir. The other Pandavas never bring this up and Draupadi is a past life they cannot imagine living again. They all have other wives, whom they visit occasionally, and they never return to Draupadi. She is Yudhishthir's holy consort when he performs the Ashwamedha Yagna, the overwhelmingly bloody horse sacrifice, and Draupadi wonders at the men's insatiable appetite for spilling blood. At the end of the sacrifice, when Draupadi must lie down in obscene mimicry next to the dead horse, the Pandavas avert their eyes when they see her and she is the lonely rani of Hastinapur.

⁀

Meanwhile the Kuru widows are an immaculate aberration in Yudhishthir's life. He is never able to fully inhabit the role of samrat when their sorrow, and his role in it, is so constantly arrayed in front of him. More prosaically, they are a drain on the royal treasury and there is no conceivable end to this as many of the widows were young women at the time of the war.

A year after Dritrashtra and the others have left for the forest, Vyasa comes visiting Hastinapur and he immediately understands Yudhishthir's quandary. He approaches Bhanumati and the other senior widows and proposes a visit to the old people in the forest and a holy dip in the Ganga.

'So it will be a pilgrimage, punditji, for me and my sisters?'

Bhanumati searches Vyasa's cracked features for some explanation but he thumps his walking cane impatiently on the earth floor.

'Yes, of course, a pilgrimage, it will bring you all closer to the loved ones you have lost. Gather your sisters together and follow me.'

So Bhanumati reluctantly agrees and she calls for all the widows and it is not an easy task for many of the women have not left the palace in decades and they are tearful and confused. But finally they all leave Hastinapur, blinking at the morning light and dazzled by the colours in the hibiscus shrubs. They follow Vyasa and they arrive at Dritrashtra's hermitage where they find the old people living frugal but contented lives. But Vyasa does not let them stay there very long and soon he is hurrying them along to the Ganga, accompanied by Dritrashtra, Gandhari, and Kunti.

'The Ganga is a holy river,' he tells the women. 'She will cleanse you of all your sins and grant you your hearts' desires.'

'Cleanse us? How so, punditji?' Bhanumati looks at the lashing, imperious river and the truth she sees there is stark.

Vyasa nods and stands in front of the widows.

'There is nothing left in this mortal world for you now, daughters. Consign yourself to the Ganga and you will be reunited with your beloved husbands and sons and fathers,' he tells the women succinctly.

Kunti is appalled and tries to reason with the ancient, cadaverous Vyasa.

'Surely there is no need for this, punditji. Yudhishthir will look after these women, it is his dharma and his duty.'

But Vyasa waves her away, his rudraksha beads clicking against his gaunt arm.

'Your son cannot look after these women forever. He has done enough. It is time for them to lighten the earth's burden.'

Faced with this barren order, the women give up hope then and sigh and walk towards the river. The older woman go first, having a more tenuous grasp on life and its pleasures and as they step into the heaving water, their frail bodies are quickly swept away, like so much husk.

Others follow then, alone or in groups. Some are dragged screaming by sisters who don't want to abandon them to Vyasa's frightening mercy. Soon the water is full of swirling white clothes and garbled screams as the loamy water fills the mouths of the widows.

Finally, Bhanumati also walks into the river, her walk still the swaying seduction it was when she was a young woman. Two of the younger girls cling to her in fear and she slowly walks into the middle of the river, holding the girls in her arms. She is so stately and strong that it looks for a moment like she might cross over to the other side, to freedom and a wild, feral life. Kunti, who has been watching the women in shocked silence, now runs towards the river when she sees Duryodhan's rani.

'Bhanumati, no, come back,' Kunti screams into the wind, hopelessly.

Bhanumati turns for an instant, her dark shoulders bare above the warm, muddy water, long hair swirling around her and her lips parted as if she is speaking to Kunti. Kunti strains to hear what she is saying, and to read the expression in her luminous eyes but Bhanumati slips and the three women sink into the churning water.

Vyasa turns away towards Dritrashtra and Gandhari and only Kunti remains by the water's edge, mute spectator to the hundred women's deaths, and soon the screams are hushed and all that remains is the breathy roar of the murderous river.

Epilogue
Fire and Ice on the Last Journey Home

~

Another twenty years pass in the lonely palace of Hastinapur. The Pandavas step quietly into old age, surprised at their weary hearts and their arms which are frail and betraying. In faraway Dwarka, the intemperate Yadav clan kill each other in a series of senseless squabbles over wine spilt and honour challenged and Gandhari's curse comes to pass.

It is surprisingly easy for Draupadi and the Pandavas to walk out of Hastinapur palace for the last time. In its echoing corridors, the dead are so much more demanding than the living. Kunti, Gandhari, Dritrashtra, and Vidura are all long gone and when news reaches them of Krishna and Balaram's deaths, their grief is mute and arid.

They leave behind Subhadra and Uttara and they crown Parikshit Raja of Hastinapur. They lay down their iron-tipped arrows and their golden waistbands and return to the familiar forest roads to the north. They walk for weeks and months and reach the lower Himalayan mountains where Bheem does not remember his swift love for Hidimbi and the first time he held the wonder of his son in his arms.

They continue to walk, into the furling blue air that fills their lungs with sweet and aching breaths. The forest falls away, the sal and the deodar trees, and life becomes elusive and flitting. At last they reach the high passes where their steps are measured in painful exhalations and every sound is a muffled whisper and the ceaseless snow slows down their relentless thoughts.

One day, after a bitterly cold night, they walk out onto a vast, whispering plateau where Draupadi knows she can walk no further. The Pandavas leave her behind, without a qualm. They have come here to die and renounce their traitorous bodies and to die quickly is a blessing and they would not thwart Draupadi now.

Draupadi settles into the icy embankment with a sigh and shuts her eyes against the evanescent dawn. She is so tired suddenly with a lassitude that weighs down her limbs and frees her spirit. She collects what little thought remains tightly into a warm thing and is surprised to notice she is looking down on herself, her lashes powdery with soft snow. Panic flashes through her for an instant till she realizes there is no Her any more and she scatters like motes in the sun.

In the distance Draupadi senses the fire and heat of an olden, primal time and the greasy flames call her name. The dancing specks and atoms that were Draupadi start to coalesce and swirl into a shadow, a girl-shaped figure, each speck illuminated by the rising dawn, and the pull is inexorable. Draupadi knows with a certainty that she has done this times without number into the deep, deep past and this clear knowledge catapults her into the high, blue-black sky. The fires recede, the greasy smoke clears and is replaced by the fresh green smell of earth and grass. With a feeling that is like relief, but also something more, the atoms that were Draupadi scatter down into the earth, the blessed Prithvi, from where she emerged at the dawn of time and the last conscious thought Draupadi has is:

I have been here before, I am the earth
Here before,
Forever

And then all memories fade like shadows in the night.

Far away to the west, the ocean is rising and submerges the eight-sided city of Dwarka and fish nibble desultorily at the huge gates set with copper and bronze panels and the tales of the Yadav clan are forgotten in the waving currents. The Khandava forest rises again and the tall grass grows over the broken tiles of Indraprastha.

And, finally, the dream fades and the worlds return to the deep, pulsing sleep beyond time, and beyond maya.

Jaya

Acknowledgements

~

Song of Draupadi is my fourth published work but it is in fact the very first manuscript I ever wrote.

My gratitude, therefore, is specifically directed at all those who encouraged me to write in the first place, who did not dismiss my attempts as the work of a misguided dilettante.

To my parents, Gobind and Nicolle Mukhoty, the first feminists in my life, who staunchly believed I could do anything I put my mind to, and who would have been very proud.

To Caroline Juneja, whose lassitude over hearing me moan about having a story to tell provoked her one day to thrust a brand-new notebook into my hands with a single, terrifying word: 'Write'.

To my brother, Ashoke Mukhoty, easy to please, who was so delighted with the prologue itself.

To my first readers, fondly tolerant and encouraging—Ayesha Mago and Anjuli Bhargava.

To my first editor, Simar Puneet, who took this text to her heart at once.

To my publisher, David Davidar, for taking a gamble.

And to the others, Mohit Jayal, Air Marshal Brijesh Jayal and Mrs Manju Jayal, Yashoda and Devaki Jayal, Rachna Davidar and the Aleph team, Pujitha Krishnan, Isha Banerji, Vasundhara Raj Baigra.

Thank you.